Hot Flashes
COLD CASES

Sue Hawley

SUE HAWLEY

Cover designer: James Price, The Author Market

Interior Layout: Deena Rae; E-Book Builders

B

Dedication

Dedicated to my husband, Jack. Not only was his encouragement priceless, but his vast knowledge of local history was invaluable.

Acknowledgements

I want to thank my sister, who is always the first to read any manuscript. She laughs in all the right places. Janine is the last person to read all manuscripts before they depart for the editor and ensures my characters stay true to themselves. EW, who answers any and all questions pertaining to law enforcement. And finally, to my kids. Without them, I probably wouldn't have the sense of humor I have developed in order to survive raising all five of them.

E

Hot Flashes COLD CASES

Chapter 1

I woke up suddenly, sweat pouring down my back. *Damn. When are these ridiculous night sweats going to end?*

I was miserable and extremely tired of menopause. "Crap, now I have to pee," I muttered. As I swung my legs over the edge of the bed, I shuddered; the cold seeping through the century-old windows in my husband's and my farmhouse was brutal. Being only just an inch over five feet, my feet didn't quite reach the floor unless I scooched a bit closer to the edge of our king-size bed. Whoever had decided it was a good idea to make king mattresses this deep had probably been tall and lucky enough to have long legs. As my feet hit the cold floor, I winced.

Stumbling back from my nightly visit to the toilet, I stopped in my tracks. There were two people, two women, standing in our bedroom. Glancing quickly at my husband, Andy, I dared to hope—absurdly, I had to admit—that he was awake. I quickly realized that he would be no help at all, and my eyes darted back to the figures. Heart pounding, I was frozen in place.

Some part of my brain was actually working, though, and I recognized one of the figures: my long-deceased grandmother. Funny the thoughts that raced along the pathways of the brain when it was trying to make sense of an absurd situation. Squinting, I recognized her steel-gray hair, curled with a fresh perm and even shorter than mine. She hadn't changed a bit. Well, except for the being dead part. My facial muscles contorted into a puzzled frown.

"Nana?" I finally ventured once my voice worked. A huge smile appeared on her face. "Peg, sweetie." Now I knew I must be in the middle of a major stroke. To my way of thinking, when you started seeing dead people, the probabilities of your imminent death were rather high.

"Well, at least I am finished with menopause," I told her spirit.

Her familiar ornery laugh echoed in my ears. "Oh, babe, you're not dying. You're merely seeing all of life fully for the first time."

My heart finally started to slow down enough that the pounding in my ears was no longer the bulk of the sound. *Does that mean I'm hearing my nana with my ears or my brain?* I wondered, my mind reverting to a type of logic I could wrap my head around. Here was a bizarre situation right in front of my eyes. Was I really trying to figure out what part of my head had the ability to absorb her words? Just went to show how much we craved normal, whatever "normal" might be at any given time.

"Fully? What the hell does that mean?" I asked, a part of me convinced I was experiencing a brain malfunction. I knew menopause could cause breakdowns; was that what was happening to me? Just because I had to pee in the middle of the night? Jeez.

Before Nana's death, her skin had been soft and smooth, despite her age, and I had loved it. That soft face now smiled before me. "You are fine, Peg," she assured me. "You're just seeing the spirit world for a moment. Enjoy the experience."

"Nana, I can't afford to go nuts at the moment." All I wanted was for the sensation of imminent throwing up to recede.

Laughing once more, she shook her head, amused.

"Who's your friend?" I asked, jerking my head in the direction of the other ghost. I say "ghost" because I had no idea what else to call them.

"Friend of mine I met here." She smiled.

"So you socialize on the other side? Parties and such?" I asked with maybe just a touch of sarcasm. "Really?" Partying didn't fit in with my idea of heaven.

"You'd be surprised what goes on over here," she said with an impish grin. Ornery. Cocking her head to one side, Nana studied my face. Then her eyes drifted to my hair. She sighed. "You really should quit dyeing that head of hair," she said, referring to my habit of twenty years. "Are those wrinkles I see?"

I glared at her. "It's not my fault that menopause ruined the color of my hair. The mousy brown was *horrible*, so I dyed it."

Shaking her head, she chided, "Mousy had nothing to do with it; you spotted a few stray gray hairs and panicked, plain and simple."

I took a deep breath. "True, the gray didn't help, but it really was the crummy color." I wasn't in the mood to argue, knowing I would lose any argument. She was giving me a more critical once-over, making me squirm.

"You've put on weight too. Shame on you; at your age, weight is hard to get rid of, you know."

"For Pete's sake! Ten pounds is all! Problem is, every ounce settled around the middle. Those pounds could have had the decency to spread around a bit!" I pouted.

Throwing back her head, she laughed. The sound was rich and deep. Okay, so I was short, pudgy, and graying. Not many options open at this point in my life.

Tired of my body being analyzed, I decided a change of subject was in order. "Is there something you want, or are you just dropping by for a visit?"

By now my nerves had settled down. I looked over at my husband again, annoyed that none of this seemed to disturb his sleep in the slightest. Here I was in the middle of either a huge psychotic moment or having a bizarre nightmare—and the snoozy stinker was snoring away in his own never-never land.

My nana's face still held that irritating smile as she said, "Visiting and introducing you to your new way of life."

"What new way of life? I like my old way just fine. Remember—boring is beautiful!"

She shook her head again, her smile giving way to her mischievous grin I remembered so vividly. She said, "You and your love of tedious life. I failed you somehow."

"Nana, you were too much for me at times. Exhausting! That's probably why I love dull and predictable now," I retorted as memories flashed through my brain. She had been exciting, but it had been a bit much at times. It had been like having my very own Auntie Mame down the street. So draining.

However, she had been able to provide an emotional stability I had needed. "Well, I'm introducing you to a new way of seeing life. Trust me—it will be good for you. It's time for you to experience exciting new pathways. Anyway, the boys are grown; what else are you going to do with yourself?" she asked. "I've been watching over you for years, Peg. I know you better than you know yourself."

The second ghost nodded as Nana spoke, which concerned me. The woman didn't need to encourage her. Couldn't she talk? I looked at the unfamiliar woman with new interest.

"Do I know this person?"

Seeing me study her friend, Nana said, "Meet your spirit guide. I selected her personally just for you. She will help you become accustomed to our realm. It works a little differently than you probably think. Takes a bit of getting used to, I would imagine."

"Really?" I hoped my new guide could still recognize sarcasm, because I laid it on pretty damn thick with that one word.

Looking over at the alarm clock, Nana raised an eyebrow. "It's getting late, and you need to get back to bed; tomorrow is a busy day for you."

"You're worried about time? I thought heaven had no time," I replied, sarcasm still in place.

"Time? That's for the living. I'm aware of your love of a good night's sleep. Love you, sweetie."

Nana and her friend slowly disappeared.

I was alone again. I sat on the bed wondering if I had imagined the scene. *Did that really just happen?* Hormones were nasty buggers and could wreak havoc on the best of us. Deciding it had to be another major drop in my hormone levels, I slid back into my warm bed and eventually convinced myself to sleep.

I'd figure it out in the morning.

Enjoying my first cup of coffee the next morning, I convinced myself the events of the night before had been the work of a bedtime snack consisting of salami, pepper jack cheese, and crackers. I sure wasn't indulging in that combo again. However, it would have been a bit cool if it had really happened. I'd never heard of spirit guides outside of Native American culture. Did that mean (if it had been real) the ghost with Nana was an Indian?

Andy had left for work, thank goodness. My mornings went better when I could wake up slowly with no chatter from him. Brewing my second cup of coffee, I started planning my day. I enjoyed looking out the window as I put my thoughts into an organized pattern. I had such a great view of the woods at the edge of our property. This hill at one time had been an Indian village. Thickly wooded areas had surrounded the village, and the trees still stood as though given the task of never-ending surveillance. We had families of foxes and deer and nests of hawks each year to enjoy. The deer had a nasty habit of eating my tulips each spring; my neighbor called tulips "deer candy," and boy, was she correct. Beautiful as they were, deer could munch through flowers faster than I could eat through a box of Malley's Chocolates. Turning from the view, I realized I was no longer alone in my kitchen.

Okay, so last night wasn't the salami.

"Hi, sweetie," Nana said with a smile. She quizzically looked around my kitchen and then finally said, "So you haven't changed this kitchen at all? That wallpaper looks pretty tired."

She was referring to my favorite piece of redecorating done many years ago. With its cream background and small blue cornflowers scattered through a field of tall green grass, this wallpaper had immediately caught my eye the moment Nana and I had spotted it among the gazillion samples in the store down on Exchange Street near downtown.

After forcing my heartbeat to slow down with deep-breathing exercises I had learned at a stress-relief class, I found my voice working again. "Hey, Nana." I was surprised I sounded somewhat normal. Glancing at the wallpaper,

I said, "You picked it out for me. Couldn't make myself change it after …" Fighting back tears, I stopped.

Nana smiled knowingly. "It's all right, babe; I never went far."

"Well, I didn't know that, did I?" I snapped. Ah, there I was. It was nice to feel normal and not afraid. Never one to back down, I continued, "Why now? All those years when I needed you, I never saw you. Why can I see you now?"

Nana was watching me closely. "Well, you really didn't need me much. You don't need me now, not really. But I need you."

I stared at her in shock. I was a little skeptical of her need of a mere mortal. Since when did the spirit world need us to help? I wasn't exactly sure how to respond to this morsel of news. Wanting to clarify the situation, I asked, "You need *me?*"

Still inspecting my kitchen, she nodded. "Yep."

I realized she had noticed the spot above the stove where the worn-out wallpaper was peeling. Hoping to redirect her attention, I pressed her for more information. "How?" Not the greatest interrogation skills.

Finally turning her gaze to me, she said, "Well, I'm in a bit of a pickle." She turned back to the issue of the wallpaper. "I think a change is in order, don't you? Ever think about ripping it out and painting instead?"

"Nana, forget the damn wallpaper. I'm not changing it till it falls off on its own accord."

Still inspecting, she smiled. "I'd say that will be sooner rather than later."

"Why exactly are you here?" I asked. She looked so real, so solid. A lump formed in my throat. God, how I had missed her through the years.

Glancing out the window before turning back to me, she said, "Well, I can't really tell you much about my side of the equation. We aren't allowed, you see, but I do need your help."

I frowned. "Okay. You mentioned that before. What you aren't telling me is how and why?"

She searched my face as though hunting for a clue of some sort. Finally, she nodded. "Yes, well, it isn't too complicated."

I waited for her to continue. It seemed an eternity, but I supposed she had no fear of time slipping away; however, my coffee was getting cold.

"We have assigned tasks here," she began slowly. "The task I was given should have been simple but has grown a little knotty."

I raised an eyebrow. Tasks? Wow, I had no idea we had to work on the other side. This news was unsettling.

"You need to help the police a tad," she finally said with a sigh, sending my raised eyebrow to historic heights.

"Help the police?" I snorted. "I have no background in police work."

"Hm?" Her tone indicated she was dodging the issue.

"Nana!" She turned back to face me.

One look at her expression and I knew what she was trying not to tell me. "You mean become one of those psychics? Like the TV show?" I asked, horrified.

Slowly nodding, she said, "Sort of."

"How 'sort of'?" I demanded. "I can't have ghosts popping in and out of my life! At least I know you, but it's disconcerting at the very least."

"I was sent here to help you get used to the fact," she said. She was back to inspecting the wallpaper. Nana had been an exuberant woman when alive but had been known for her ability to ignore pieces and parts of life she found distasteful, including anything that made her uncomfortable. Even death hadn't cured that part of her personality. I thought we became perfect with death; wasn't that what life was all about somehow? Jeez.

I suddenly remembered an earlier statement of hers. Suspicious, I narrowed my brown eyes and asked, "What pickle are you in exactly?"

Her inspection of my wallpaper became intense. Uh-oh! Something really big must be up with her. I kept my mouth shut, determined to outwait her. It paid off a minute later.

"Peg, my assignment was to clean up Akron and surrounding areas. The situation got away from me a tad," she said, sighing slightly as she shifted her stance, diverting her eyes again.

My husband and I lived approximately twelve miles from the old Rubber City, Akron, Ohio. Akron was only about thirty-nine miles south of Lake Erie, one of five considered the Great Lakes. Surrounded by smaller cities, along with various townships, the total population was close to three hundred thousand people. Our township, Bath, clocked in at a whopping ten thousand, so we were little fish compared to Akron's other local communities.

"Clean up Akron? Why? This isn't New York City or Chicago. This township is just a speck in the world."

Clearly frustrated at the limitations of her jurisdiction, she turned to face me, disappointment written on her face. "There's a big push to get the world prepared for the next step, and cleaning up the crime is the number one goal at this point," she said.

I decided to ignore her inner struggles with the situation. Let's face it: I was dealing with my own struggles and didn't have energy to help her.

"So some hierarchy decided to send you to clean up an entire city?" I asked in disbelief. "That's a tall order."

Shaking her head, she said, "Not just me, but we all screwed it up. Akron may be small potatoes in your eyes, but we have to start somewhere. They've been trying to clean the bigger cities for decades—putting the right politicians in office, making sure good judges are in place and the police forces are effective. It hasn't worked for a variety of reasons."

Heaven was in charge of politicians? Good luck with that!

"And?" Nana sighed heavily. "It appears that no matter how honest a person is, once in an office of authority they seem to fall off the rails. Human nature being what it is, keeping politicians honest is hard work. Judges are the worst in my opinion, though. Too much power in some cases, not enough in others. A big mess."

I thought about this bit of information. Heaven can't even control this stuff? Hells bells, we were in trouble.

"I can't make people stay honest! If you guys can't do it, what makes you think I can?" I said hotly.

"Calm down. You'll have help. Lots of it, actually."

The hairs stood on the back of my neck. Uh-oh, this didn't sound good. "Nana, no."

"It wouldn't be hard." She smiled. "Might put a little excitement in your life."

"I don't want excitement. I like dull," I pouted. It was a true statement. Raising four boys, Adam, Bryan, Christopher, and David, and trying to make sure they stayed out of trouble had been enough excitement for me. Andy liked life's surprises, not me.

"You won't be the only one involved. You could make new friends," she told me patiently.

"I like the friends I have now," I said. "I'm not interested in making new ones," I said with more than a little heat. I could feel my eyes narrowing again. "What do you mean, I wouldn't be the only one?"

She returned to inspecting the wallpaper. I sat back in my chair to wait her out again. Until that moment I hadn't realized I had been sitting forward, leaning with anticipation, during the conversation. Had my subconscious figured this mess out before Nana had told me? No, I decided. But somehow I had known this was going to be a situation I didn't like.

I didn't have to wait long. Turning back to me, she said, "There were a few of us that had this assignment. All of us grew up in Akron at different time periods." She smiled at me. "Some as far back as the mid-1800s, a few much earlier."

"Interesting. But what does it have to do with me?"

"At one time, Akron was an important city. The Ohio and Erie Canal helped the city grow, the school system used across the country started here, and then there was the boom of the rubber companies."

"I don't need a history lesson," I snapped.

"Yes, actually you do," she told me.

Sighing, I nodded, rolling my eyes. "Fine."

"Believe it or not, Akron has been more vital through the decades than you may realize. But that importance also invites the unsavory elements," she said, frowning.

"Like crooked politicians and lousy judges?"

Slowly nodding, she added, "People react to the corruption in different ways. Some try to clean it up; others decide to make a profit from the corruption. Then, of course, some ignore it altogether. Crime isn't only muggers, murderers, and mayhem. It rots the soul of a place."

Okay, she had a point.

Looking straight into my eyes, she emphasized, "Our job is to make sure the world is prepared for the next step, and cleaning up the mess is important."

Her intensity was unnerving. "Nana, I can't clean up an entire city, even with help."

She smiled again. That smile was starting to get on my nerves. "I'm not asking you to do the impossible, just your corner of the world."

I sat quietly thinking about her information as she went back to looking out the window toward the wooded area.

"Okay, let's say I'll help. What exactly does this entail?" Seriously, I couldn't believe those words actually left my mouth.

Keeping her gaze on the woods, she said, "Working with law enforcement. Helping to solve crimes."

Was she nuts? "Nana, there is not one bone in my body that can solve a crime."

She smiled, still watching the woods. Her attention to that area made me curious. Was she waiting for something or someone? I decided I'd rather not know if anything was back there. Those were *my* woods, and I refused to allow the thought of them being infested with more entities to ruin my years of enjoyment.

"You won't be working on your own."

Time to take the bull by the horns. "Who exactly would be helping me?" I asked, determined to get an answer.

Turning toward me again, she said, "Other spirits."

Wow. Just slap that information out there to hit me in the face. I could only stare at her. Not one word came to mind. My greatest fear justified.

Finally finding my voice with words to go with it, I said, "Not sure I can handle any more spirits than I'm dealing with right now." I gave her my most stern look.

"Sweetie, you can deal with much more than you realize. What's a few more spirits? No biggie."

No biggie? Who was she kidding? Jeez.

Chapter 2

Over the next few days I kept my mouth shut concerning my recent encounters with the otherworld; no sense everyone knowing I was having some type of breakdown. However, the following Saturday Andy looked at me and said, "Sweetie pie, I've minded my own business for a few days now, but you look like a truck hit you. What is going on with you?"

Apparently trying to sleep with one eye open waiting for the next group of spirits to visit was taking its toll on me. For Andy to mention my appearance meant it was pretty gruesome. Since we had an unwritten rule between us concerning comments on weight, hair, and looks in general, we seldom made such remarks unless they leaned more to the positive. I figured I looked as though I were ready for the next world myself.

Sighing in dread of his reaction, I heard myself say, "Here's the deal. Nana visited me a couple of times earlier this week telling me she needed my help."

To his credit, he nodded. "Okay. What type of help? Don't see what we could do that she wouldn't be able to handle on her side of things."

I could only stare at him a moment before I burst into tears. What a champ he was to take the news so matter-of-factly. No questions or teasing, merely took my statement as truth. My hero.

He wrapped his big arms around me, patting my back softly. "Peg, none of this should surprise you. You watch programs with people that can connect to the spirit world; we both believe it is real. I'm only surprised she took so long to contact you considering how close the two of you were." He was silent for a moment, deep in thought.

I nestled deeper into his clutch, feeling the safety of his arms surrounding me. God, I felt so much better now; maybe he could figure this mess out for me.

Pulling his head back to get a good look at me, he said, "What type of help are we talking here?"

I craned my head back to look up at him. "I'm not entirely sure I understood. Something to do with the police," I said slowly as I tried to grasp Nana's information. "It really doesn't make sense to me. She knows I have no knowledge of detective stuff."

He continued watching me carefully, as though I was about to impart some wonderful revelation. Hell, I had no idea what was going on with all of this.

"That's it?" he asked.

"Yep, I'm pretty sure. She did mention something about getting the world ready, but who knows what she meant by that."

"Ready for what?" he asked.

I could tell by his expression he was as confused as I was, which was, quite frankly, nice. At least I wasn't alone in thinking this was screwy.

Shrugging my shoulders, I pulled slightly away from his comforting embrace. "Who knows? You remember how squirrelly Nana could be at times. She obviously hasn't changed with the whole dying experience."

He kissed the top of my head. He was a foot taller than me, which made for an odd-looking duo, but it worked for us. With eyes the color of clear blue water, firm jaw, and a nose fit for royalty—straight and perfectly aligned—he wasn't handsome, but he was good-looking. Sometimes I believed that perfect nose had been a big deciding factor in my decision to marry him. His once- auburn hair was now lightly streaked with gray, making him more appealing than ever. I, on the other hand, colored my hair whenever I remembered and hadn't been a natural color of any sort for at least twenty years, as Nana had so kindly pointed out to me. Having a house full of sons had a habit of graying mothers early in life. By some cruel twist of fate, Andy had so far escaped any sign of middle-age bulge, while mine was expanding. Life was so unfair.

"When was the last time you, um, saw her?"

"The other morning. A few nights ago, she had another person with her that she called my spirit guide. I didn't recognize her; Nana met her over there somehow."

He nodded again, lost in thought. "Okay, let's go back to the police thing. What are you supposed to accomplish?"

I frowned, trying to remember exactly what she had said. Why hadn't I written it all down so I wouldn't forget anything? Damn, it had never occurred to me before this second.

"Something about cleaning up the world." After a second's pause I added, "And her assignment was Akron. But since we don't live in the city, I guess her mission includes the surrounding communities."

He raised an eyebrow. "Cleaning up the world? Assignment? Gosh, it never dawned on me we had homework in heaven."

I grinned. "Yep, that's pretty much what I told her. Guess there is quite a bit of work to do once you're dead."

He laughed. "Sounds like it." He gave me a quick squeeze before releasing me to finish his coffee. "So, are you going to work with the police for her?"

Disgusted, I shook my head. "I don't think she will leave me alone until I agree to help. I tried to warn her I know nothing about legal stuff, but she told me I'd have help." I frowned as I sipped lukewarm coffee. "Yuck. Let me nuke this stuff," I said, heading for the microwave.

"Help? What type of help are we talking about here?" he asked, watching me decide how long to nuke the coffee. I tended to take warming to a whole new level with microwaves. I had even been known to blow up a couple of them, but we didn't discuss those adventures often. I mean, who knew they were serious when the instructions said not to use foil?

Testing the heat of my coffee once the microwave had done the job, I continued, "Something about other spirits helping me. I have no idea what she means." Pausing a moment to think, I said, "Maybe the spirit guide she had with her—makes sense."

"Are you going to tell the boys about your new life?" he asked.

Emphatically shaking my head, I said, "No way! They already think I'm nuts because of decreasing hormones. This would prove their point!"

Andy grinned before draining the last drop of coffee from his mug. "Okay, just asking."

I threw my hands in the air. "Can you imagine their reaction? I don't think I could bear the teasing at this point."

Patting my back as he walked by, he said, "I'd whip them into shape!"

"Since when?" I laughed as he walked back to the bedroom. I could tell he was grinning and stuck my tongue out at him.

"I saw that," he teased before disappearing through the door.

After the last kid had finally left home, we had knocked out a wall connecting our bedroom to the room next to ours. It hadn't doubled the size of our room, but it had made it a heck of a lot more livable. Old farmhouses weren't famous for oversized bedrooms. When we had first bought the house, we'd had to build a closet in one of the bedrooms. The room had only had wooden hooks on the wall to hang clothes. I suppose the late nineteenth-century farmers hadn't been big on wardrobe choices. You had work clothes and Sunday-go-to-meeting clothes. Period. Yuck. The kitchen and dining room had started the original cabin with each generation adding rooms as needed. I marveled at the thought of families once living in only two rooms; the lack of privacy made me shudder.

I sat at the table enjoying the view as I drank my last cup of coffee. I loved the way the morning sun radiated the mass of trees out back. The woods were in the west, so as the sun rose in the east, it slowly illuminated the wooded area. During the winter months, the sun was farther down the horizon, which made the snow sparkle like thousands of tiny diamonds. For right now, I was happy there was no snow. The fresh leaves of spring caught the light, playfully bouncing the rays through the trees.

Movement off to my side caught my eye. Before turning, I felt my stomach knot, which should have given me plenty of warning. Obviously, I was still not taking Nana's words seriously. There they were, two people I didn't know, a man and a woman, standing square in the middle of my kitchen. I gave a short but loud scream. They didn't disappear but continued to look at me expectantly. Damn. Hadn't Andy heard my yell? Where was he?

Once my breathing calmed down and became closer to normal, I asked, "Who are you?" They looked at one another before the man cleared his throat (*You can do that when you're dead?*) and said, "We were told you would help us."

"Really? Who told you?" I asked, irritated. I wasn't even comfortable thinking about ghosts, and now they were being directed to my house? Jeez Louise.

The woman with him said, "She told us to say 'Nana sent us.'" Her impatience was obvious. I took a deep breath and refused to allow the words forming in my mind to fly out of my mouth. Where the hell was Andy?

In spite of myself, I was intrigued. The woman was well dressed, wearing a two-piece mint-green suit. The cut reminded me of the many snapshots of Jackie Kennedy during her White House days. Her makeup was perfection, hairstyle reminiscent of the midnineties—bottle blonde, shoulder length, but a bit poofy, in my opinion, for a woman her age, which I placed about mid- forties. The earrings and necklace were subdued but beautiful stones, making me wonder if they were her birthstone.

I shifted my attention to the guy with her. He was nice enough as far as looks went—average height and slender, not athletically built but not skinny, a bit nerdy to be honest. His wavy, dark hair definitely needed a haircut. His clothes were a little unkempt but of good quality. Pleated Dockers, button-down plaid shirt, and expensive loafers couldn't hide the disheveled air of him. He gave me the feeling he was constantly rumpled. These two people had little in common based on their sense of fashion.

Well, might as well tackle the situation. "Fine. What's the problem?" I mean, how hard could it be? Listen to their story; figure out a solution; move on with life. Right? Wrong.

"We were murdered," the man answered. He looked embarrassed for a moment. "Sorry, we should introduce ourselves first. Don't know where our manners went." He shook his head. "We are new to this ourselves."

"New to what?" I asked suspiciously.

"Being dead and talking to live people," he answered bluntly. "It's a bit different than we expected."

"We didn't expect to be dead!" the woman hotly added.

I held up my hands, flustered. "Wait a minute. Who are you?"

The man gestured toward the woman. "This is my wife, Elaine. I'm Bob. We were murdered—" He stopped suddenly as his face squished in thought. "What's the date?" he asked.

"The date? May 9, 2010," I answered slowly. *He needs to ask the date? Don't ghosts know what the date is over there on the other side?*

"I told you it wasn't last week!" Elaine snapped.

"That many years? I hadn't counted on that being the case," Bob said, sounding perplexed.

Elaine looked at me. "He never listened when we were alive! It's no different now!" she said in disgust.

I sat there looking at them, not knowing what I should say or do next. Something in the back of my mind kept bothering me. I continued to study their faces, wondering why they looked so familiar. Suddenly, it hit me. "Is your last name Bradley?"

Bob looked surprised. "Yep, that's us. How'd you know that?" Looking at Elaine, he said, "She's pretty good."

Elaine shook her head at him. "I bet we were in the papers, and that's why she knows our last name."

Bob looked back at me. "We were in the papers?"

I nodded as the memory of the coverage in the Akron newspaper flashed through my mind. Weeks of their images on the front page must have seared into my subconscious. But that had been years ago! Why had Nana sent them to me now?

"Your pictures were in the paper for quite a while. I don't remember if they caught the murderer though."

Bob thought over my last statement. After a few moments he said, "I don't believe they did. I think that is why we are here."

"To bring justice!" Elaine spat. "As if that will help us—a little late for that."

Bob looked at Elaine, then back at me, embarrassed. "She's been pretty upset since 'the event,'" he explained apologetically.

Elaine glared at me. "Well, wouldn't you be?"

I had to agree. Being murdered would probably piss me off a great deal.

"We were close to retirement and looking forward to traveling a little. House paid for, money not as tight, relaxing. Then some jackass decides to rob our house and murder us in our own beds!" she snapped.

Boy, was she indignant about their outcome. Thinking about their situation for a moment, I decided she had a right to be mad.

"I understand your anger, but what am I supposed to do about the situation?" I asked.

"Beats me, ma'am. We were told to come see you; figured you'd know what you were doing," Bob answered.

Taking a deep breath, I decided to be honest with them. "This is all new to me. Nana only came to me last week. You're my first, um, ghosts to appear other than her and one of her friends."

Bob appeared to be thinking this over. This news was apparently not satisfactory to Elaine. "Great! On top of everything else, we get a beginner!"

I was starting to dislike Elaine. *Not my fault they showed up. It's not like I invited them!*

"Do you have any idea how this works?" Bob eventually asked, avoiding Elaine's eyes.

Shaking my head, I answered shortly, "Nope. Don't even know the first thing about police work. Nada, zilch."

Elaine made a nasty noise I pretended not to hear. I kept my eyes on Bob since he seemed to be more sensible about the situation we all faced.

"Well," he started slowly, "why don't we give you all the information we have, and you can take it from there?"

Agreeing with the wisdom of his idea, I asked, "Do you have any idea who did this to you?" Subtle, I was not.

"Of course we know!" snapped Elaine.

She was truly getting on my nerves. I continued to ignore her as I asked Bob, "Okay, who?"

Bob opened his mouth to answer, but Elaine beat him to the punch. "Alexander Hayes!"

"Hayes?" I asked, stunned. "As in son of Bennet Hayes, the mayor?" If I had knots in my stomach before, now you could moor a ship with the knots that had formed.

"Now, Elaine, we don't know that for a fact," he said soothingly to her. Looking back at me, he said, "But he was in the house the night it happened."

"I'm telling you, he was the last thing I saw before …" She couldn't finish her statement. She looked out the window to collect her emotions.

I sat there, sweating slightly, hoping this mess would go away. I mentally swore at Nana, hoping she could hear me wherever she was right now.

Bob stirred uncomfortably. "Listen, I'm real sorry, but we were sent to you for help."

I waved his apology away. What good was it anyway? Elaine started to comment, but I threw her a look that she correctly interpreted as a warning not to open her mouth.

I was totally out of my element, and I knew it. What was Nana thinking? Frantically trying to come up with a decent idea, I shrugged as I looked at Bob. "I promise I'll do my best. Give me a few days to think it over. Maybe Nana will visit and give me some type of direction."

Bob's face cleared instantly. "That's a great idea! So, what, we come back in a few days, and you will have it solved?"

"Ha!" Elaine said. "You can't figure out time from our perspective, so how do we know when to return? I'm not leaving until this is concluded!" She sat down at the kitchen table determinedly. Great.

"Oh no you don't!" I said. "Leave me alone to work. How about I yell your names or something? Would that work?"

Bob thought this over for a minute. "It might. Wouldn't hurt to give it a try." He looked hopefully at Elaine.

She sat there, shaking her head. "Nope. Not leaving. It took all these years to contact someone, and we get an amateur. I'm not moving from this spot."

I glanced toward the bedroom door. Where was Andy? Had he drowned in the shower?

"Fine, but I don't want to see you. Make yourselves invisible!"

"Uh, we don't know how to do that," Bob said, embarrassed.

"Then you have to leave. Shoo!"

Suddenly, I found myself alone. Wow. It had worked! So I'd learned a tidbit that would come in handy. If I told ghosts to leave, they had to leave. One thing working in my favor!

17

As I sat down, contemplating if it was too early for a margarita, Andy asked from behind, "Sweetie, you alone?"

"You knew ghosts were here? And you let me deal with them by myself?" I asked furiously.

"I couldn't *see or hear anyone*, but I heard you talking to people. I thought it best to let you handle it since Nana made it your job," he answered logically.

Men were a pain, and engineers were the worst. Sadly, my husband *was* an engineer. I shook my head, reminding myself that his engineering logic didn't always match my emotional needs.

"Who were they?" he asked after a moment.

I was so furious I had a hard time satisfying his curiosity. Staying silent allowed him time to figure out that I didn't find his antics amusing. I glanced out the window to ensure he got the message.

Watching my face, he said, "Okay, I'm sorry. But I saw no reason to interfere with the process." He looked so hopeful that my anger would vanish that I had to laugh out loud.

"Jerk."

"Yeah, I know." He grinned.

I filled him in on the situation and waited for him to digest the information. After a few minutes of silence, I asked, "So what do you think I should do next?"

Now it was his turn to gaze out the window. When he finally brought those blue eyes back to mine, he asked, "Did Nana appear with a manual of some sort?"

"Ha! No such luck. She sent a couple to me but gave no indication of what steps I was to take to be of any help." I felt useless and very put upon in this deal.

"Well," he said, "you could always go talk to Jack. You know him pretty well, don't you?"

Ah, Jack. I hadn't thought of him. Jack Monroe was our township's police chief. We had all been in PTA together while the boys were growing up and had gotten to know each other through the years. Well, I knew his wife better than I knew him, but at least there was a history I could count on with him.

"That's not a bad idea at all. Wish I had thought of it." I smiled at Andy. My spirits rose a bit at the thought I could dump this problem in someone else's lap. I was in for a surprise.

Chapter 3

Sitting in Jack Monroe's office, waiting for him to get out of a meeting, I had a chance to look around the room. I spotted the graduation pictures of his three children, two girls and a boy. His son and Adam had graduated the same year. I remembered the gratitude I'd felt when he and his wife, Lori, along with Andy and me, had been chaperones for the senior prom the year our boys had graduated. Having the police chief on duty at the prom and after-prom party had kept most of the seniors under control. We'd happily piled them on the buses the next morning for their day up in Sandusky at Cedar Point, an amusement park on the shores of Lake Erie. Not being a roller coaster fan myself, I had been glad I didn't have to attend that piece of prom weekend. Never could figure out the attraction of rides whose main goal was to make you puke. Andy and I had gone home and collapsed.

I hoped Jack's and my thirty-year friendship would count when I filled him in on what this meeting entailed. Let's face it: telling someone you've started seeing ghosts will more than likely send them to the phone book to look up a good psychiatrist for you. Surely he knew me well enough to give me the benefit of the doubt. Maybe.

I looked up as Jack walked into the office, only to see a frown on his otherwise good-natured face. Not having seen him for a few years, I was surprised at the graying hair and expanded waistline. Jack was a big man, a little shorter than Andy but not by much. He had always had a hefty build, like a linebacker on a pro football team. Beefy but fit. Age was catching up with him if those love handles told the story. Concerned at his expression, I asked, "Hey, bad meeting?"

Startled to see me, he grinned. "I hate those damn things. Township politics can be brutal. Who let you in my office?"

I smiled. "Big fish in a little pond?"

Township politics were tricky; you were neighbors with other board members, and heated arguments in the building could lead to nasty arguments out of the building.

He laughed. "Yeah, you know how it is around here. Seriously though, no one should be in my office, even you."

"Owen told me I could wait for you in here."

Officer Owen Wells had graduated with my son Brian, in 1995, so he most likely had put me in the boss's office as a courtesy. "I've only been here a few minutes; didn't sneak peeks at any of those papers piled on your desk, if you're worried."

"Peg, I trust you, but the council is antsy about allowing people to mill around the station."

"What are you talking about?" I asked, surprised. "I don't remember the police station being some sort of hangout for the population."

Shaking his head, he answered, "Never happened in my time here, but I guess Owen's sister was waiting alone in the hall one day. Talk about a stink!"

He pointed to the coffeemaker, raising his eyebrows at her. I waved off his offer of coffee and said, "Don't let them get to you."

Nodding, he asked, "What brings you down here?"

I watched fascinated as he prepared his coffee. Six sugars, three creamers, and two stir sticks. Wow. "You need to slow down on that sugar, Jack. It'll catch up with you," I kindly informed him.

He glanced down, surprised at his pile of empty sugar packs. "Damn it!"

He stomped out to the hall and dumped his coffee down the watercooler drain. "I wasn't even paying attention, just so irritated about the meeting. Sorry about that," he said sheepishly when he returned. Standing in front of the coffeepot, he turned to me. "Sure you don't want any?"

I smiled uneasily. "Nope. Not this time." The last thing I needed was caffeine; my nerves were shot, and coffee would send me over the moon.

He started his coffee process over, adding only one sugar and creamer. Much better.

Getting comfortable at his desk now that his coffee dilemma was situated, he asked, "What can I do for you today?"

I squirmed in my chair, not sure how to start.

He raised an eyebrow before saying, "Peg, it can't be the boys; they are grown and out of the house. Surely, it isn't Andy?"

Shaking my head, I finally gathered enough courage and blurted, "I see dead people!"

You could have heard a pin drop. Then we both burst into laughter. "Good movie," he said with a grin, referring to the Bruce Willis movie *The Sixth Sense*. "Now tell me what's going on."

The sudden laughter had helped calm me down. "This is a recent event, never happened before. Doesn't seem to be going away, though," I sighed. He looked confused, and I didn't blame him. I was confused.

"Start at the beginning, and bring me up to date," he said patiently.

As I told him about Nana appearing a couple of times, plus the Bradleys, his face became unreadable. Must have been his cop face. Part of my mind was fascinated. I had never seen him perform official duties before, but his blank look was probably why he was the chief of police. Talk about a poker face! My chair became increasingly uncomfortable the longer I talked. His expression suddenly changed, and I could see sympathy in his eyes. Uh-oh.

"Jack! I'm not kidding!"

"Peg, I live with a woman going through the change. It isn't easy, and you are probably experiencing some type of side effect from it," he said. His face became a bit red from the embarrassment of discussing hormones, but my face was thunder.

"Jack Monroe! If I thought for one second this was all in my mind, do you honestly believe I would humiliate myself by coming down to the station?" If looks could kill, my friend would have dropped stone dead in front of me.

Throwing his hands up in front of him, he sighed. "Okay, okay. Settle down. But you have to admit this is a little weird."

"Weird? I almost peed my pants the first night Nana dropped by for a social visit!" I retorted angrily.

He continued to study my face. What he saw must have convinced him I was being honest. Running a hand through his thick, graying hair, Jack gathered his thoughts.

"Let's just assume for a moment that what you're saying actually happened." He put a hand up to quiet my reaction. "Give me a second here." He cleared his throat before continuing, "What exactly do the Bradleys expect you to do? Or me for that matter?"

"Good question. Nana told them I could help them. They seem to want their murderer to pay for his crimes."

"Did they at least give you a hint as to who killed them?" he asked.

Oh boy. I didn't want to get into that arena yet. He noticed my hesitancy and read it correctly.

"I'm not going to like this at all, am I?" he asked, resigned to the situation.

"Nope. It was Elaine who threw out the name, and she's a pain in the ass. But it could be a beginning," I said.

One of his eyebrows rose, but he didn't say a word and waited me out. Fidgeting in the chair, I was stalling, and we both knew it. His patience won, and I said, "Alexander Hayes."

Jack closed his eyes, and they stayed closed for more than a minute. Finally, one eye opened, and he asked, "You sure? You didn't misunderstand them? They are ghosts, right? Maybe you couldn't hear them well through the mist."

"Mist? What mist?" I asked, confused. "You watch too much TV."

"No mist?"

"Not a drop. The other strange bit: they appear as solid as you or me. That was a shocker, let me tell you." I shuddered at the memory.

He looked skeptical. "All those famous mediums don't see ghosts. They hear voices in their heads, or something along those lines. Why do you see them?"

"If I came in here and told you I heard voices in my head, would your reaction have been better?" I asked hotly.

He conceded the fact and said, "Yeah, that would have been easier to ignore." He studied me a minute before continuing, "Peg, if anyone but you were seated in my office chair right now, I'd have already thrown them out of here. We've known each other a long time. Gone to dinner as couples and raised our kids together. I've never known you to exaggerate a story. But you have to allow me the courtesy to be cautious here, especially with the township council crawling all over me right now."

I breathed a sigh of relief. He believed me. "I would appreciate it if we could keep it between ourselves for now."

He looked relieved also. "I was hoping you'd say something along those lines. I can dig around quietly and see what pops. Sounds like a plan for the time being."

I nodded. "Pretty much what I had in mind."

"Who else knows about your new abilities?" he asked.

"Andy is the only person I trusted," I answered.

Some of the strain left his face. "Good, let's keep it that way. Now tell me everything again from the beginning," he said, reaching for his notepad.

Glad to hand the problem over to him, I repeated the entire episode, which took about five minutes.

"How are you getting into contact with them again?" he asked once he was finished with his notes.

Shrugging, I said, "God only knows. I told them to get out, and they did. I figure I'll call their names and see what happens." I thought a moment and added, "Did I mention Elaine is a pain in the ass?"

Grinning, he said, "Only about a dozen times. I don't remember much of the incident, but all the neighbors interviewed were sorry to hear about Bob's murder. Elaine? They figured she had it coming."

"So we don't improve on the other side?" I asked, disappointed.

"Guess not. This doesn't sound anything like what we learned in Sunday school, does it?" he said sarcastically.

I sat watching him sip his coffee, lost in thought. He hadn't changed much through the years, just the usual—little more gray, little more width, and a lot more life experience. "So what do we do now?" I asked.

He looked startled at the question. "Do? How the hell do I know? This is your rodeo," he said, shaking his head. "I've been a cop my entire adult life, never heard of this type of situation before. Well, maybe on TV, but those shows don't count."

"Think I should head over to the library and do a little digging through old newspapers, you know, to refresh my memory of their story?" I asked in a moment of inspiration.

He looked at me for what seemed an eternity. "Peg, I honestly don't see how that will help," he said finally.

My shoulders slumped. Should I ignore the ghosts and risk Nana showing up again to scold me for not taking her seriously? Sighing, I looked out the window; I was doing a lot of that lately.

Seeing my expression, Jack relented. "Okay, I'll pull the files. They were murdered here in the township, so the files will still be in the basement. I don't think that part of the basement was damaged by the flood a few years back."

Crap, the flood. I had forgotten about that blasted thing. A few years ago we'd had biblical-proportioned rains in July, causing massive flooding. Thank God Andy and I lived on a hill; we didn't have any problems as long as we *stayed* on the hill. Our entire little village, Ghent, had flooded to the point that every basement along Wye Road, including a high-priced restaurant, had been knee-deep in water. They had been replacing the bridge over Yellow Creek at the time, and the machinery the county had left close to the edge of the work area had come close to falling in, which would have eventually landed in the Cuyahoga River downstream. It had been a mess, but I hadn't realized the police station had suffered any damage. So much for paying attention to events in the township.

"I can't believe we had a murder here; I've never considered Bath a hot spot for crime," I said. "I know there are drugs here, but murder is a big-city crime."

Jack laughed. "People are people wherever you live. Greed, jealousy, and hatred exist as long as people are in the picture."

I nodded sadly. Home was my safe haven, and it was hard to imagine such ugliness in our small township.

He suddenly became serious. "Peg, we had Jeffrey Dahmer. Along with being a media nuthouse, it was serious as hell."

"He grew up here, but those murders were done elsewhere," I shot back at him.

Shaking his head, Jack said, "Not the first one. We worked with the FBI on that case." He cringed at the memories. "We never found an intact body, but we did find bits and pieces. Had to run DNA to confirm, but turned out it was human. Steven Hicks." Turning to stare at the pictures of his kids, he continued quietly, "It took all of us here a while to clear the images of the scene from our minds."

Remembering the huge media mess those murders had caused for the township, I shuddered. *Silence of the Lambs* had recently been released in theaters; the story line in the movie had been too close to home for comfort. That scenario had been the talk of every PTA meeting for months. Gruesome.

I threw my hands up in resignation. "Fine, but it was years ago."

He shook his head at me again. "We also had those murders back in the '70s. Some love triangle if I remember correctly. I was away at college in Columbus and recall being disappointed I wasn't here for the excitement," he told me ruefully. "Bath Township isn't insulated from the world."

I looked out the window again to avoid his gaze, keeping him in my peripheral vision. He sighed, shaking his head at my stubborn refusal to believe our hometown was full of crime. I didn't consider myself a denier necessarily, but I didn't like the underbelly side of life. That was probably why the idea of "cleaning up" my piece of the world didn't sit well with me.

As I was staring out the window, I saw figures standing by the parking lot of the station. Leaning forward in the chair, I recognized the couple. For Pete's sake.

"Crap," I said aloud.

Jack followed my line of sight. "What's wrong?" he asked.

"You don't see them?" I asked, irritated. "I didn't think they'd show up unless I called for them."

"Who?"

"The Bradleys. Damn it."

"Wow, they're out there?" he asked, suddenly excited. Quickly getting up from his well-padded office chair, he made it to the window in one second flat. "Where?" He scanned the view, clearly full of anticipation.

"Right there by that red car," I said.

"I don't see anything," he said, disappointed.

"Not surprised," I told him wryly. "*I* see dead people, remember?"

"Well, I was hoping I could get a glimpse at least," he said. "Ya know, maybe see some mist or something."

"I told you there was no mist!" I snapped.

I looked back at the couple. Bob was waving enthusiastically; Elaine had her arms crossed, and her face was sour as a lemon.

"They still there?" he asked.

"Yep. Bob is waving like mad, and Elaine's expression is her normal nastiness," I answered.

"That's it? Waving and being a pain? Doesn't sound like much of a visitation," he said.

"What exactly did you expect?" I frowned at him.

Jack shrugged. "Not sure, but more than this."

"Go away," I mouthed to the couple. Bob kept waving frantically. Jeez.

"Hang on a minute," I told Jack, getting up from the chair. "I'll be right back."

Stomping outside, I wondered what they could want. "Well?" I asked Bob when I got closer.

"Hey! We thought we'd drop by and see how you're doing." He had a huge smile on his face.

"I thought I told you two to go away. I will call you when I know something," I told him.

"See? Didn't think she would do much," Elaine snarled. God, she was such a misery.

"I'm at the police station, or didn't you notice?" I asked, hoping she caught my sarcasm.

Bob looked at Elaine smugly. "See, I told you she'd be working on our case." He turned his attention back to me. "We figured out how to come back when we want, so we don't have to worry about the whole time frame problem. Did you notice we didn't interrupt your conversation with that man? We were careful!" The pride in his voice could almost make me like him. Almost.

Nodding, I said, "Yep. Figured that one out, did you? What's the story with that?"

25

Cocking his head to one side, he replied, "It's not as hard as I thought. We merely have to watch events, you know, like a newspaper or something. Gotta be on your toes, though."

"God," Elaine muttered, rolling her mean little eyes, "what a moron."

Okay. It was official. I hated her. It wasn't like *she* had figured it out years ago; Bob was the one who had finally caught on to the process. What had she been doing all these years? Making his life hell, I bet.

Ignoring Elaine, I turned to Bob. "I've got my friend, the police chief, looking into this for you."

Bob's grin got even bigger. "Wow. You're friends with the chief of police! That's awesome. He can help."

"Not to burst your bubble, but we have to be careful." Forcing myself to look at Elaine, I said, "Hayes is a big power name. You can't just throw the name out there. We need to tread carefully."

"I don't see why! The little creep murdered us!" she snapped.

I remembered the stories through the years about the Hayes boy. Trouble seemed to follow him wherever he went. Until now, I had never heard anything as serious as murder attached to his name, but I reminded myself I really didn't know much about the kid.

"Maybe. Just because his is the last face *you* saw doesn't mean he killed you himself. Also," I added with a touch of my own sneer, "we can't take that to court. Just imagine my telling the jury a dead woman gave me the information." Shaking my head at her, I said, "It won't fly. So we need to carefully and quietly do our research."

She didn't say anything, for which I was grateful. Looking back at Bob, I said, "Hayes Sr. is now the mayor of Akron. Surely, you can see the PR problems this could cause."

He was listening attentively and nodded. "Yeah, politics being involved could complicate the situation. I get that." He quietly thought for a moment. "When'd this guy become mayor?"

I had to think for a minute. Bath wasn't part of Akron, and we didn't vote concerning the city's elections, so I was unsure how to answer.

"Around the time you were murdered," I finally said. "I've never really paid much attention to Akron's elections."

"He's crooked," Elaine said.

I cocked an eyebrow at her. "Really? How do you know that?"

She stared at me a moment and looked away. I figured she had decided for some reason silence was her friend, which worked for me.

The newest cold front was making itself known. The wind was picking up, and I had been so focused on the Bradleys' arrival that I'd left my jacket in Jack's office. "Go away and let me work on this without interfering. Okay?"

"You sure? We could help maybe," Bob said.

Emphatically shaking my head, I said, "No way. Let me figure this out; if I need you, I'll call you somehow."

Disappointment covered his otherwise cheerful face as he nodded and looked at Elaine. "Ready to go?"

She didn't answer, but they both began fading. Thank God.

I turned and stomped back into Jack's office. He had been standing at the window watching the entire conference. "You know how weird that looked? You talking to no one but yourself, obviously irritated out there!" He started laughing. "It was great! I couldn't hear what you were saying, but body language said it all!"

I glared at him. It had never dawned on me how it would look to anyone watching. People were going to think I'd lost my mind.

"I told them not to come back until I called on them."

Still laughing, he asked, "Really think that will work?"

I thought a second before answering, "Nope. Elaine will goad Bob into appearing, not that she will have to push too hard. He's ridiculously excited about talking to me. It's pathetic."

Wiping tears out of his eyes from his laughter, Jack said, "Well, next time try to find a safer place to carry on a conversation with them. At least you could sit in your car! It could be embarrassing for you in the long run."

"Long run! Hell, the short run isn't doing me any good either!"

He laughed. "You've told Andy the whole story?" "Yep. He thinks it's cool, but then it isn't his butt dealing with Bob and Elaine!"

"How about the kids?" he asked mischievously.

I moaned. "Nope. None of their damn business."

Jack threw back his head, roaring with laughter. Personally, I didn't see anything funny about my present predicament. Not having any worthwhile comment to toss at him, I merely glared. Hoping to steer his attention away from telling the kids, I asked, "What can we do about these murders?"

Wiping his eyes for the second time, he grinned. "Peg, I'll do what I can, but don't get your hopes up. This could be dicey, and I'm not sacrificing my job for it. Let's see how it plays out."

I nodded, knowing it was a fool's errand. *Nana, what were you thinking?*

Chapter 4

The next morning, my left leg jiggling with nerves, I sat in the county library in the middle of downtown Akron, reading newspapers from 1998. The database was available online; too bad I hadn't called ahead first. If I had known this could be accomplished at home on my own damn computer, I would have stayed put this morning. But since I was there, I made the executive decision to hog their computer instead. It was boring as hell, but guilt wouldn't let me walk away from the case. Guilt and the fact I wanted to get rid of Bob and Elaine quickly—well, at least Elaine.

I had forgotten most of what made up the news from that year, which was a lesson: what seems important today probably won't be in ten or twelve years. Good to know. An article discussing the possibility of adding a third lane to I-71 headed toward Columbus was interesting considering they still hadn't done much to make the two-hour drive any easier. Reading the story reminded me there had also been talk of a train between Cleveland and Columbus, with one stop in the Akron area. Needless to say, that had never happened either.

After scanning a few days' worth of newspaper articles, I was trying not to get distracted. I was pleasantly surprised to finally see Bob and Elaine's story. It must have been a few days after the murder judging from the lack of detail. I searched for an earlier issue for a complete account of the story. Finding the article a week earlier, I was relieved that it was fully two columns. I hoped there would be tons of possible suspects mentioned.

There was a good deal of information about Bob and Elaine. He had owned a successful Porsche car dealership off Market Street near downtown

Akron. He sold to the bigwigs of the area at a time when we still *had* bigwigs. Most of the tire industry had been facing hard times, but some businesses had still been cashing in on the economic bubble that later burst. His sales volume had allowed him to buy a massive house off Revere Road, not too far from the high school. I was convinced that Bob would have been happy living in a nice, friendly neighborhood, but Elaine had wanted to live in Bath for reasons unknown. Bath had its fair share of upscale homes, but many families had been around here since the 1800s. The township had a certain reputation concerning wealthy homes scattered throughout the community, but there were surrounding townships that could also claim the same flavor to their own small slice of the area.

Research had never been my strong suit, but I felt I owed it to Nana to do my best. I finally found another article pertaining to the murders, but it had no real information other than Bob's background and Elaine's charity work. That certainly wasn't going to do me much good in finding their killer. I had decided I couldn't take Elaine's word concerning Alexander Hayes. Let's face it: when you're being murdered, can you truly identify the guy trying to kill you? Maybe, maybe not. I would probably have my eyes shut as tight as a drum hoping the guy would disappear.

I suddenly felt a chill and looked up, surprised to find Bob sitting with me. Narrowing my eyes, I hissed, "Don't do that!"

"Do what?" he asked, innocent as a lamb.

"Sneak up on me!"

"I'm still getting used to all of this," he said sheepishly. "Had no idea I was sneaking." Looking around our surroundings, he asked, "What is this place? Looks like a library."

Rolling my eyes heavenward, I said, "It is the library, you idiot."

His face came back to look at me. "Gosh, you don't have to be so mean." Glancing around the room again, he looked confused. "This doesn't look familiar at all. I mean, when did they redo the Fairlawn branch?"

"We are downtown!" Seeing his sad expression, I relented. "Okay, this is the main library downtown. But now that you mention it, they recently replaced the Fairlawn branch a few years ago. Tore the entire building down and started from scratch."

"Wow," he said, surprised. Shaking his head, he continued, "I sorta liked that old building. The second floor was the best part."

Sighing, I replied, "Yeah, well, it's one story now."

"A mistake, in my opinion," he said sadly.

"You aren't alone there," I said, agreeing with his analysis. "The new building has a cold feel to it. Large windows everywhere—no snuggly places to sit and read."

Nodding, he said, "See, told you the second floor in the old building was great."

I glanced around, expecting to see Elaine floating close by. "What did you do with your wife?"

Grinning, he answered happily, "I figured out how to see you without her tagging along! Great, isn't it!"

Great? Was he kidding? A knot formed in my stomach. If he could appear without her, what kept her from doing the same? This was getting increasingly complicated, and I didn't like complicated.

"What are you doing here?" he asked, leaning forward to see what I had been reading. "Working on our case?"

I looked at him a moment before answering, "Bob, you need to leave, so I can work. I'm trying to do a little research, and you are distracting me. I'll never solve the murder if you and Elaine keep interrupting me."

Rubbing his hands together in anticipation, he said excitedly, "What'd you find out? Anything helpful?"

Sighing, I asked, "How'd you know where to find me?"

"Oh, this is the really fantastic part! I think of you, and wham! I'm here!" he announced gleefully.

Was he out of his mind? Awkward as it was at the moment, this could really become a serious issue. Worrying constantly, wondering when these two would pop in for a visit, was not my idea of fun.

"You need to quit it; don't think about me at all. I told you I would call you somehow," I said between gritted teeth.

Noticing my anger, he pouted, "Just wanted to help."

"Showing up and startling me is not helping; it distracts me." Glancing at my watch, I said, "I've wasted time dealing with you that I could have been researching. Now get out of here!"

His face filled with sadness as he slowly disappeared. "Thank God he's gone," I muttered to myself. I glanced around quickly, suddenly realizing I had yet again stupidly argued with myself as far as anyone watching was concerned. I grew dismayed when I spotted a middle-aged man in the corner, well dressed in a suit and tie, a briefcase on the floor next to him. His expression alerted me to the fact he had been aware of my conversation. Oh well, too late now. Realizing I had noticed him, he returned to the books on the table in front of him. I needed to learn to at least take a quick scan of the area when either of those two idiots showed up, literally out of thin air.

Deciding it was time to get back to work, I swiveled back to the computer screen. And there it was—the complete article describing Bob's and Elaine's murders. How had I not seen this earlier? This one had all the details omitted from my previous finds. Scanning quickly through the background information about both of them, I finally reached the actual police analysis of the crime. Apparently, the murders were estimated to have occurred at around two in the morning on a Thursday. It had been steadily raining for a week prior, but there had been no evidence of footprints anywhere outside the house. My favorite TV shows tended to be mysteries, so even I knew there should have been prints somewhere with all the soggy ground. April was a funny month, though, here in northeastern Ohio. I wondered if I should check somewhere to find out if we'd had freezing temperatures at night that week. If the daytime rain had been freezing at night, that might explain the lack of footprints. Kinda hard to find prints in ice. Taking notes in the spiral notebook I had thankfully remembered to bring with me, I felt a sense of satisfaction. Maybe I could decipher this mess with enough digging. I finished the article, making a few notes as I read, knowing I would forget little details.

When I got to the end of the article, I was surprised there were no suspects mentioned. Hayes had been mayor a long time, and I was pretty sure 1998 was about the beginning of his reign as czar of Akron. My stomach started knotting again as I wondered if the old fart knew his family had been involved and was keeping a lid on the situation to save his political butt. I sat there for a few more minutes thinking through the information I had read. It wasn't much; I would need far more to get to the bottom of this case. I hoped Jack had been able to find something noteworthy for me. How was I going to make headway with this crap if professionals hadn't been able to solve it years ago? Sighing, I knew I would have to call on Bob and Elaine for firsthand knowledge. My trust of Elaine's version of the incident wasn't strong; hell, it didn't exist at all. She had been hanging on to her perceptions for over a decade, so I was pretty sure she wasn't going to back down anytime soon. Bob, however, might have data he didn't even realize his brain had registered. That could be wishful thinking on my part, but with no other easy leads, I was going to give it a try—at home. No more conversations with dead people in public; just the thought of people thinking I was nuts made me sweat.

I switched the computer off and gathered my notes. Stretching, I felt another chill but didn't want to turn around. Hadn't I told Bob to leave me the hell alone? I stood there, frozen like a popsicle, willing whoever was behind me to leave. No such luck; the hairs on my neck were standing at attention. Slowly turning to face whatever, I saw the spirit that had been with Nana that first night. Taken by surprise, I opened my mouth to talk, but the spirit shook her head and looked around the room. Finally! Someone from the other side who understood how awkward it looked for me to have a conversation with no one around others could actually see! I sighed with relief. The spirit beckoned me to follow her, and after a few steps I realized she was taking me to the garage where I had parked. Yeah! We would talk in my car with no witnesses. I relaxed and followed contentedly, thinking this one might have my best interests at heart instead of the mission to clean the world.

When I had parked my butt in the car and locked the door, I turned to the passenger seat, where the spirit was patiently waiting for me to get comfortable.

"Now we have some privacy, and you don't need to worry about what others are thinking," she said kindly.

I drew a deep breath of relief and smiled. "You are the first one to consider me in this mess," I said.

Nodding in agreement, she said, "I've been around for a lot longer than your nana. Bob and Elaine are relative newcomers, so they are quite wrapped up in their own problems. Once you've been on the other side for a century or so, you stop being so attached to the physical world and start paying attention to the people you are helping. It takes longer for some than others." She smiled.

"So how does this all work?" I asked. "I'm out of my league with this case and have no idea what I'm supposed to be accomplishing."

Her kind expression brought tears to my eyes. My frustration had built over the past few days; her understanding kindness was almost too much to bear.

"You are actually off to a good start, better than most. You became proactive and dove right into the problem. We rarely see that happen; usually a person takes months to accept the truth of us, then months more to act upon it. You are doing quite well." She smiled again.

I took a deep breath to calm myself and think. My small amount of experience had taught me some of these ghosts didn't hang around as long as you would like, though the irritating ones never left unless I made them.

I became acutely aware of the smell of my leather seats for some reason. I looked over at the spirit; with a nod, she indicated the surrounding air. Somehow, at some point it had turned gold. What the hell? Eyes narrowing, I asked, "Are you a spirit or an alien?"

She playfully threw her head back and laughed. Her gaze coming back to meet mine, she said, "I haven't had a good laugh in centuries! Thank you for that."

I continued to study her; she hadn't answered the question, now had she? Let's face it: all those episodes of *Ancient Aliens* Andy had made me watch with him might actually pay off.

"Please answer the question," I said.

With a gleam in her eye, she said smiling, "I lived on earth for seventy-two years a long time ago."

I thought about that for a moment, not good enough. On the last episode of Andy's favorite show, the theorists had guessed that aliens had been living among us for centuries, hiding themselves in our societies. So that declaration of hers was not an answer. Now the big question was, did I really want to know? Nope. Spirits were enough to deal with; no sense complicating the issue even more. I merely shook my head to let her know that while I didn't necessarily believe her, I didn't really want that piece of our conversation to continue. I had bigger fish to fry.

I looked her square in the eye and asked, "How do I make Bob and Elaine leave me alone?"

She said with a smile, "You have no power over *when* they appear, but you have already realized how you can make them *disappear*. Isn't that enough?"

Shaking my head angrily, I answered, "No! They pop up all over the place and at the most inconvenient moments. I have entire conversations with them in front of people who probably think I'm nuts!"

"You will learn to move to a private area before beginning to speak. These situations are new for you and take time for you to reach a level of comfort. Give yourself credit for what you have accomplished so far."

A level of comfort? Was she out of her mind? If my eyes narrowed any more, I wouldn't be able to see at all. "Isn't there some magic word to keep these two nuts under control?"

"To my knowledge, their contact with you is the first they've made since they have arrived on our side." She paused before continuing, "Murder victims usually have the most difficult adjustment. They aren't ready for actual work for many years."

Work? Heaven expects those two to do actual work up there? I thought. *Good luck with that one.*

"Shouldn't *you* know who murdered them? Why don't you tell me, and we can wrap this job up nice and easy," I said. I snapped my fingers as a new thought entered my tired brain. "Actually, why don't *any* of you people from the other side know this stuff? Can't you see what's happening down here?"

Smiling, she shook her head as you would when dealing with a three-year-old. "Peg, that's not how it's done. You must accept we have rules and must follow them precisely. But to relieve your mind about your nana, none of have the answers. We have limited access to earthly matters; it is better that way."

Trying to appear smarter than I was, I nodded as though I understood. What was really going through my mind ran more along the lines of *Give me a break!* This spirit must have been a mind reader, because she burst out laughing again. "You are quite fun to work with, and I appreciate your present situation. However, you are the one who needs to solve this—the quicker, the better. Bob and Elaine must move to the next level; concluding this episode in their lives will help their process."

"Level?" I asked. There were levels in heaven? For Pete's sake. This piece of information was not making me feel all warm and fuzzy. "How many levels are there?"

"Seven," she answered with surprising frankness. I had anticipated more fudging with specific information.

"Good to know," I said with a touch of sarcasm. "Too bad we didn't learn these facts in Sunday school."

"You probably did, but most humans don't pay attention to details," she said, smiling. Her smile was beginning to get on my nerves.

"Really?" I sniped.

Still smiling, she nodded, amused. Glad I was able to offer cheap entertainment.

"I must leave you for now, but I will be back to help where I am able," she continued, her glowing smile on full blast.

Before I could come up with a snappy retort, she faded away, leaving me alone in my car. I continued to sit, drumming my fingers on the steering wheel, wondering what to do next. The little information I had been able to find in the old newspaper article wasn't going to get me far, and I had a hard time believing the police department was going to open their files for me. Realizing my bladder was in total revolt due to my ignoring the obvious, I started my car and headed for the parking garage exit. Home, especially the bathroom, sounded heavenly.

Chapter 5

A few days later I found myself again staring out the back window facing the woods. This was becoming a habit, and I wasn't sure it was a good sign. Neither Bob nor Elaine had shown up the last couple of days, for which I was extremely grateful. While Bob was not as obnoxious as Elaine, neither one of them was welcome company. My spirit guide hadn't much help either; she hadn't really given me tons of information other than the fact she had been around heaven for hundreds of years. What had she been doing all that time? Floating around in the ether amassing time for some sort of point system? Okay, I realized my snottiness was increasing as the days flew by, but let's face it: I wasn't thrilled with my new lifestyle.

I had done research downtown and had searched more on the Internet at home, digging through everything I could think of for new information concerning Bob's and Elaine's murders, but zip, nada, nothing. I dreaded calling Jack at the police station; there was only so much you could ask of a friend and remain friends. I wasn't sure how far I could push him to hunt down facts, especially considering his concern that any of this could become public knowledge. He recognized political suicide when he saw it.

I swallowed the last sip of my coffee and sat looking down at the now-empty cup. I missed those dredges of leftover coffee grounds from my old coffeepot. I had bought one of those newfangled brewers that made one cup at a time. The coffee was great, but those last few thick, sloppy coffee grounds were a thing of the past. They tasted like crap, but for some stupid reason, I missed them. Go figure.

Suddenly, I felt the hairs stand up on the back of my neck. Bob. I turned around angrily to face him.

Holding his hands up in front of him, he quickly said, "Don't get mad. I'm only here to check in with you. My wife is in a snit, and I promised to come by and ask you how it was going. That's all."

"Bob, we have had this discussion before," I said.

"Give me some credit: I was careful to show up while you were at home," he said before I could continue.

That made me stop in my tracks. He was right, and I hated to admit it, but I was intrigued.

"True, I'll give you that. How did you know I was home?"

His smile was wide as he answered, "I decided to do some snooping of my own! If you think of the person you want to see, you pop up in their world at that moment. Right?"

I nodded since he had already given me this information before. "So how did you pick when I was here at the house?"

"That's the really cool part," he said excitedly, rubbing his hands together. "I have to visualize *where* I want to visit them, and that helps me control when I show up to talk with you! Isn't that great?"

"Hmm. How'd you figure that out?" I asked, hating myself for being so intrigued.

"This is where the snooping comes in. I watched how other spirits were doing it and realized they were controlling the *where* part. I didn't want to ask them, because I was embarrassed to admit, after all our time dead, I hadn't figured it out for myself."

I swear he was blushing.

"Which brings up another point I've been meaning to talk to you about," I said. "What exactly have you and Elaine been doing all these years? The way I see it, if she was so mad at being murdered, why haven't you two been busy trying to contact someone here to help?" My real thought was *If only they had done this earlier, I wouldn't be involved with these morons today.*

He looked down at my worn tile floor. His ears turned beet red, which was interesting; I hadn't realized we could be so embarrassed when dead. This was twice in five minutes. Learn something new every damn day.

"Well?" I finally prodded after watching him stare at my floor long enough. Time might mean nothing to him anymore, but I sure wasn't going to allow him to waste mine.

He eventually looked up, his lopsided grin in place. "We've been arguing."

"Arguing? For all these years?" I shouted. "What the hell about?"

He winced, then shrugged. "I told you, Elaine was pretty upset about being murdered."

"So," I said between gritted teeth, "you've been arguing for over a decade about the murder. In all that time you could have actually been haunting someone else to help you solve it." I shook my head, disgusted.

He looked shocked. "Oh, no. Elaine wasn't just angry about being murdered." He continued, looking around the kitchen, "She brought up every annoying thing I'd ever done. Turns out, everything but breathing irritated her. I had no idea." He moved over to the kitchen sink. "You realize this place needs an overhaul?" Seeing my expression, he threw his hands up in surrender. "Just making an observation." He looked at the wallpaper and couldn't help himself from adding, "It's peeling. Did you know that?"

Before I could make my normal snotty remark, I heard a voice scream from my right side, "So this is where you've gotten to! How dare you leave me alone!"

Oh God, Elaine. Too early in the morning. Heaven help me.

Turning to face her, I opened my mouth to demand she leave, but Bob beat me to it. *Miracles do happen,* I thought.

"Elaine, I've had just about enough of your attitude," he said. "I didn't invite you because you don't have any manners whatsoever!"

Apparently, Bob had never spoken back to her. The shocked look on her face was worth a million bucks.

Bob was on a roll and kept going. I had no idea what had gotten into him. "Nothing was ever enough for you! I wanted to sell Fords, but you insisted I own a Porsche dealership. I never even liked Porsches! Ford trucks are fantastic; we could have had a nice life selling Fords. I wanted to live in Wadsworth, but you nagged until we bought a monstrous house in Bath."

Wadsworth was a small community south of Bath and was more along the lines of country living.

Turning to face me, Bob said, "Bath is nice; don't get me wrong. I merely wanted to live in a different type of community. I wanted kids. Not her." He pointed an accusing finger at his dead wife.

I'm not sure what triggered Bob at this point in time, but boy, it was some trigger. If they hadn't already been dead, I honestly believed he would have killed her. Maybe over a decade of listening to her bitch nonstop had finally pushed him over some sort of ledge. Did they have ledges in heaven?

After the shock wore off her face, Elaine's expression turned nasty. I could read revenge all over the place. Poor Bob—his one moment of releasing built-up frustration would cost him for eternity.

Unless he could get away from her. Was that possible over there? This situation was bringing up tons of theological questions I was not about to delve into at this point in my life. If ever.

I decided to defuse the situation in a simple manner. "Get out of here, both of you. Now."

Elaine glared at me as Bob threw me a pleading look. His brain had finally registered the look of rage on Elaine's puckered, bitter face. I had a pang of guilt as they faded slowly. Not a lot of guilt, but some.

I took a deep breath of relief. God, those two were bad enough at any point, but first thing in the morning was more than I could handle.

Glancing at the clock above the stove, I decided I would gather enough nerve to get my butt to the police station and talk to Jack. He hadn't called to inform me if he had been able to find information for me, but I was at a standstill and needed something, anything, to get me on the right track. I'd deal with any political fallout for him later. It was worth the effort. I headed for the shower, convinced talking with him was my only option.

Later, I sat in my car in the back lot of the police station. I could see Jack's office windows and knew he was at his desk. He must have felt me staring at him, because his head came up from the paperwork he was reading and swiveled in my direction. I wiggled my fingers at him in greeting; his shoulders slumped when he recognized me. Not a good sign. Grabbing my purse, I opened the car door and stepped out right in the middle of a puddle. It hadn't rained last night, so where had so much water come from? I looked around the lot and spotted Owen Wells, the newest recruit on the force. He had worked his way through college and, after earning his master's degree, had applied to the department. They were thrilled to have a homegrown boy. He had been on the force less than a year. I smiled, realizing they had him washing the police cruisers—must be some sort of rookie job. He spotted me watching him as he did his chore and waved, a huge grin on his handsome, young face.

"Hey, Mrs. S. What are you doing here?" he asked, turning off the water.

I walked the ten steps over to him. Grinning, I said, "Hi, O. Gotcha washing the cruisers I see. No big-time crime to solve?"

Shaking his head, he answered, "Not a lot of crime here in the township. Mostly teenagers racing down Bath Road. The hills on that road make it a popular spot."

Laughing, I said, "You should know. I seem to remember a couple of boys getting into trouble for doing exactly the same thing not that many years ago."

His face turning red, he answered with another famous Owen grin. The kid's entire face lit up like a Christmas tree when he smiled. It didn't hurt he was the most handsome boy in the township. Their senior year, every girl had wanted to be on his arm for homecoming. He'd solved the problem easily by taking his younger sister; no hurt feelings and made her feel like a million bucks. Another reason he was so loved by the community. Too bad I had a gut feeling he was destined for bigger things than staying in our small township. I'd bet money that his present job was a career-building move and not a permanent decision. Jack would miss him when he left.

"Jack in?" I asked diplomatically. Since I had just spied him in the office, I was well aware he was there. But it was always nice to use manners, something Elaine had obviously never figured out either here or on the other side of life.

Owen glanced over at my parked car sitting smack-dab in front of Jack's office windows. He turned back to me, grinning again. "Yep. He's in there."

He walked me over to the back door to let me in using his swipe key. "You know the way," he said. "Gotta get back to important work." I laughed as he turned to head back to scrubbing the cruisers.

Walking down the hall to Jack's office, I felt my gut knot. I was aware the mayor's name in this mess was a major concern for Jack. Mayor Hayes had accumulated quite a bit of political capital his ten years in office and was one of the most powerful men in the city. He was a real piece of work, but it didn't seem to hurt him. He won each election easily, though no one could figure out why, considering taxes had risen, city services were terrible, and potholes were everywhere but in the downtown area. He had a line of bullshit a mile long; obviously, people still believed him. Even though we didn't live in Akron and he had no jurisdiction over Bath, he could still make life miserable for Jack. The police department in the township partly depended on backup from Akron PD; if Jack pissed off the wrong people, he could kiss that backup good-bye.

I knocked on his open office door and heard him sigh. Wow. He wasn't looking forward to seeing me this morning. Sticking my head through the doorway, I said, "Gotta minute?"

He looked up silently, nodding. Okay, this didn't look promising. I gathered my wits and entered smiling. "How's your day so far?"

"It's been better. Got a phone call earlier asking why we are poking around a ten-year-old case. My ass got chewed out royally," he said.

My eyebrows rose practically to my hairline. "Really? Who called?" I asked.

"Some damn lieutenant downtown. Seems they got wind of this somehow." He shook his head. "*How* is the question."

"I haven't said one word. Went to the library earlier this week, but nothing really popped at me in those articles," I said.

"I did go through our files from the basement. Like I thought, those boxes were tucked away in the area that didn't see any damage." I waited for him to continue. Didn't want to give him a reason to clam up on me.

"Someone had cherry-picked reports to discard. There was definite evidence of tampering." His lips formed a thin line. His steely eyes met mine. "Peg, we have stumbled into an unbelievably huge mess."

I stared up at the ceiling fan and watched the blades turn for a minute before asking, "How old is the mayor's son?"

Jack drew a quick breath. "Shit."

"Yeah, that idea has been swirling around my brain the last couple of days. I wonder if a teenage prank simply got out of control," I said.

"My God," whispered Jack. "The mayor is considering a run for state representative this next election."

My mouth dropped open. This was news to me. "I haven't heard that bit of gossip," I finally said.

Looking out the window, he answered, "Yeah. Just heard it a few weeks ago. I didn't believe it at first. Let's face it: he isn't the cream of the crop. But turns out it's true." He threw me a sneaky look before adding, "The mayor isn't the only one with spies out there."

If my eyebrows rose any further they'd be at the back of my head. "Really? You have spies in Akron?"

"Hell yes!" he exploded. "Can't trust that son of a bitch as far as I can throw him."

I frowned, finally bringing my eyebrows down into their normal territory. "Why the hell do you have to spy on the mayor? We don't have much business with Akron, do we?" I asked.

Shaking his head disgustedly, he said, "More than I like. We have newer subdivisions here that use Akron water. That's a problem for us every time he raises the sewer and water fees. The homeowners call the trustees screaming, but it's not our fault. Most homes out here still have wells in their backyards, but the EPA is clamping down. Mayor Hayes sees the handwriting on the wall and knows eventually many people are going to cave in and run city water to their homes. He is charging a fortune for the service to surrounding areas. Don't get me started on the police situation."

"I know they are backup for us," I said. "Is it a problem?"

"Most of the time, it works like a charm. But piss off the mayor, and the charm's gone. What should be professional courtesy becomes a damn three-ring circus."

I thought about that for a moment. "So somehow he found out we are looking into a situation he thought he had under control and long buried."

"Yep," Jack said.

"What did you say when the lieutenant called?"

"Told him we were cleaning out the basement. When I found the files, I read through them out of curiosity. You know what the sucker said?" he asked, furious.

I shook my head.

"Told me curiosity killed the cat! Can you believe that shit?" Jack's face was beet red. "That was an outright threat!"

It didn't take a genius to recognize we had really stepped in a poop pile. Did Nana realize what a mess she had brought to my door?

"You want to quit? I wouldn't blame you at all. Ruining your career isn't worth Bob's and Elaine's murders being solved," I told him.

"Let me think about it for a couple of days. I don't like being pushed around, but I'll talk with Lori and get back to you."

I nodded, understanding this investigation could be a career buster for a good man. I needed to figure out my own involvement with this situation. Was it worth the trouble? Probably not.

Chapter 6

I woke up late the next morning. Andy must have been unusually quiet for me to sleep through his morning routine. I stared at the ceiling for a few minutes, allowing myself the luxury of consciousness arriving slowly. It was a rare treat, and I enjoyed every second.

Finally deciding my bladder wouldn't hold any longer, I swung my feet onto the floor. There was a slight chill in the air, and the floor was too cold to let my feet linger long. I sprinted to the bathroom and was thankful that it was still warm and damp from Andy's morning shower. After taking care of business, I made the decision to go ahead and get dressed instead of slobbing around in a house robe for my morning coffee. It was already later than normal for me, no sense dragging it out any more.

Once coffee had done its work, I wondered what I should do with my day. Bored with Bob and Elaine's problems, I decided to head for the mall. The truth was, when I was dealing with a problem, my favorite place was the mall. I didn't like to shop, but boy, did I like the cosmetics counter at Dean's department store. The store in our mall usually hired gay guys to man most of their makeup counters. Smart move on their part; gay guys were fabulous when it came to perking up a gal's day with a makeover. I only indulged when my two favorite fellas were working. The women were so busy trying to sell me crap, which I never bought, that I always felt my blood pressure rising. My special guys didn't give a hoot if I bought anything; they merely wanted to ensure I looked good. Worked for me. Then there was the food court. As far as I was concerned, free makeup at the cosmetics counter and the choices at the food court were the main attractions at any mall.

My step lightened as soon as I walked in the store. I heard my name being shouted before I spotted either one of my guys. "Hey, Mrs. S!"

I looked over to their counter. Brian smiled sweetly as he held out his arms for our ritual hug. After squeezing me till I almost peed, he reared back and studied my face.

"Well, you certainly didn't give it much of a try today!" he scolded. "Did you decide that waving makeup in front of your face would get the job done? Sit down right this minute! I can't have you walking around town looking like an old lady."

I winced at the old-lady remark, but I knew he had diagnosed my face correctly. I had barely taken makeup out of the cabinet, much less spent any time using the stuff, this morning. It had been one of those weeks. His remarks didn't anger me; how could they when I knew by the time he finished, I'd look like a million bucks? At least my version of a million bucks. Okay, so maybe only a hundred bucks. But I'd walk out looking better than I had walked in the place.

As Brian got to work removing what little makeup I did have on, Sean came up the aisle. "Holy smokes! What happened to you?" He inspected the gray peeking through my hair color, tut-tutting as he examined my roots. "Time to get these taken care of," he said. I noticed the two of them exchange looks, shaking their heads. God, I must look horrible. Sighing, I let Brian do his magic and enjoyed being pampered.

"Okay, so what's going on with you?" Sean asked as he watched Brian expertly apply a layer of foundation to my face.

I cut my eyes over to him; I knew I couldn't move much while Brian was working his miracles on my face. "Why do you ask?" I mumbled as Brian fought the wrinkles around my mouth. Smile crinkles, I liked to think of them. You gotta deal with the hand you were dealt; a smooth face as I aged was not in the cards for me. Obviously, I hadn't inherited Nana's smooth skin.

Sean studied my face for a moment before replying, "Something is up with you. We can always tell, so you might as well spill the beans."

Brian stood back to ensure the color was even, then added to Sean's remarks, "I knew it the second I saw you. Mrs. S, we can read you like a book; you know we'll get it out of you eventually."

I had been coming to these guys for years, and they knew the ups and downs of most of my life. I didn't mind informing them of my most recently acquired acquaintances. They'd understand. As I began explaining, they pulled up stools from other counters, ignoring glares from the owners of them—ladies from other cosmetic companies.

They stayed quiet for the most part during my entire dialogue. When I finished, I sat back and looked at them. "So, you think I'm nuts?"

Shaking his head, Brian said, "Not you—if someone else tried to tell me this, I would ignore them. But you are a straight shooter. This couple sounds crazy."

Sean was deep in thought. I poked him with my foot, startling him, and asked, "Well? What's your verdict?"

"I actually recognize some of this story. The couple, Bob and Elaine? Yeah, it strikes a cord."

"Really? You are too young to know about them," I said.

Shaking his head, he said, "No. I was in school back then, and we lived in Akron. I remember my parents talking about the mayor and his involvement. Wish I could recall exactly what their discussions were about."

Brian picked up his wonderfully soft brushes and began applying eye shadow. "What is your next move?"

"I'm stumped. This could turn out to be a real mess; I don't want to drown in this crap," I answered.

"Sounds as though you aren't being given much of a choice," Sean said thoughtfully.

"It's nice to know you two haven't decided I'm off my rocker." I smiled.

Sean grinned. "We'll let you know when that happens." I kicked him, making sure I didn't move my face as Brian got the mascara wand to work.

Once done working on my lashes, Brian sorted through the lip colors, searching for just the right one. He settled on a creamy brick red and grabbed it, turning back to me. "Look, Mrs. S, if anyone can figure out what to do, it's you."

I sighed. "Wish I felt your confidence. I really am stuck."

Carefully applying the lip color, he said, "What I find hard to believe is that neither Bob nor Elaine knows who killed them. I thought spirits always knew that shit." We'd known each other long enough they were secure in their free use of language.

"Elaine knows who she saw last, but that won't stand up in court. I need proof, and as far as I know, any proof has long disappeared."

"Yeah," said Sean, "a jury won't accept your word that ghosts told you."

"I wouldn't blame them, would you?"

He laughed, "Hell no!" Brian stood back and inspected his masterpiece. Satisfied, he handed me the mirror.

"Wow, you did a great job!" I smiled at him.

Turning to Sean, he said, "Now do something with that hair!"

Sean had been a hairdresser for a short period of time before he'd made the career change to makeup. He grabbed the comb he kept hidden away for special customers, and within five minutes my hair was decent.

"Thank God for you two! I needed you both today," I said, inspecting myself in their mirror. "At least I can face the world knowing I look good."

They beamed at the praise. Those smiles wore down my resistance, and I actually bought a compact of eye shadow. Hugging them both, I told them I'd see them later. Deciding to walk the mall for a while, I headed out of Dean's and started browsing. Though I hated shopping, strolling around the stores at least gave me an excuse to visit the food court before I left.

I was inspecting the purses displayed in the window at one of the swanky stores when the hairs on my arms rose at least a foot in the air. For Pete's sake! Now what?

Before I could turn, I heard Elaine snort beside me. I refused to respond or face her. I was not going to be caught in public again having any type of conversation with people no one but myself could witness. See? Even old dogs could learn new tricks.

My silence for some reason encouraged her to talk more. "I always wanted an Italian purse. Bob refused to spend that much money on anything he considered useless," she said. "We could afford any purse in this store, but oh no! It was a waste of money in his mind. What a tightwad!"

I couldn't help myself from hissing at her, "You think eight hundred bucks is affordable?"

"Of course it was affordable!" she shrieked. I winced, thankful I was the only one who could hear her bitterness spewing. "The bastard didn't think I was worth a nice purse. He was happy with O'Neil's. You remember that store?" She looked around the mall. "Where did it go?" she asked, confused.

I nodded my head at the mention of O'Neil's. It had been a lovely department store that had disappeared along with other local stores at the mall. It had been at one end of the mall, with Higbee's at the opposite end. Back then we'd had a theater right in the middle of all the stores, the only theater in this part of town. All of it was gone now, replaced with stores that were pricey, much like the expensive shop I was sharing a view of with the bitch Elaine.

"What do you want?" I asked as quietly as possible. I even tried not moving my lips much, but I'm pretty sure I looked ridiculous.

"I want to know why you are wasting time getting makeovers instead of solving my murder!" she screamed.

Closing my eyes, I sighed. Turning, I headed for the door, hoping to get to my car without trying to smack her, which I was pretty sure wouldn't work anyway. Sure enough, the old cow followed me, stomping all the way.

Once I was safely locked behind closed doors, I turned to face her. "Elaine, I don't answer to you. I needed a break from this mess, and I don't want you following me around."

She glared at me, saying, "You need to get busy. Too many years have passed with no answers. I demand you find out who killed me."

"You?" I asked between gritted teeth. "You? What about Bob? He was murdered also!"

She waved a dismissive hand. "Whatever."

Heated blood coursed through my system. God, my blood pressure must be ready to blow through the roof.

"Not to mention the fact that it is not my fault you wasted these years arguing with Bob instead of appearing to other people long before now! That's your problem."

Her glare was enough to melt rocks, but I didn't give a damn. How dare she blame me for her mess. Did I mention she was a bitch?

"Go away!" I said, teeth firmly clenched. I could feel my jaw locking as I sat there. "Go now."

The vision of her as she faded was that damn glare. Jeez, I'd have nightmares for life if I didn't solve this murder soon. I hated her.

Chapter 7

I was surprised to find Andy standing at the kitchen sink when I walked in from my mall excursion. I glanced at the clock to ensure I hadn't lost a chunk of time somehow. Nope, it was only three in the afternoon. I raised a questioning eyebrow at him as he took another lazy sip of coffee.

"Took the afternoon off," he said, grinning. "Figured you needed some living company; the dead ones aren't much fun."

"That's an understatement!" I said, plopping my purse on the oak table we had bought in Amish country years ago. I had kept Andy up to date on each spiritual visit; he was highly entertained, but I didn't see what was so damn funny.

He stood there inspecting me a moment before saying, "I know you aren't enjoying any of your situation, but boy, oh boy, do you look great today."

I reached up to touch my face in surprise, suddenly realizing that my encounter with Elaine had wiped the memory of my time with Sean and Brian completely. I cherished those times with my guys and resented the fact she had ruined my afternoon.

"Yeah, needed a break from life. I went to the mall," I said.

"The guys outdid themselves this time." He smiled. He paused before asking, "You tell them about your new friends?"

Since the aroma of his coffee had hit me as soon as I'd walked in the door, I started making myself a cup as we stood in the kitchen together. I didn't answer till my cup was full of french roast coffee and I had taken that first lovely sip. The first taste of a fresh cup of coffee was one of the best moments in life. I allowed myself a few seconds of pure ecstasy and then said, "Yep, and they believed every word!"

Nodding, he replied, "I'm not surprised. They would assume anything you told them was the absolute truth."

I looked at him over the rim of my coffee cup. Was he implying they would trust me even if I was lying?

Seeing my expression, he threw a hand up defensively. "I don't mean you could tell them lies, but they do trust you to the bone. You've known them for years."

Backing off the ledge of unreasonable reactions, I shrugged. "True. It made me feel better knowing they believed me."

He put his arms around me in a long hug. "Honey, no one would dream this scenario out of thin air for the hell of it."

I allowed myself to snuggle in his embrace for reassurance.

"When are you telling the kids?" he asked innocently.

I sighed. The boys. Thankfully, they lived all over the country now. College educations had taken them away from our little hometown to bigger and better opportunities. At least that was what I comforted myself with when I missed them—well, most of the time I missed them. It was nice to have my life back now that the child-rearing years were firmly behind me. Since I was not ready for the grandparent scenario, I was fine with the boys building their careers before the next step in life. Smart kids.

I shook my head as he set a piece of cake from the local bakery in front of me. "Not planning on saying anything to them," I said. "Why worry them?"

Andy looked surprised. "Really? Any special reason?"

"Nope. They don't tell me every piece of their lives; I don't have to tell them mine!"

Andy grinned. "Stubborn to the bone!"

I kept quiet for a few moments, then looked Andy square in the eye. "What do you think their reactions would be? Hmm. They would decide either I had lost my mind or dropping hormones were making me hallucinate. I have enough on my plate without their interference."

Thoughtfully, Andy nodded as he said, "You are probably right. They would worry and then meddle."

"If it becomes a lifestyle, I'll say something. But I hope once I solve Bob's and Elaine's murders, I'll be done with spirits!"

We sat in comfortable silence, sipping our coffee and looking out the back window at the birds fighting over the feed in our feeder hanging from the apple tree. Our oldest, Adam, had made the feeder in seventh-grade woodshop class. It was the only project he had finished correctly, and he considered it a masterpiece. It had been hanging in the old apple tree ever since.

I looked around the kitchen and realized Nana might have a point about the need for an upgrade. Funny how I'd never noticed how tired it had become: wallpaper faded and peeling, appliances old and outdated. Not to mention flooring worn to smithereens. To me, it had looked exactly as it had when Andy and I had refinished it soon after moving into the house. We had been thrilled we'd actually accomplished the task with little knowledge of what we were undertaking. Thankfully, he had bought a book on home remodeling. We'd followed instructions and, with only a few mishaps, finished the kitchen the first summer. That had been over thirty years ago, and the poor old kitchen had survived the kids, many meals, and time.

"We may want to change this room," I said.

Andy looked surprised as he said, "I didn't think you'd ever consider tearing into this kitchen. I've been trying to talk you into new appliances for over ten years!"

I shrugged, not wanting to admit he had been right all along. No sense letting that information go to his head. "I'm still in the thinking-about-it mode; don't rush me."

"Rush you?" he laughed. "Ten years of pointing out the problem areas is not rushing!"

I looked around the tired kitchen again; it was a mess. How had I let it get this bad? I shook my head at my own blindness. Suddenly, the air grew cold. My throat constricted. Who now? Turning, I saw Nana's smile and relaxed somewhat. I glanced at Andy, wondering if he sensed the change in the atmosphere. He was frowning.

"What?" I asked, intrigued.

"Do we have a breeze from an open window in here?" he asked, getting up from his chair to check the windows.

I raised an eyebrow at him. "Why?"

"All of a sudden, I felt cold." His frown deepened as he glanced my way. "Uh-oh. Is this ... you know?" he asked.

Nana laughed as she watched his expressions.

"It's just Nana," I said. "Nothing to fear."

He stared at me for a moment as the information sank in. "Wow. Had no idea you could feel them this way," he said, shaking his head. Looking around the room, he said a bit too loudly, "Hey, Nana. Wish I could see you, but I'm glad you're here."

Her laugh filled the air again, and she said, "Tell him it's good to see him too."

I relayed the message, and Andy's eyes teared up a bit, which surprised me.

"It's a bit overwhelming, isn't it?" he said, looking over at me.

Nodding, I said, "Nana is easy. When Bob or Elaine show up, the feeling is horrible. Sorta like electricity zipping along your body. Sucks."

While Andy thought about that piece of information, Nana said, "Bob and Elaine are the least of our problems."

"What? They are a huge problem," I shot back at her.

"Who?" Andy asked, hearing only my side of the conversation.

Waving a hand at him to hush, I continued, "They are all I want to deal with, thank you very much!"

Smiling sadly, she looked at me with those huge, beautiful eyes of hers. "Sweetie, I told you from the start we have to clean up this area. Bob and Elaine are merely the beginning."

I stomped over to the sink and dumped out my lovely cup of coffee. This conversation had soured my stomach, and coffee was making me want to puke. Damn, I enjoyed that flavor, and now it was ruined for the time being. Turning to face Nana, I said, "They are horrible people! Well, maybe not Bob so much, but Elaine!" I shook my head in disgust. "She is really terribly rude and nasty. I don't believe I've ever met anyone quite like her."

Nana sighed, "I agree."

Well, that admission stunned me. Why the heck were we helping Elaine if the heavens realized what type of person she was?

As if reading my mind, which I was pretty sure she couldn't, Nana said, "We see situations differently on this side of life." As if realizing that her explanation wasn't calming me one bit, she continued, "Our job is to help Elaine move forward in her spiritual development."

"I don't give a damn about her spiritual development! She thrives on her selfishness!"

Nodding at my assessment, Nana said, "Yes. That is part of her problem and why we have been assigned the task of helping her realize she is holding herself back from a successful journey. Bob is ready to move on and has been for quite a while. But because he feels so attached to her, he won't budge without her alongside him."

I looked at her, stunned at this piece of information. "You mean Bob could move along whatever highway of spiritual life but refuses to because he feels beholden to Elaine?"

"That's pretty much the long and short of the situation," Nana said as she glanced over at Andy.

God! Andy! I had forgotten he was sitting at the table, listening to only part of the conversation. I looked at him, wondering how he was handling this scene with only partial information; it must have seemed odd to say the least. So imagine my surprise when, with one look, I realized he was having a grand time. Obviously, he had been able to figure out the gist from my reactions to Nana's part. I raised an eyebrow at him.

He nodded in response to my silent question and said, "Yeah, I can follow you pretty well. Maybe have a few questions later, but for now, I'm getting most of what's happening. This is amazing!"

I snorted. Amazing? It was a bloody nightmare. I'd just been informed I was not stuck with only those two lamebrains but more to follow. *I'm too damn old for these shenanigans!* I thought.

Nana quietly watched my expressions, as if able to decipher my thoughts precisely. Creepy.

I turned away from both of them and stared out the window. This had become my form of a passive-aggressive attitude, but I knew myself well enough to realize it wouldn't last long. I wasn't exactly what could be described as *passive* in any area of life. Not really aggressive either, sorta in the middle, I guessed. Was there a middle? There must be, because that was where I lived.

Turning back to Nana, I said with a sigh, "Fine. So could you explain to me why you are here this time?"

Nana had been inspecting the kitchen again, but at my question she turned to look out the window. Was this behavior genetic? I couldn't remember her paying much attention to windows when she was alive, so why now? Ha! I'd bet money it was for the same reason I did it, to avoid pieces of our conversations she wasn't thrilled about.

Still looking out the window, she said, "It has been noticed that Elaine has become rather trying for you." She stopped; I waited. No sense replying to the obvious. After a few moments, she continued, "We understand this is a difficult situation for your first time aiding our side of things. Look at my visit as reassurance it is worth the trouble." Turning to face me, she smiled. "And we do understand how infuriating Elaine can be; remember—we have dealt with her for years," she said with a small shake of her head. "Some circles here consider it a miracle that Bob stayed married to her all those years."

"He isn't the brightest bulb in the package," I snapped at her.

Smiling, she shook her head and said, "Don't be fooled by his natural enthusiasm; he is actually quite bright. He ran a very successful business until the local economy sank and was well thought of in the business community.

He may appear to you as a bit goofy, but that is merely his absolute love of life. Even in death, Bob has maintained his enthusiasm and endeared himself to many on our side."

I stared at her as I thought about this new information. "If he was so successful, why is Elaine so bitter about their life?"

"Do you remember the story I told you years ago about one of the Rockefellers? The one who, when asked how much is enough money, answered, 'Just a little bit more'?"

I nodded; it had been a lesson Nana had taught me about becoming too greedy in life.

"Well, that was Elaine. She never had enough; no matter how much money or prestige Bob had, she wanted 'just a little bit more.' Never satisfied, she became bitter."

"Wow. Okay, but that doesn't help me now," I said.

"I wanted you to have more of the picture. Elaine's personality propelled her to this point in her life while living," said Nana. "But you are correct: it doesn't solve the murder." She looked me fully in the face and said, "Researching files and newspapers won't help either. Talk to the people involved. A few of the main players will refuse to see you, but they will come around once you make headway."

"You mean people like the mayor of Akron?" I asked, stunned. "He isn't ever going to agree to talk with me!" How on earth could Nana believe the honorable mayor would stoop to tell me one thing? Honestly!

She smiled before saying, "I think you'll be surprised the people who will finally come forward and admit to having information."

"Okay, smarty-pants, who do I start with exactly?" I snapped.

She arched an eyebrow to a height that meant I had overstepped my allowed boundaries. I had seen that look my entire life, and it held consequences. But what could she do to me now? Ground me like she did when I was a kid and spending enormous amounts of time at her house?

"Don't believe for a moment I don't have certain abilities you would regret knowing about should I have to use them," she said in her grandmother tone that could make my toes curl.

I held up my hands in defeat. "Fine, but I could get into major trouble asking the wrong questions to the wrong people."

"Then be careful not to ask the wrong people those questions," she said as she faded away.

Really? That was no help at all. I was silent in thought for so long Andy finally asked, "Is she gone? Or are you giving her the silent treatment?"

Startled at his question, I jumped a bit. "Oh crap, I forgot about you! Sorry."

Grinning, he said, "It got a little heated there at the end, didn't it?"

"Yeah. She didn't give me any helpful information but did tell me I had to keep going." Looking around the kitchen again, I realized remodeling would be a hell of a lot easier than the job Nana insisted I accomplish. Poor Jack Monroe was not going to be a happy camper when I called him next.

Chapter 8

A fter an enjoyable evening with Andy, I decided not to bother Jack at home. I figured it would be easier to tackle him at his office. So then I just had to decide whether to call or go there. I needed to think so made the decision to sleep on it. I did, but sleep didn't help one damn bit. I didn't want to make a nuisance of myself, but I needed his help. If I called, he would see my name and number on caller ID and could ignore me completely. But showing up at the office could start tongues wagging, considering I'd been there a few times recently.

I marched into the bathroom and threw open the shower door to see Andy lathered up, stunned at my intrusion. "Peg! What the hell?" His shower time was sacred, and I seldom bothered him during it.

"I need your opinion. Do I call Jack and take the chance he will ignore me, or do I go to the station and risk starting gossip?"

"You couldn't wait until I was finished here?" His tone was a tad grumpy, so I conceded the point.

Sighing, I closed the shower door and drifted back to the kitchen. As I stared at the many scars on our oak table from years of babies, teenagers, and forgotten coasters, my eyes welled with tears. I remembered how every mark on that table had gotten there, and the memories flooded my senses. God, I was a mess. Suddenly, I felt a hot flash begin, which added insult to injury. "Damn it to hell! Things can't get any worse."

Wouldn't you know it? The doorbell rang, which proves if you make stupid statements, you are asking for trouble. Of course life could get worse, and glancing out the window, I realized it actually was getting worse. A black limo was parked smack-dab in the middle of our driveway. I didn't know anyone who rode around in a limo, unless it was prom night. Every parent in Bath hired one then to keep their kids safe.

Fanning myself through the hot flash and totally exasperated, I walked to the front door to see what new mess I was facing. Imagine my surprise when my least favorite official of Akron stood staring back at me. None other than the Honorable Bennet Hayes. With his graying hair, pudgy face that matched the rest of him, and fake smile in place, the word *honorable* didn't necessarily come to mind. I couldn't for the life of me think of one word to say, so I stood there like an idiot.

Sticking his hand out, he said, "Hello, Mrs. Shaw. I'm Bennet Hayes. Nice to meet you."

I stared at him and then his hand, unsure of what to do. I mean, what was the protocol in the situation? Shake, not shake? What the hell!

I came up with a brilliant opening line: "What are you doing here?" See? Told you it was brilliant. I blamed it on the hot flash I was experiencing; the bloody things had to be good for something.

He seemed a bit taken aback by my attitude. He wasn't alone; I was struck by my own rudeness. How do you fix a blunder of that magnitude? I shrugged mentally as I thought, *He isn't a king, God, or president.*

He had obviously made the decision to continue talking, which wasn't necessarily a good idea on his part. "Are you the little lady digging around in old murders that aren't any of your business?"

"Little lady"? Were we in an old episode of *Gunsmoke?*

"What makes you think I'm digging around or, if I am, it isn't any of my business?" I snapped. Okay, maybe I was more aggressive than I previously had thought.

Andy came out of the bedroom with his towel wrapped around him. Obviously, he had not heard the doorbell. "Okay, Peg. I'm ready to talk now." He stopped short as he spotted our distinguished guest. Both men turned an interesting shade of red, which I found fascinating.

"The mayor stopped by to threaten me, I believe. Should I ask him in for coffee?" I said as sickly sweet as I could muster.

Andy's stunned expression was priceless. The mayor winced as he listened to my words. "Now listen here, little lady—"

I held up my hand to stop his irritating voice.

Out of the corner of my eye, I noticed Andy scamper back toward the bedroom, holding on to his towel for dear life. The mayor was so stunned at the idea of someone telling him to stop talking, his mouth dropped practically to the stone sidewalk where he was standing.

"You want to start again? This time with a different opening line?" I asked him. Never screw with a woman during menopausal hot flashes; it might be dangerous to your health.

"Maybe if you invite me in, we could talk?" he asked in the oily manner his political enemies had learned to hate. For some unknown reason, it won votes from his faithful followers. Go figure.

"What makes you think I'd invite you into my house?" I asked. "If you are here to badger me about something I may or may not be doing, you are wasting your time and mine." I started to slam the door shut, but he quickly stuck his foot in the doorway. Wow, talk about pushy. I looked down at his Italian shoe and calculated how hard I would have to slam my solid oak door to tear the leather on his very expensive loafer. He must have read my expression correctly, because he hastily retreated the offending foot. I shot him a quick smirk and let the door fly. The sound of a solid wood door slamming is quite impressive. I stood there, heart pounding, and had to steady myself by leaning my overheated forehead on the door.

Andy came up to me, fully clothed in jeans and a sweatshirt, and asked me, "You okay?" Looking at the door, he shook his head. "Might not have been your best idea."

I fell back into his arms and started crying; this was becoming overwhelming. I sobbed uncontrollably for about two minutes. All the while, Andy was watching the black limo maneuver out of the driveway. He wasn't stupid; he had heard the same rumors I had concerning the mayor's questionable connections. But let's face it: when you stand up to bullies, you take the risk of backlash. Oh well, worry about those possibilities another day.

Blowing my nose on a tissue I dug out of my pocket, I looked up at my husband. "This is ridiculous."

Nodding, Andy said, "I agree slamming the door in his face was not good."

"What! I'm not talking about the door! This entire situation is way beyond me," I said, waving my arms around to indicate, well, everything.

Hugging me, he said, "Your nana seems to think you can handle it, or she wouldn't have asked you to help her."

"I'm not so sure," I said slowly. "What if I am the only person she could think of merely because I live in this area and faintly remember the murders?"

"Could be the reason she was given the assignment in the first place," he said, using logic only a man would consider. Jeez, I wasn't in the mood for logic. "Or," he said thoughtfully, "it's quite possible your connection to Nana *is* the reason she appeared."

I frowned. "You've lost me."

"Well, you miss her, even after all these years. Maybe your memories pulled her back into your life."

I opened my mouth, ready for a snotty reply, but slammed it shut when I realized his idea had some merit. After a few moments of silence, I decided to ignore his statement and plunged ahead with my own questions.

"That brings up another point. Who the hell is handing out assignments in heaven? Isn't that supposed to be a place of peace and rest?" I stomped my foot in frustration. "Give me a break!"

Andy had learned through our years of marriage that once the foot stomping began, he should remain quiet and allow me time to sort through whatever crisis I was facing. He had become pretty good at it, I have to admit.

I broke away from his arms and stormed into the den. It was a peaceful room, now that the kids were gone. The old TV had been replaced last year with Andy's dream of a forty-eight-inch flat screen. Since neither one of us was a big TV watcher, it had been a complete waste of money. It looked quite nice in the room, however. I had also conceded to leather furniture, which I would never have done while the kids were still living at home. Leather wasn't too attractive with mud prints, slashes from safety scissors, or Magic Marker drawings on it, not to mention disrespectful teenage attitudes that would have added to the destruction. Empty-nest syndrome wasn't as bad as people might believe.

At some point in the deep recesses of my brain, the question arose that I hadn't minded the den being refurbished after the kids had left home, so why not the kitchen? I had been perfectly willing, excited actually, to throw out worn furniture, repaint, and purchase items replacing memories of our children's years of family time in that room. Why had I been unable to tear into the kitchen with the same excitement? Because Nana had helped me with the kitchen before she'd died? Was Andy correct assuming my emotional tie to Nana had someway opened a door for her to return? I mentally sighed as I pushed the thought further into the deep pit of my brain.

I plopped my butt into my recliner, which was the only piece of furniture in the den not leather, and pouted. Andy had followed me and stood in the doorway watching me, waiting to see if the coast was clear so he could add his two cents. It wasn't, but he spoke anyway. "Okay, what's going on? Is it the hormone thing, or is the murder upsetting you?"

"The 'hormone thing'?" I asked with enough acid to burn through steel. "Really?"

He waved his hand, dismissing my snottiness. "You know what I mean."

I glared at him a moment and realized it wasn't fazing him in the least. Obviously, he knew me too well. Taking a deep breath, I said, "I'm not sure.

The hormones are driving me nuts, I'll admit. But Nana has blown apart my idea of afterlife. I don't want assignments when I'm dead. What happened to 'streets of gold' and all the usual stuff?"

He laughed as he came over and kissed the top of my head. "Sweetheart, go with the flow. You have to admit we are learning quite a bit of information about what comes next. I honestly find it, well, fascinating."

"You would!" I sniffed.

"Why don't we work together? I'll do some research online and see what I can find. You can tackle talking to people who still live around here and remember the story. I'm sure your old PTA gals would be a great help."

I looked up at him in shock. How had I not thought of the idea myself? The murder had been the talk of the township that year at meetings, and most of the gals still lived in Bath. "I never considered them!"

Grinning, he said, "See, two heads are better than one."

At that moment, the doorbell rang. We looked at each other, stunned. Now what? Andy glanced out the side window and smiled. "It's okay," he said. "Jack's here."

Jack? What was he doing here? Well, one problem solved: Jack had shown up, so I didn't have to be sneaky trying to talk to him. Andy went to the door as I kept my tired butt in the recliner. I heard the normal chitchat as they came down the short hall toward the den. As Jack turned into the room, I was surprised to see the weariness on his face.

"What's up?" I asked, motioning him to make himself at home. "Want some coffee?"

Shaking his head to the coffee question, he sat down on the couch and turned to face me. "You slammed the door in the mayor's face?"

I raised an eyebrow. "Wow, news travels fast."

"Where do you think he went after he left here? He was so mad I thought he was going to have a heart attack right in my office. You should have seen his face!" Jack sighed.

It hadn't dawned on me His Highness would pick on Jack. It wasn't Jack's fault I wouldn't talk to the mayor.

At that precise moment, the hairs on my neck stood on end. Damn. Bob. I quickly glanced around the room. I couldn't detect him, but I knew he was there somewhere.

Suddenly, his voice boomed out, "Isn't this great? I'm here, but you can't see me! Gosh, this is the greatest trick I've learned yet!"

Oh my God! He was *invisible* now when he showed up? Son of a bitch!

Jack noticed the change in my expression and immediately began looking around. "Who's here?"

"Bob. And he's invisible," I moaned. "Damn it, Bob, show yourself!"

"Um, not sure exactly how to do that," he replied.

"What? You've got to be kidding! I can't have you popping in here and be invisible! It's bad enough when I can see you, but not seeing you is worse!"

"Invisible?" Jack asked. "That's new?"

"Yes, it's new!" I hissed at him. "I don't need this shit!"

"Don't swear; it isn't nice," Bob said from a different part of the room.

I groaned as I let my face fall into my hands. Bob had been dead for over a decade, and he was just now learning tricks? This was getting out of hand.

"What do you need, Bob?" I asked wearily.

"Did I hear you say the mayor was here?" he asked distractedly.

"Answer the question, please," I said.

"Hm, wait a sec. I think I figured out a way you can see me," he said.

I watched in the area his voice was emitting from, and sure enough, I eventually could see his faint outline.

"Congratulations, I can make out where you are," I calmly said. It was taking a lot of control not to snap at him, but I had learned that Bob got his feelings hurt if I pushed too hard.

"I did it!" he said excitedly. "It's harder than you would think once you become invisible."

"Why exactly did you want to be invisible?" I asked in spite of myself.

There was a moment's silence before he whispered, "Elaine can't see me either."

Ah, there was a method to his madness.

He cleared his throat before adding, "The little episode the other day when I lost my temper didn't sit too well with Elaine. She's made death a living hell. Acquiring a new maneuver to avoid her seemed wise."

Well, that explained the current state of affairs. I'd thought he was going to pay for his unwise outburst.

Back to my original question. "Bob, why are you here?"

"Wanted to see how you are progressing. Didn't have much else to do."

I glanced over at Andy and Jack. Somehow they were getting the hang of following conversations with only my side available to them. This was getting a tad creepy.

"You're bored? Are you kidding me?" This was the reason he showed up so often? Just my luck to have a ghost with nothing better to do than drive me nuts. "What have you been doing all these years to keep yourself occupied? Surely there was something you were involved in before I came into the picture."

Silence. Finally, he said, "You need to understand the situation; we lose track of time. I sorta got used to listening to Elaine complain. I figured visiting you was more interesting, so here I am."

He sounded rather proud of the fact he now had someone to irritate other than Elaine, or maybe he sounded proud because he realized he could avoid her totally. Don't misunderstand; I truly got why he was tired of Elaine. Hell, I'd only known her a few days, and I hated her. But he needed to find some worthy endeavor to pursue other than popping up in my life. Being Bob's new best friend was not a situation I was happy about one bit.

"Bob, I'm sure you could find more-important tasks to involve yourself with other than driving me to the loony bin," I said to the rather shadowy figure in the far corner of the room. His outline moved closer to the window. What was he doing?

"Bob! Pay attention!"

The outline froze in place. "Did you know you have deer in your backyard? We used to have deer in our yard; I miss them to be honest."

I sighed. "Bob, stop trying to change the subject."

His outline began moving closer to the window again. "What did the mayor want?"

"None of your business," I answered sharply. The last thing I needed was input from Bob concerning the mayor.

"It was his son that Elaine saw that night. You know that, right?" he said quietly. "Is he involved?"

"I have no idea." I sighed again.

After a few moments of silence, Bob said thoughtfully, "I could watch his movements and report back to you."

I opened my mouth for a smart-ass reply and quickly snapped it shut. Why hadn't I thought about this possibility myself? It could be a solution to a couple of issues. Bob would be busy somewhere other than my life, and he could also be my inside man snooping on the mayor's conversations and whereabouts. Making a snap decision, I said, "You may have a point."

"Really?" he said excitedly. "He'll never even know! This could be my new career!"

"You need a career?" I asked.

Andy raised an eyebrow at my remark. Jack shook his head. They had no idea what we were discussing, and I wasn't sure it would be a good idea to detail the new plan of action. But, hey, let's face it: Bob would be in absolutely no danger; the mayor couldn't order a hit on a dead man. It would solve the problem of what exactly the mayor was hiding if Bob could listen to his conversations. It was a win-win.

"You want me to start right now?" Bob asked, his outline quickly moving through the room.

I thought about his offer for a split second. "Wouldn't hurt. Let me know what you find out," I said as he started to fade. "And hey, Bob!" I shouted. The fading figure paused, listening. "Don't you dare show up in the middle of the night!"

"Roger that!" he said as he faded completely.

Chapter 9

After Bob left, I turned to face Andy and Jack. Their expressions indicated they had followed most of the conversation but were lost concerning the end of my little talk with Bob. Now came the decision of whether to tell them exactly what Bob had gone off to do. It wasn't illegal, so what could Jack object to? And Andy wouldn't care as long as I wasn't in danger.

"So when did Bob learn to become invisible?" Andy asked, one of his eyebrows raised. Bob could do that to a person. One day eyebrows stayed put. Then you met Bob or Elaine, and the damn things roamed freely around your forehead.

"Recently, I gather. He's rather proud of the fact, especially since Elaine can't seem to find him when he does it," I answered, smiling. I realized I felt a sense of deep satisfaction that, after all these years, Bob had found a way to avoid the bitch. Maybe Nana was correct: there was more to Bob than met the eye. I'd have to think about it, though. His new maneuver could be a fluke.

Jack sat watching me carefully. "What's he gone off to do, and why would you warn him not to visit in the middle of the night?"

Damn, Jack had instincts. I hadn't counted on those popping up at all, never even entered my mind. I looked at him with what I hoped was an innocent expression. By the way he shook his head, he wasn't buying it. Sighing, I decided on the truth. At least I wouldn't have to remember whatever lie I dreamed up.

Nonchalantly, I said, "He's off to spy on the mayor."

Jack shot out of the chair he had been perched on, screaming, "What? Are you nuts?"

"Why not?" I asked, ignoring his rising anger.

"At least a million reasons!" he shouted.

"Name one," I said calmly.

His mouth opened, closed, opened again.

"Uh-huh. Exactly what I thought," I said, totally self-satisfied.

"There must be some law he is breaking," Jack grumbled.

"He's dead! What law could he break?" I asked.

Shaking his head, Jack said, "There must be a code of some sort up there!" He pointed heavenward.

"Trust me: all the stuff we learned in church does not hold water!" I snapped. "Nana has *jobs* to do! What's with that? They have *missions* and damn *chores*. So don't go on about 'up there.' It's about as bad as down here as far as I can tell!"

I'll admit he was on the receiving end of my disappointment concerning the afterlife. I should have been ashamed of myself, but I wasn't. He might as well have his bubble burst alongside my torn beliefs.

Jack's shock showed clearly on his face. "You mean"—he swallowed hard—"we have to work there too?"

"Yep," I answered shortly.

Jack fell into the chair with an expression that clearly showed his devastation. My heart fell. Damn it, I hadn't meant to destroy his hopes, just bring a little reality into his life. Let's face it: I wasn't any happier. Andy, on the other hand, seemed intrigued.

"I, for one, am glad to hear it," he said flatly. Jack and I looked at him, surprised. Seeing our faces, Andy grinned. "Think for a moment. How boring would that have got over the centuries? Sitting around playing harps and smiling at each other for eons? *That* would have been hell!"

I had to admit there was a certain amount of logic in Andy's analysis of the situation. I hadn't thought of it quite in those terms. Obviously, poor Jack was having none of Andy's ideas.

Shaking his head emphatically, he said, "I have to believe there is rest at some point! If not here, then it needs to be there, wherever there happens to be, and you are right, Peg: right now there is beginning to sound a lot like here." He sighed deeply. I really was beginning to feel sorry for my old friend.

Andy walked over to Jack, nudging him gently on the shoulder. "Hey, bud, it's gonna be all right! Think of the adventures we'll have over yonder way! It will be grand."

Jack looked at the floor; I followed his gaze, wincing at what I saw. I cringed as I saw fully the condition of the house for the first time in years. I wondered if he noticed the faded and worn spots in the carpet. Trying to see it through his eyes, I realized it was another thing needing to be updated. Hell, my entire house needed an overhaul. How had this happened? I'd thought we were keeping up with repairs through the years. How many others little things had I ignored that had grown into big things? Redecorating wasn't a cure all; things got overlooked. Was this what happened when you got older? Just comfortable with things as they were?

Jack finally looked back up at me. Apparently the carpet was no longer interesting. "Back to your idea of spying on the mayor," he said after a moment.

I kept my mouth closed, hoping he wouldn't get snarky due to his present mood. His gaze left my face and studied the ceiling. I followed his eyes, hoping like hell they wouldn't lead me to more home repairs.

"This could be a bonus in the long run," he said and stopped, gathering his thoughts. Looking me in the eye, he continued, "Peg, we still have to be careful. The mayor's not somebody we need to piss off and bring any more attention to ourselves than we've accomplished already. Let's get off his radar quickly."

"I never knew I was on his radar until this morning when he showed up at my front door!" I said.

Nodding, he returned his gaze to my ceiling. I once again followed suit, inspecting for problems. Nope, didn't see any, thank God.

Eyes still heavenward, he said, "Remember, the mayor's son is probably his biggest concern. That doesn't diminish the problems this could cause for his political career. He is more than likely protecting both, and getting in his way isn't healthy. He's been mayor of Akron for so long he wouldn't know how to be anything else; he is going to protect his position with every ounce of power

he can muster—which is a lot of damn power. He may seem like a buffoon to you, but he has nasty friends and knows how to use them in a pinch."

Our little township had had problems with Akron for over twenty years. They'd tried to annex this area more than once, and we had barely held onto our independence from them. It had been, at one time, a huge fight. It had died down in recent years but had left a bad taste in the population's collective mouth. We might be tiny, but that didn't give the bigger cities the right to own us along with every other inch of land they could gobble up along the way. Somehow, we had lost portions of the township land, but we were holding on to what we had left to the best of our ability. Overall, our taxes were lower here, most of us had water wells and so free water, and we didn't have the crime rate the surrounding cities dealt with daily. The township was still considered rural, but with the building up of the Montrose area only a mile from here, I wasn't sure how rural we would stay in the years to come. The mayor was angry he had lost those battles, and who knew how much longer he would hold a grudge? Probably forever.

"Yep," I said. "I get it; we need to be careful."

Jack got up from the chair and began pacing around the den. "More than careful! He has to believe we are no longer looking into him or his son." He rubbed his hands together. "I'm beginning to warm to this idea of Bob doing the spying for us. You may have hit upon a great solution regarding our investigation."

Our and *we*? Wow, Jack now considered himself totally involved and part of the hunt. I slumped back into my chair, relieved.

I smiled. "It was Bob's idea, not mine. I can't take credit, since I never thought of it."

"Really?" he asked, surprise clearly showing on his face.

"Bob?" Andy said. "Odd from your shy friend."

Grinning, I said, "It's an easy way for him to stay out of Elaine's line of fire."

Andy grinned back at me, and Jack shook his head.

"Poor guy. I barely remember them, but she was not easy in life. I can't imagine what she's like in death," Jack said.

"Funny, I don't remember them at all," I said.

"You were busy with the boys," Andy said as he walked toward the kitchen. "Anyone for coffee?"

Jack perked up and asked, "Any of Peg's pie to go along with it?"

"When have I had time to bake?" I asked indignantly. "I did buy one at the bakery, though."

I was started toward the kitchen when I heard, "Psst." I stopped cold. Now what?

"Peg."

I turned to see my mother standing in the middle of the room, looking exactly as she had when I'd been in high school. I felt my blood leave my upper extremities and had to use the wall to hold me upright. Andy turned around, mouth open to say something, but promptly froze upon seeing my expression. After a moment, he asked, "Peg? Sweetie, what's wrong?"

Shaking my head, I said, "I'm fine. I'll be there in a minute."

Studying my face, he clearly didn't like what he saw.

I waved him away and said, "I'll be fine. Tell you later."

After a quick survey of the room, he nodded and turned, heading to the kitchen. He glanced back at me, concerned. I smiled tightly and shooed him on his way.

It took a few deep breaths before I was able to face my mother. When I did, she was hesitantly looking around. Needless to say, our relationship had had more downs than ups.

"I always did like this room. Glad you redecorated, though," she said as she inspected the room carefully. "Could use a new carpet."

Thanks, Mom. "I'm pretty full up concerning dead people," I said with a hint of sarcasm.

"I'm fully aware of exactly what you've been up to young lady," she said condescendingly. Her arched back slumped, and she said, "I'm sorry. I shouldn't have used that tone."

If I hadn't been leaning against the wall, I would have fallen over from shock. She had never apologized for a single thing her entire life. Maybe the afterlife could improve a person's disposition.

Seeing my face, she sighed. "I've been working on my attitude. My mother thinks it should be adjusted."

Ah, Nana to my rescue. She had done that as far back as I could remember concerning my relationship with Mom.

"You look pretty good for a dead person," I finally said. Nana looked as I remembered: gray hair, glasses, a little pudgy around the middle. My mother looked like a damn fashion model and twenty years younger than when I last saw her right before she died.

"Well," she said as she straightened her skirt and smoothed down her blouse. Were those high heels she had on? For Pete's sake.

"We have the choice of how we appear to people. I looked the best in my forties, so that's the way I wanted you to see me." Clearly, she was proud of her appearance, and I had to admit she looked fantastic.

"Surprised you didn't pick your twenties," I said sarcastically.

She shook her head and then threw it back and laughed. "Oh, dear, no! When a woman is in her twenties, she has too much of a carefree attitude. It's the forties where a woman shines—mature but still young enough that what shows is her wisdom and confidence."

Wisdom? Since when did this woman possess wisdom? I thought. *Never.* I arched an eyebrow. "Really? Good to know."

"I'm here to give you advice," she said smugly.

This ought to be good. "Okay. Let's hear it," I said. I no longer needed the wall for support, so I made it to my chair and sat with a plop.

"You'll ruin the cushion in that recliner," she said, watching me.

I nodded. "Thanks. So what's the advice?"

Her eyes narrowed as she said, "You need to stop this investigating. Stirring up old crimes isn't healthy. Leave it alone."

I studied her face as she spoke. Every line and expression brought back memories I would rather forget. She had never been a loving mother nor especially kind. But she had been a beauty and had known it. *Narcissistic* was the term that popped into my mind. Even dead, the woman was something else again.

"Why?"

She began pacing around the room, inspecting every knickknack I owned. "It will lead to big problems. The wrong type of people will notice, and you will regret your decision."

"Who are the wrong type of people?" Might as well ask.

She stopped pacing and turned to face me. "You know damn good and well who!"

"That's not an answer; that's evasion." She was getting on my nerves. I had actually thought for a split second she was trying to improve herself on the dead side of things.

"Nellie? What are you doing here?" a voice asked from the other side of the room. Thank God, Nana had come to save me.

My mother abruptly turned, her skirt swirling around her in a way that showed off her legs. "Don't call me that! You know I hate it!" She faced her mother with iron grit and determination that was all too familiar.

Shaking her head in quiet despair, Nana said, "Fine. Nell. What are you doing here?"

"I've come to save my daughter from your interference," she snapped.

A thought suddenly flew into my head. "Mom?" I asked.

She turned to me with a questioning look.

"Which side of the fence are you on?" I asked with as much innocence as I could muster.

Her face turned hard, and she was seething. "How dare you ask me!" she snarled.

Okay, question answered. She was batting for the other team. I glanced at Nana with a "Now what?" look. Maybe the afterlife couldn't change a person as much as I had hoped.

Nana winked, then raised her hands out in front of her. "Be gone!"

Damn if it didn't work. Mom was gone with just a hint of something rancid in the air.

"So there is a hell?" I asked, looking over at Nana.

Shaking her head, she said, "Not exactly. More like a way station until they get their act together. It takes a while, to be sure, but no burning and scorching."

"Too bad," I said.

"Peg!" Nana said in shock. "She is your mother!"

Chagrined, I said, "Well, not only her. There must be millions of people deserving somewhere nasty."

Sighing, she said, "It is complicated, but never wish anyone that type of afterlife."

"Fine. But why was she warning me?" I had to admit that Mom's warning had given me goose bumps.

Nana waved her hand dismissively. "Being dramatic and wanting to be involved, I suppose."

Uh-oh. Nana wasn't telling me the whole story. I decided to dig my heels in and get the truth. Shaking my head at her, I said, "Tell me all of it! And what was the smell when she left?"

Nana sighed again. "It was your mother's drama. Maybe a tad of selfishness thrown in to boot."

"No way! Elaine is as selfish as they come, and she doesn't stink as she disappears!"

Looking out the same window Bob had enjoyed, she said, "Elaine didn't have children."

I raised an eyebrow, then nodded for her to continue.

"Your mother's self-centered attitude didn't change when you were born. She didn't want to grow up and be an adult. Elaine never allowed herself the chance to put someone ahead of her own desires. Children usually do that, not always, but usually."

I have to tell you, this news was a revelation. Children *had* changed me. You worried about them for years, and about the time you thought you could stop worrying so much, they left home, and you worried even more since you couldn't keep your eye on them. Go figure. But this was big news; having children was supposed to make you a better person? And if it didn't, you must be so selfish your afterlife would smell?

"So Mom is in more of a pickle than Elaine because one of them had kids and the other didn't? Doesn't it mean at least Mom tried to be a better person and Elaine didn't even give it a go?" Come on here, I didn't necessarily like my mother, but I knew I didn't like Elaine one bit! These heavenly rules were getting on my nerves. Better to get back to solving a murder. It was sure as hell easier than figuring out the universe.

Nana shook her head. "Nothing's as easy as you may think."

Really? Didn't she think I had sorta stumbled across that fact as soon as she'd showed up in my bedroom? Jeez.

"Look, Nana, I don't know why Mother showed up; it doesn't matter. What I want to know, is can you help me solve this murder? I need to get rid of these two before I lose my mind. Bob has figured out how to be here *and* invisible; even he is trying to hide from Elaine!"

Nana smiled that little irritating smile of hers. She looked behind me, and I realized there was a cold breeze in the den. Not wanting to turn around to see who or what had caught her attention, I walked over to the window in the back of the room. It overlooked the woods, facing the same direction as the kitchen. I stared out into those woods and felt my arm hair stand at attention. Now what? Nana's voice startled me, but I refused to look back toward her. No telling what new person was visiting along with her this time.

"Peg, I want you to meet one of your helpers. He has come a long way in distance and time but is willing to help as much as possible. Please come meet him." Her voice was all honey and spice. When I was a kid, I'd called that tone her company voice. She could turn on charm like a light switch when people came to visit her. Don't get me wrong; she was a great lady, but the minute you heard that particular tone of voice, someone was getting conned. Not conned out of money—Nana wasn't that type of person—but conned nonetheless. Now I was the one getting her special treatment.

I closed my eyes and took a deep breath. Who or what was behind me? Only one way to find out. I slowly turned, dread filling every cell of my body. Imagine my surprise when I saw an Indian standing quietly, a slow smile spreading across his face. My mouth had dropped open, and I was thankful he hadn't burst out in hysterical laughter. He gave me one nod, as if any more acknowledgement of my existence was beneath him.

I stared a moment longer before turning to Nana and asking, "So I'm in a TV western now?"

Okay, there was a little itty bit of sarcasm in that question, but cut me some slack. I was hanging onto reality by a slight thread, and she introduces me to a full-blooded Indian, in total historical garb? Really?

Nana looked nervously at our new guest. I suppose my question was in bad taste; I'll concede the point. I looked back at the Indian and raised an eyebrow but stayed quiet. Two could play at the silence game. The truth was I didn't have any idea what to say to him. Did he even speak English? He was dead, and maybe on the other side they gave language lessons; I wouldn't be surprised at all.

Then he surprised both Nana and me; he threw back his head and laughed. Nana looked confused but relieved also; I hadn't pissed the guy off too much. I opened my mouth to ask a question, but Nana shook her head quickly. I snapped my lips together and waited until his laughter had subsided. I must have really hit a funny bone with the man, because he laughed for a good minute. I didn't think my snotty remark was so funny.

When he finally got himself under control, he turned to Nana, nodding. "She will do."

"You speak English." I had to admit that statement wasn't stellar, but I had nothing else.

He shook his head. "No. You *hear* your language."

"I have somehow landed in an episode of *Doctor Who*?" The sarcasm was back; it was my relief valve, I guess.

Nana frowned. "*Doctor Who?*"

I cut my eyes in her direction. "A British TV show. They can understand all languages because of the police box they fly around the universe inside of …" I trailed off, realizing I was complicating the discussion rather than helping.

"Ah. British. They are still in existence?" our new friend asked.

"Don't you know this stuff?" I asked, surprised.

"What's a police box?" Nana asked, obviously trying hard to make the connection. For Pete's sake, why did I have to bring up the TV series?

Sighing, I said, "Nana, don't worry about it. It's not important."

The Indian answered my question; at least he knew how to stay focused. "We do not concern ourselves with the physical world, unless necessary."

I narrowed my eyes. "But you are here, in the physical world." See? I could stay on task too. Occasionally.

He looked over at Nana. "I am doing this lovely lady a favor."

Nana actually blushed. "You two dating?" I asked. I was having trouble keeping the sarcasm at bay. Shoot me.

Nana's eye flashed hotly. "Peg! Your manners!"

I cocked an eye at her. "So you *are* dating."

"We don't date here. I met him at a meeting."

"You have meetings? In heaven?" The more information I got about the other side, the less I believed it was a better place than right here on planet earth. "This is beginning to sound a lot like a corporation and less like a heavenly environment." I could feel whatever faith I had left sliding toward the door, on its way out of my life.

Nana began tapping her foot on the floor. I ignored the obvious irritation growing in her and turned back to our visitor. "What do I call you?" I asked.

He smiled again. Why did all these spirits keep smiling? It gave me the creeps.

"You would not be able to pronounce my name." That was probably a true statement. I had trouble pronouncing French names, Spanish names, any name that wasn't firmly English.

"Doesn't answer my question."

He cocked his head to one side, studying me. "Logan," he finally answered.

"Logan? As in the Indian chief?" Well, that one stunned me, I have to admit.

He laughed again. "You know your history?"

I shook my head. "Not as well as you may think. But I do remember that bit." I thought a moment before saying, "But he wasn't from Bath."

The Indian, Logan, looked out the window. The windows must have some sort of magnet; we all seemed to spend a great deal of time staring out of the darn things.

"I did not say I *was* Logan, merely that you could call me by that name," he said, still watching the woods.

Ah, so this was the guy Nana had been on the alert for that day she'd seemed preoccupied with the woods behind our house. She must have already enlisted his help at that point. So nice when a few of the pieces started coming together.

"Does the chief know you have stolen his name?" No sarcasm here. Honest Injun. But I did remember reading somewhere that names were highly important to Native Americans.

I noticed a twinkle in his eyes when he glanced back at me. "He is aware I use his name on occasion. It is easier to say for whites."

So I was a white. Fair enough.

"I'll buy that. So why exactly are you here?" Nana opened her mouth to answer, but Logan quickly put his hand up to silence her. Surprisingly, she nodded at him and actually took a step back. Gosh.

He looked over at Nana and studied her face for a moment. "Thank you for the introduction. I am sure you have many other duties requiring your attention."

Nana's eyes grew big, but she nodded and slowly faded away. Great. I was stuck with Logan all alone.

Chapter 10

I eyed Logan warily but refused to comment on his dismissal of Nana. No sense revealing how ignorant I actually was concerning protocol of afterlife hierarchy. It was confusing at best, ridiculous at worst. Watching Nana defer to his authority was unnerving. I had never seen her back down to any living person, but she sure as hell backed off with Superchief, um, Logan.

He turned back to the window, scanning the woods for something or someone he expected to see there. The hairs on the back of my neck were standing straight as rods as I watched him. I decided right then and there that Bob and Elaine were a piece of cake to deal with next to this guy. Suddenly, his shoulders relaxed as his gaze stopped in one area. In spite of my decision not to follow his lead and look at the woods, I found my curiosity too strong to ignore. I couldn't see anything significant along the tree line, but once I allowed myself to study deeper in the woods, my heart started racing. Shit fire! There were at least twenty Indians stoically standing there, their eyes locked with Logan's. My eyes darted back to Logan, and I watched as he acknowledged each one individually with a slight nod of his head.

By this time, my stomach was roiling. What the heck were all these men doing in my woods! I opened my mouth to make a smart-ass comment when Logan's hand shot out and grabbed my wrist. Electricity flew up my arm, and I jerked it away. My eyes narrowed as I examined my wrist for burn marks. None were visible, but my entire arm was now tingling. How on earth had a spirit made physical contact? Either I was losing my mind, or

Logan had major powers. I hoped my mind was shot to hell instead of the alternative, which scared me spitless.

I quickly glanced toward the door, wondering where Andy and Jack were. Why hadn't they come back to check up on me. You would think they would have become concerned, at the very least, that I hadn't made it to the kitchen.

Logan turned to face me, smiling. "Do not worry about your husband and Mr. Monroe. They will not be bothering us."

Oh God. Had he killed them? And how did he know what I was thinking?

"They are fine, but we do not need to be interrupted," he told me.

"So you didn't hurt them with some mojo?" I asked, breathing fast. If I had a heart attack over this crap, I was going to be pissed.

 Laughing as he shook his head, he said, "I do not have mojo. But I do have power." He sighed as he continued, "Our people had great spiritual abilities for many generations. As time continued, they lost their way. I am fortunate I lived during the peak of our cultures' power and awareness. What Europeans would call a golden age. I gained great strength during that time and retain the powers even in death."

I thought about his words for a moment before asking, "So, as time went by, your people lost magical powers? Why?"

Sadness covered his face as he returned his gaze to the woods. "They became lazy. It is the same with all cultures eventually. But it is not only 'my' people; you also are among us."

I frowned. What did that mean?

"Your Indian heritage," he said, answering my unspoken question. His mind reading was getting on my last nerve. My brain might not be the brightest, but it sure as hell was *mine!*

His manner became quite serious as he continued, "I could not be here to protect you if not for your genealogy."

Oh, that. But why did I need his protection?

"I have a very small amount of Indian blood in the family line. It's not much," I said.

Nodding, he said, "Cherokee."

"It is very far back. I don't even think about it," I told him.

"It does not matter how much or how little Indian blood runs through your veins. One drop would be enough to call upon our help."

"Help? What help? I didn't call upon anyone," I said.

"No, but your nana did," he replied calmly.

"Why on earth did she ask you guys to come here? This makes no sense. You don't know Bob or Elaine, and I don't think you want to meet them. They are a pain in my ass," I said.

Turning to face me, surprise clearly showing in his expression, he said, "They have not warned you of the dangers?"

Sweat began to trickle down my back and even between my boobs. Damn it, I *knew* there was more to this mess than Nana had admitted. Bloody hell. My head began to swim, and I was pretty sure I'd be vomiting any minute now.

"Sit," Logan commanded.

It was an order that I was very willing to follow. I stumbled over to the nearest chair and plopped down, hard.

"Drop your head between your knees, and take slow breaths," he ordered.

I did as I was told and began feeling better immediately. I stayed put for a few minutes as I gathered my emotions and thoughts. Finally, I raised my head a tad, just enough to see him, and asked, "How much danger are we talking here?"

He looked at me and gently said, "Enough to warrant my presence."

Well, he certainly wasn't making me feel better. I slammed my head back between my legs but did not have the earlier results. I was going to pass out, and Andy wouldn't be able to help. I could see stars before my eyes and knew blackout was next, but then I felt a strong hand on my head. Logan was humming some Indian-sounding song as he rubbed the base of my neck. Within seconds, I felt totally fine. Wow.

"Thanks," I mumbled.

He continued with whatever ritual he was performing, and I wisely sat still and let him. Let's be honest: when someone had major abilities to this degree, you damn well respected it. When he finally finished, he stepped back and looked at me. I sat up, amazed at how fantastic I felt. "Gosh" was all I could think of to say.

Smiling down at me, Logan said, "It will continue a few moments longer. Then you will feel normal. Enjoy it while it lasts."

I had to laugh. So I was feeling this fabulous, and it was only going to last a few minutes? Sounded about right, the way my life had been going lately. Little by little, I felt the familiar aches coming back to life in my menopausal body. At least they were recognizable. I sat back in the chair and looked up at Logan.

"I feel better, so how about telling me the truth about this entire mess Nana has dragged me into."

He walked around the room, studying every nook and cranny. He was going to find a lot of dust, and he wouldn't have to look too damn hard. So scrubbing wasn't my joy. Shoot me.

"When we have the desire to fight evil, we face opposition. It is the balance. Evil does not tolerate much interference." He stopped strolling around my den and faced me. "Dangerous work at any time in history."

I frowned. "My job is to find one murderer; that's it. I have no desire to fight evil—just one guy."

He smiled sadly. I wasn't thrilled at his expression; it meant there was more going on here than I cared to know. I resented that I was receiving information in bits and pieces, but if Nana had told me the entire truth from the get-go, I sure as hell would have said no. The situation was getting way beyond my comfort zone.

"So," I started slowly, "you are here to protect me against 'evil,' which means there is more to this story than anyone so far has been admitting to me. Right?"

He nodded silently.

"What exactly am I facing?" Might as well find out and be prepared. The alternative didn't appeal to me much. I didn't like surprises, and this was beginning to feel like one big-ass surprise.

"Danger. The amount of danger depends on how committed you are to finding your one murderer. We," he said, spreading his arms out to include the guys in the woods, "are here to protect you and your family."

"How good is your protection squad?" I asked. "I mean, can they stop a bullet coming my way?"

He smiled. "Bullets were after my time, but I think we can manage." He pointed to the guys out in the woods and said, "They are more familiar with bullets than I am, but you should be safe." He grinned at me.

Should? I would rather have words like *positively, without a doubt, guarantee. Should* and *probably* weren't going to make me sleep better.

I continued, probing the situation, "You fellows are going to follow me everywhere I go?"

He thought about my question before answering. I was beginning to sweat again, and I had to pee. Go figure.

"One of us will escort you every time you leave this property. They will be guarding this hill constantly."

"Why?" I asked. This didn't make sense to me.

He cocked his head and said, "There was once a village at the crest of this hill. The men in the woods were part of that village and are here to protect what was once theirs."

I nodded at his answer, but it still wasn't hanging together. "Why?" I asked again.

He studied me a few moments more before answering. This guy made me believe he was weighing his words exactly. I stayed quiet and let him do the studying.

"The facts are not enough justification?" he asked.

Oh, he was getting fancy now. *Justification*? His pulling out the ten-dollar words made me itchy.

"Nope. You guys have been dead and gone for, what, around three hundred years?" I asked.

He nodded and motioned for me to continue.

"Why protect land that hasn't been yours for centuries? It isn't adding up," I said.

His study of my face was making me nervous. If he was measuring me for something, I was not so sure I was making the cut. I wasn't sure I even wanted to make any cut. But I sure wanted answers, and I figured he was the one willing to give them. As I sat there, wondering how far I wanted to push him, a thought flew into my head. Uh-oh.

"How does my mother fold into this mess?" I asked, suspicion building.

Logan sighed. "We are not entirely sure. But your grandmother is concerned."

"Anytime my mother is involved, we should be concerned." I frowned. "She's a bit nuts, you know."

He cocked his head and frowned. "Nuts?"

"You know, crazy."

"Ah." His expression cleared. "Crazy, I understand. If that is all we are dealing with, it is easily handled."

"Really? Let me in on the secret of coping with crazy!" I snapped. He laughed. Mom was no laughing matter, but if he knew how to handle her, that was fine by me. She could be his problem. I'd thought when she'd died that I wouldn't have to be concerned with crazy again. When she had shown up today, that idea had been blown to hell and back. No pun intended.

I returned to my earlier line of questions. "The land? Why protect land that isn't yours?"

His gaze returned to the window. "They lived there at one time. The land has their mark on it and is their responsibility."

"Mark? What mark?"

"The mark of life," he said simply.

The lightbulb went on; I got it. "Women of the village giving birth."

He nodded. "The life-giving water from birth filters deep into the ground. It is a type of record, binding us to the land."

Well, this was getting way too damn complicated. I liked simple, boring, and no complications. What had happened a few weeks ago causing a need for me to be protected by a bunch of dead Indians? I'd started off with a handful

of dead people to sort through, and now I had dead people everywhere I turned.

"So," I began slowly, "you and your merry band of followers out back"—I jerked a thumb in the direction of the woods—"are here to protect me from evil spirits. Fine by me. What about solving the murder? You know, Bob and Elaine. This mess started with them."

He looked at me a moment before responding, "It may have begun for *you* with Bob and Elaine, but the problems in this world started long before they existed on earth."

Damn, more mumbo jumbo. I had been happy before all this creepy spirit stuff had bloomed into my life.

"Well, let's stick with the problem nearest to me, which *is* their murder. I need to solve this, so how can you help me?"

Shaking his head, he said, "My job is to protect, not solve murders. You are on your own in that regard."

Somehow, I had expected that answer.

Chapter 11

Andy walked down the hall toward the den calling my name. "Peg? Where did you put the pie? Jack and I have looked everywhere!"

As he turned the corner, he got a good look at my face and stopped in his tracks. "Um, sweetie, you okay?"

I glanced over at him and nodded. When I returned to face Logan, he was gone. I wasn't shocked at his disappearance, wasn't even surprised. The question lingering in the back of my mind, however, was, is the guy still here but, like Bob, invisible? I'd bet dollars to donuts the guy could mask his presence whenever he darn well felt like it. Since I couldn't prove it one way or the other, I decided to assume he was hovering nearby and act accordingly. Which basically meant I would behave and follow his lead.

I hauled my tired butt out of the chair and motioned Andy to head for the kitchen. "The pie is in the refrigerator, safe and sound."

"The fridge? Didn't think to look there," he said, walking down the hall.

"Obviously," I laughed.

Andy stopped before we made it to the kitchen doorway. Turning, he asked, "You sure things are all right?"

I sighed. "Mom showed up, then Nana, along with a band of Indians."

Leaning against the wall, he patiently waited for more. Thank God for his peaceful demeanor; I needed his steadiness to calm the rough seas in which I found myself.

"That's about it," I said.

He watched my face for a moment, then shook his head. "Nope. There's more." He reached over and tugged my hand playfully.

I hesitated, wondering how much to tell him. There was no sense in worrying him, but my need for his support eventually overrode any need for secrecy. I bit my lip before continuing, "I think Mom is playing for the other side."

"Other side?" Andy asked. "There actually *is* good versus evil? Wow." Andy's view of the afterlife had never involved heaven or hell, more like a place where he could nap to his heart's desire.

"I'm not sure it's as cut and dried as we would like to think. Nana is being pretty damn vague about this stuff." I sighed again. "But Logan made it bloody plain there was evil to deal with, here and there."

"Logan? Who's he?" Andy asked.

I waved a hand dismissively. "The Indian guy."

"Okay, tell me about the Indians. Their appearance is unique." He grinned at this new information.

I decided leaning against the wall was a good idea and followed suit. He was still holding my hand, and my head found that comfortable spot on his shoulder. "Yeah, it seems every day I meet new dead people. I don't even know this many living ones, and now I'm facing Indians!"

"That doesn't tell me why they're here," Andy said.

I bit my lip some more, thinking about Logan. "Peg?" Andy said, nudging my foot with his.

I took a deep breath and said, "Logan isn't the *real* Logan, you know the famous chief?" Andy nodded, and I continued, "Well, he told me they were here to protect me." I paused for a moment before adding, "From evil."

Andy's face stayed neutral, but his eyebrows moved a fraction. My own hiked up a bit to match his, just to show him we both agreed the situation was weird. We stood staring at one another for a few moments before Jack interrupted us, yelling from the kitchen, "Hey guys, the pie? My coffee's getting cold."

"On our way," Andy said, pushing off from the wall. He patted my hand and led me down the hall toward the kitchen. "We need to tell Jack the new developments."

I pulled him back sharply. "Why? I think it is strange enough for Jack as it stands. Why muddy the waters by scaring him with the whole evil stuff?"

Andy looked down at me. "Because he has a right to know. Face it, Peg: this is getting serious."

"Why, because we have Indians now?"

"Nope, because those Indians are worried," he said as we continued toward Jack.

"It's about damn time," Jack said as we entered the kitchen. Noticing our expressions, he shook his head. "I'm not going to like this, am I?"

Shrugging, I said, "Depends."

"On?" he asked.

"On how creepy dead Indians seem to you."

Jack frowned. "Now we have dead Indians?" Turning back to the counter, he said, "Found the pie. Who keeps pie in the fridge?"

Andy and I exchanged glances. Jack was more worried about pie than the newest addition to our merry gang?

"You don't seem at all surprised," I told him.

He shrugged. "I'm not." He turned to face me. "Once you accept dead people visiting and parceling out jobs, nothing else seems out of order." He turned back to the pie, lifted his freshly cut piece, and plopped it on a paper plate. Bless his heart, I wouldn't have to wash plates!

Andy joined Jack at the counter and pushed another paper plate toward him. "Make mine a little bigger than yours."

Jack nodded and started operating on the pie.

"The main Indian guy mentioned evil," I said.

"Stands to reason," Jack said as he turned again to face me. "Look, think about it. Good versus evil is classic human experience. Forget religions; think about any great story in history. Hell, even Superman is based on good versus evil."

"So it doesn't worry you?" I asked.

Holding up the pie knife, he grinned. "I never said it doesn't scare the shit out of me, merely that I figured evil would show up eventually. I'm not stupid."

Well, hell. I must be dumb as a damn brick. *I* never gave one second's thought to evil being introduced in the equation. I knew murder was evil but didn't consider Evil, with a capital *E*, as another factor adding to my misery.

Andy looked at me, rolling his hand, encouraging me to tell Jack more. I frowned, trying to figure out what he was referring to. Wasn't Logan enough? He mouthed, "Your mother." Oh yeah, forgot about her.

"Another little detail: my mom showed up."

Jack paused before handing Andy his plate. "That worries me more than the Indians. I remember your mom; she scares the hell out of me."

I had to laugh. He wasn't that far off the mark being scared of Mom; she had issues alive and dead.

Andy glanced in Jack's direction. "You remember Peg's mom?"

"That woman raced around this township like she owned the place. Chief Jackson had strict orders not to ticket her. Never figured it out, but something screwy was up regarding your mother. She was untouchable and knew it—made her a pain in the ass." He glanced at me. "Sorry, Peg. Didn't mean to sound so bitter."

I waved a hand to show no harm done. "Believe me: she was hell on wheels. I was safer with Nana than her."

"What did she want?" Jack asked as he filled his mouth with pie. "How does she figure into this murder?"

"I'm not sure she does figure much in the murder," I said after a moment's thought. "She wanted to warn me away from investigating."

Jack stopped chewing, swallowed hard, and then said, "Uh-oh. What do you think she means?"

I wasn't having pie, so I chewed on my bottom lip instead. "Not sure." I paused as a thought struck me. "She was always flirting with danger in some fashion, which makes me wonder how she is involved in this. Whatever creep she's hanging out with in Deadsville doesn't want the murder solved. But *who* that is?" I shook my head before finishing, "I have no idea."

We sat at the table in silence, each lost in own our thoughts. Mom being connected to this case, if she was, only spelled trouble. The problem was I had no idea how she was tied into this mess. I wondered if Bob would know any useful information. Long shot but worth a try.

"Bob!" I shouted. Jack and Andy jumped in their seats and looked at me as though I had lost my mind. Calling for Bob surprised even me, so I understood their expressions.

Damn if it didn't work. Bob popped into the kitchen, surprised as we were that I had called him.

"Wow, didn't know you could do that!" He sounded excited. "That was awesome. One second I'm watching the mayor eat a humongous cherry cream Danish; the next I'm here with you!"

"Other than his eating habits, have you found out any info?" I asked.

"What kind of pie are they eating?" he asked, noticing the paper plates, now empty of all but crusts of pie. "And no about the mayor. He's been eating for hours."

"Peach. Forget the pie. I have a question," I said.

He tore his gaze away from the pie and waited for my query.

"How does my mother fit into this murder?" Might as well be blunt; never know what answers you'll get.

"Your mother? I don't know her," he said. "We haven't met too many people over there ya know." He looked sheepish as he added, "Elaine isn't the nicest person and tends to be rude."

"What's he saying?" Jack asked. "Any good news?"

I waved at Jack to be quiet.

"You need to spy on my mother as well as the mayor. Think you can watch both of them? One's here on earth; the other is …" I stopped. Well, hell, where was my mother? Damned if I knew. "I'm not sure exactly where she is, but she's dead. You should be able to find her somehow."

Bob was quiet, thinking. "Hm, we haven't joined any of the available groups, so I haven't much in the way of sources to ask."

"You have groups you can join?" I asked, surprised.

"Oh yeah. If it weren't for Elaine's, you know, personality, we could be involved in lots of activities." His voice was full of sorrow. I had to feel sorry for him at this point, but let's be honest here: he was no picnic either.

"They have groups to join?" Jack asked, shocked. "My God, what next?"

"This is absolutely fascinating," Andy said, awed at the thought of social gatherings in the afterlife. I, on the other hand, found the entire situation ridiculous and extremely irritating. Did religions get *anything* right? Jeez.

"Bob! Focus! Can you keep an eye on both sides? On two people at once?"

"Well, not at the same time," he said, thinking through the problem. "But I'm pretty sure I can spy on them both. I'm learning new stuff every day!" he finished proudly.

I eyed him cautiously, not sure how far to trust his newfound abilities. Bob had basically sat on his ass for over ten years, learning nothing. Now, all of a sudden, he was gaining skills at a rapid pace. Would he be able to handle these powers? I had a headache forming and suspected Bob was the cause. Well, not just Bob. The entire ensemble of afterlife revelations, along with trying to solve a murder, was a headache.

"Can he do it?" Jack asked.

Bob looked over at Jack and Andy. "Wish they could see me; a little guy talk would be nice."

I rolled my eyes. "Meet guys on your side of things," I snapped.

Andy raised an eyebrow at that remark. "Gay?" he mouthed.

I had to laugh as I shook my head. "Tell ya later," I mouthed back.

He nodded, grinning.

"Okay, Bob. You've got work to do, so get going," I told him.

"Yep," he said before beginning to fade. Then the fading suddenly stopped. "How often do you want me to check in with you?" he asked.

I was surprised at the question. Since when did he ask to pop in? This was new.

He saw my expression and sighed. "All those years with Elaine made me forget manners. That's one of the things I've decided to correct. When this is done, I'm joining one of the organizations whether Elaine likes it or not!" he declared stoutly. I had to wonder if Elaine would self-combust over his newly acquired independence. One could only hope.

Nodding at his explanation, I said, "Once a day at least. But only stay long enough to fill me in on the news. Got it?"

"Yep. Sounds like a plan." Suddenly, he was gone. The change in the air was palpable.

"He's gone," Jack said.

"You noticed?" I asked.

"Yep. Getting used to the subtle differences when he's here and when he leaves," he answered, eyeing the pie. "Mind if I have a sliver more?" he asked.

I grinned. "Go for it."

Jack got up from the table, paper plate in hand. Turning to Andy, he asked, "Another slice?"

Shaking his head as he patted his belly, Andy said, "Better not. Trying to keep my waist down."

Grinning, Jack said, "Life is too short to worry about that baloney." He made it to the counter before the air changed again. Apparently feeling the shift, he sent a questioning look my direction. Shit fire, now what?

I quickly glanced around the kitchen, looking for the new visitor. Finally spotting the spirit tucked away in the shadows in the far corner of the kitchen, I caught my breath. God, a new one! He stepped forward, nodding silently.

I slowly let the air out of my lungs once I saw him fully. Surprised but no longer scared, I whispered, soft enough that only he could hear me, "Hey, Dad."

"Hey, twinkle toes." He smiled. He looked exactly as I remembered. A tall man, though not as tall as Andy, with bits of gray around his kind face. He was wearing the shirt I had given him one year for Father's Day, blue with little sailboats scattered around the waistline. His brown eyes were carefully watching my reaction to his sudden appearance.

My eyes filled with tears that then streamed down my cheeks. God, how I'd missed him. He'd died in a nasty car accident when I was eight. He had been my cushion of protection from Mom. His death had created a void that, thankfully, Nana had been willing to fill.

Andy's look of alarm at the sight of my tears forced me to pull myself together. "I'm okay," I told him quietly.

Jack was busy cutting another hunk of pie but asked over his shoulder, "The Indian back?"

"Nope. My dad."

Jack stopped his slicing, and Andy's mouth dropped open. Andy was the first to gather his wits about him, asking, "That good or bad?"

My dad looked at me, waiting for my answer. "Not sure" was all I could come up with.

Dad's sad expression at my answer made me ask him, "Well, which side are you on? Good or evil?"

The sadness in his eyes gave way to shock. "What are you talking about?"

"You don't know what's been happening around here the past few weeks?" I asked suspiciously.

"No, I pop in about once a month. Didn't realize you could see me."

Once a month? Dad had been popping in and out? News to me. But hearing this bit of info made tears start up again.

"How long have you been popping in?" I asked, sniffing.

He gave the question some thought before saying, "You were about twelve by the time I learned we could come back. Had no idea it was allowed, but once I did, I kept my eye on you." He glanced at Andy. "Pretty good guy you picked."

I smiled. "Glad you approve."

He nodded at Jack. "Who's that one?"

Jack had decided the pie was worth his attention more than the ghost in the kitchen and was walking back to the table to make himself comfortable while adding to his waistline. "A friend. Police chief of Bath."

Realizing he was the topic of conversation, Jack stopped midstride. "Do I need to be concerned that I'm being discussed?"

I grinned. "Nope. Dad wanted to know who you were."

Satisfied, he continued to the table. In between bites, he said to the air, "Nice to meet you."

Dad laughed. "Seems pretty comfortable with my presence. That's unusual."

I shook my head. "Dad, after the last few weeks, you showing up is easy."

He cocked his head and asked, "What exactly has been going on around here?"

"Well, Nana showed up to inform me I have been assigned a murder to solve. The murdered couple were next in line to appear and demand justice. Mom showed up earlier today, and then there was a group of Indians. It's been busy."

His face showed concern at the mention of my mother, and his eyebrows rose at the mention of the Indians.

"Indians? Peg, what's happening that you have all this activity?" He stopped and eyed me. "Since when can you see us?"

I sighed heavily. "Since menopause hit, I guess. One night I opened my eyes to see Nana and her friend standing in my bedroom. Next thing I know, it's like a parade of dead people around here." I paused, thinking. "Come to think of it, Nana's friend was supposed to be my spirit guide, whatever the hell that is. Haven't really seen hide nor hair of her since." I stopped, then added, remembering the library visit, "Once only."

He waved a hand. "Those guys play it sneaky." He held up both hands. "Don't get me wrong; they are good to have on your side, but they don't materialize often. Like to hang in the background, unnoticed."

I cocked my head, saying, "You seem to know a lot about them. What gives?"

He shrugged. "You been here long enough, you watch and learn. They only get involved when it's serious." He frowned as he gave out this nugget. "You must be dealing with some grim circumstances."

His words did not make me feel better. If Dad thought it was bad, then it was bad. Damn it.

"I thought it was just a murder I was supposed to solve. Logan informed me it was deeper than that, but he wouldn't explain."

"Logan?" Dad asked.

"The main Indian guy. He isn't the *real* Logan but said I could call him by that name. He's pretty serious about the situation."

"He wouldn't be the real Logan; that guy seldom allows himself to get involved in earthly matters. But if the Indians are visiting you, that's something to think about, babe."

"Just what I want to hear," I said. After a moment's hesitation, I added, "You seen Mom over on your side?"

His frown deepened. No surprise there; he and Mom hadn't had the best marriage.

He shook his head and asked, "What did she want?"

I thought it was interesting Dad asked that question rather than asking if Mom was helping me somehow. Apparently he knew her better than I realized.

I shrugged before answering, "Warned me not to solve this murder; said if I didn't keep my nose out of it, I would regret snooping."

He stood stock-still listening to me. Watching his manner made me sweat. Something big must be going on, and I wasn't happy to be sucked into the afterlife's bullshit politics.

"Should I be worried?" I asked him.

"What'd your nana have to say about the warning?" he asked quietly, ignoring my question.

"Not much. But she brought Logan along with her, so even she must not be happy about Mom's visit."

Jack and Andy had been quietly listening to my side of the conversation, neither one looking too thrilled about the bits and pieces they were able to hear.

"I'll come by more often until you get this murder cleared up; you know, keep an eye out for you," he said. "Let me see if I can nose around over here and pick up some useful info."

I nodded my thanks. "Appreciate it a lot, Dad."

He gave me a quick smile, then added, "Babe, listen to this Logan fella. I trust him, but your mother's involvement could complicate your investigation. She's up to no good; I guarantee it. Watch yourself."

Jeez, that didn't make me feel all warm and fuzzy. I shot him a quick nod as he started to fade. "Daddy!" I called.

The fading stopped as he paused to hear me. "Dad, it's good to know you've been around all these years. Thanks."

Smiling his million-dollar smile I remembered so well, he gave me a quick wave and faded totally.

I was quiet for so long Andy cleared this throat and asked, "You okay, sweetie?"

"Yeah, but I never expected to see him." I felt tears threaten again, so I jumped up from the table and headed for the coffee machine. I needed something stronger than caffeine but settled on black coffee. Brewing a cup, I noticed the tremor in my hand. Damn, my world had been rocked for weeks, but now it was swinging precariously. Dad's warnings had shaken me more than I liked to admit.

Watching me, Jack asked, "We in a world of trouble?"

"Could be, not sure. Odds are …" I couldn't finish the statement.

We sat silently at my scarred, well-used kitchen table. Events were running along too fast for me. I was ridiculously out of my element.

Chapter 12

I didn't sleep well that night—no surprise there. Let's face it: between meeting the Indians and seeing both my parents, the day had been jam-packed with emotion. I did, however, eventually acquire enough sleep to survive. Sitting at the kitchen table the next morning, feeling hung over from the previous day's weird adventure into dead land, it hit me I had not specified an exact timetable for Bob to check in with me. The goofball was likely to show up while I was in the shower! As if on some sort of cosmic telepathic wavelength, up popped Bob. Creepy.

Glancing at my coffee cup, Bob said, "Too early? I've been waiting, honest."

I looked at his excited expression and thought it was like seeing a three-year-old proud of himself for pooping in the toilet instead of his pants. Oh well, he was trying.

Shaking my head, I said, "Now is fine. I take it you have something to share?"

His gaze followed my cup as I took another sip of steaming coffee. "I don't miss much about the physical world, but I do miss a good cup of coffee," he said longingly.

Nothing I could do about his inability to enjoy coffee, so I changed the subject to the matter at hand. I said pointedly, "Bob, you are here before I am ready to face the day, for what exactly?"

Dragging his focus from my coffee, he said, "Oh, yeah. Okay, here's the deal. The mayor finally finished eating yesterday and made some calls." His expression changed as he said, "Peg, that man can eat! I've never seen anyone able to put away so much food at one time. He's a machine when it comes to eating."

"Bob," I said, irritated, "I don't give a damn about the mayor's eating habits. What's the information you were so hot to share with me?"

"I'm just saying," he pouted.

I glared at him; he got the point.

"Fine, but you don't have to be so mean!" He continued pouting but did at least give a report on his activities. "Once he filled his gut with way too much food, he made a ton of phone calls," he said triumphantly.

I waited for him to continue, but the smug look on his face told me he felt he had delivered the golden nugget.

"Um, Bob? Anything more?"

He looked confused by my question. Throwing his arms up in the air, he said, "I did what I was supposed to do! I spied on him!"

"But who did he call? What did they talk about?" I asked, so frustrated with him that if he wasn't dead, I might have killed the idiot.

With a wave of his hand, he said, "Oh, that. I didn't know I should have taken notes!" Was that a touch of sarcasm I heard? Jeez.

One of my eyebrows rose to great heights as I looked at him, dumbfounded. First, no decent information, and second, Bob had the audacity to be snotty?

"Do you know who he called?" I asked patiently. Well, I asked through gritted teeth, but I knew if I exploded, I'd never get anything out of him. He was already pouting and could shut down completely if I wasn't careful.

He actually had to pause and think about the question. Not promising at all. Finally, he nodded, answering, "Yeah. I'm pretty sure it was his son. Asked him a bunch of questions. Then he hung up. Well, he slammed the phone down. Is that important?"

Uh-oh. His calling his son made me nervous. Was the mayor trying to warn his kid or trying to get information out of him? I sat thinking for a few minutes, and to give Bob credit, he stayed quiet and let my brain work.

"Did he call anyone else connected to your murder?" I finally asked.

Another thoughtful expression came over Bob's face. Maybe not having to focus the past decade had fried his ability to function properly. Who the hell knew?

After what seemed to be an eternity, because Bob certainly had that kind of time, he said, "Yeah, he called some guy with an Italian-sounding name."

I frowned. Italian name? I had to admit I was as bad as the next person: my mind immediately went to the Mafia. Sue me. But it would explain how

94

he kept getting elected for well over ten years. I had heard rumors for years but had never given it much consideration.

"Do you happen to remember any of the conversation?" I asked him, again with a great deal of restraint and politeness. Didn't know I had it in me. Would wonders never cease?

Bob's thinking gears must have gotten dusted off, because he answered right away. "Yeah, I do." He screwed up his face tight as he recalled the conversation. "Said something about having to clean up a mess he thought was long ago controlled." He tilted his head, saying, "Wonder what it was about."

I laid my head on the table, groaning. God, what a total moron. I let my poor head rest a moment before lifting it up and saying, "You think it could be your murders?" Honey dripped off those words, but Bob was oblivious.

Bob's surprise was total. "Wow. Never even considered it was about us." He looked at me with awe. "You really are good at this stuff."

I gave him a quick, tight smile as I said, "You were the one who heard him talking. I'm only connecting the dots." Might as well throw the idiot a positive bone, build up his self-esteem a little. God knew Elaine had been taking potshots at it for years. Maybe it would help him pay better attention while spying on the mayor. Couldn't hurt to try.

"Okay, on to the next. Anything about my mom?"

He shook his head sadly. "Couldn't find her anywhere. Even asked a few spirits I'd seen around a couple of times. No one knows where she hangs out, and I don't really know the territory too well." He gave me an apologetic shrug. "I guess I haven't been very helpful."

Shaking my head, I said, "Bob, focus on the mayor for now. You might get lucky and hear something useful. Just pay close attention to all conversations he has from now on. He will be careful about talking in front of other people, so focus on calls when he is alone."

Nodding, Bob said, "That's really a good idea. Would have never thought of it myself."

No kidding. "Thanks for the update. Check in when you find something promising."

He began fading. "Not a problem. See ya later."

How had I gotten stuck with this imbecile? Maybe I was expecting too much from him. But honestly, you'd think being dead would sharpen a person's skills somehow.

Before I could get any further with my thoughts, the air changed, and the hairs on the back of my neck moved around. Jeez. Now what?

I swiftly scanned the room. Nothing. I knew something or someone was in the room with me but couldn't pinpoint where. Suddenly, I could smell perfume. Mom. In death, as in life, her perfume announced her arrival.

I stayed still, determined to wait her out; the woman loved a dramatic entrance. Finally, I could sense she was behind me.

I slowly turned, scanning the room as I did. Sure enough, there she was, right behind me.

"Hi, Mom," I said once I had spotted her.

"You could tell I was here?" she asked, clearly disappointed.

"Yeah, I can tell. Plus you must have doused yourself with a gallon of perfume." I frowned. "Since when does the afterlife have perfume counters?"

Her laughter filled the room. "Sweetie, haven't you watched enough of those ghost shows on TV to know we can emit fragrances we wore when we lived?" She sniffed the air. "This one was my favorite."

"Yeah, I remember. L'Air de Aroma. I always did like the scent." Just not on her, but I refrained from adding that remark.

Nodding, she said, "Yes, I remember."

Ah, she was using the scent for a reason. Trying to awaken memories? Not necessarily her best move; our relationship hadn't been stellar. If she was trying to evoke emotions, she'd chosen what I considered a big, fat, flashing warning sign. Whatever she was up to with these little visits of hers, it wasn't good. I knew her better than she realized, and I needed to keep the knowledge to myself. Might as well allow her to think her sneaky schemes would work on me. I wasn't completely stupid.

She walked around the kitchen, critically inspecting the outdated room. "You really need to gut this place and start over. The den is nice, but why didn't you bother in here?"

"I like it," I said simply.

She waved a hand in the air. "You always were overemotional concerning your projects with your grandmother. I remember when you two pored over wallpaper samples. How boring."

My eyes narrowed as I watched her continue to scrutinize my kitchen. Remembering her disdain for the decorating choices I had made then, I didn't expect her opinion to have changed. It hadn't.

"This is the ugliest mess in the world. And now it's peeling. Get rid of it!"

"I'll get around to it eventually. I've been busy. You know, raising kids, being involved in their lives, getting them graduated and on their way. Plus there's Andy."

"Ah, yes. Andy," she said, ignoring everything else I'd mentioned. She hadn't been what you would have called an "involved" parent. Homework, projects, school plays; she had ignored those parts of my life. After Dad had died, Nana had stepped in and guided me through those years. Mom couldn't have been bothered. I had taken the opposite approach with my own children and probably gone overboard—room mother more years than I cared to remember, PTA, team mother for every sport they'd played. It had been exhausting, and I'd loved every minute of it.

"I never understood what you saw in him," she sneered. "Such a boring guy."

"He's not boring!" I said between gritted teeth. Even dead, she angered me with her snide comments.

"What would you call him then? Dependable?" she asked, sarcasm dripping from each word.

"That's one word. Fun, interesting, intelligent, caring, just to name a few."

She waved her hand, dismissing my view of Andy. "Like I said, boring," she replied.

Changing the subject, I asked, "What are you doing here?"

She stopped her inspection, turning to face me with deliberation. "I am here to finish our little talk from yesterday. You must stop this ridiculous investigating."

"Ridiculous?" I asked. I had to admit I was intrigued. Why was ending this investigation so important to her? Caution was needed; no sense allowing her to realize my trust in her was basically nil, nada, zilch.

"Oh, yes, your nana has a bee in her bonnet about those deaths. *Why* is beyond me. They were so long ago. What difference does it make?" She was watching me with careful eyes.

I looked at her for a moment, then said, "They were quite a while back; that's for sure. I don't know why they seem so important to her."

With a quick flip of her hand, she said, "That woman was always a little off! She has you running around making a fool of yourself."

Her flippant remark about Nana was intriguing. Why should she care the murders were being looked at now? I'd never trusted her, so what made her think discrediting Nana would gain my confidence? Of course, there was the fact she actually believed she was the smartest person ever, so it would never occur to her I couldn't be fooled. Death had not improved her assessment of others; she was still under the allusion she could fool everybody, every time. I wasn't really surprised.

I decided I needed to be extremely careful dealing with her. I might not trust her, but the possibility she was dangerous was considerable. I wasn't sure exactly what I was dealing with and didn't want to find out the hard way.

"What makes you so sure the murders shouldn't have a fresh look?" I asked as innocently as possible.

I could tell from her expression she was appraising me, searching for clues that would give her an inkling about what was going on in my mind. Let's face it: she was beginning to scare the hell out of me.

"I warned you yesterday: stay away from these murders." Her smile was repulsive as she continued, "It would not be in your best interest to pursue them. Very unhealthy, I assure you."

"Are you threatening me?" I asked with wide-eyed wonder. Two could play at this game, and I'd taken acting classes in high school, something she hadn't been interested in forty-odd years ago. I hoped death had not given her any type of insight into our past.

She laughed callously. "Why do you assume it is a threat?"

God, I was beginning to sweat. Suddenly, the air shifted; this time, more electric.

She glanced up, shock clearly showing on her face. "You!"

I turned to see Logan standing quietly behind me. Thank God.

"Hello, Nell. How have you been?" he said softly. His low voice was more menacing than if he had yelled at her.

I was still sweating as I felt the tension between my mother and my protector amplify. This was officially freaking the hell out of me. The sweat trickled down my back, but at least it wasn't sliding down into my bra. Such an icky sensation.

My mother glared a moment longer at Logan and then finally broke their eye connection, looking at my faded wallpaper instead. Glancing quickly back at him, she asked, "What are you doing here?"

His eyes sliding in my direction, he answered, "Your daughter has my protection."

I swear my mother's face turned snow white. I mean, come on, she was dead—no blood to actually drain from her face, right? So how had she lost color? Should I care? My headache started up again.

Logan never turned a hair. He was Mr. Calm and Cool. Didn't help my headache.

"How did she obtain your protection?" she finally asked once she had gotten control of herself.

He cocked his head to one side, watching her. "Does that matter? She has my protection."

My mother stomped her foot. No kidding, a full-out stomp. "How!" she demanded.

Logan continued watching her. I wondered if he was as intrigued by her reactions and demand as I was. Honestly, he scared the poop out of me, but why would *she* be frightened of him? They were both dead, so why fear him? My head was pounding. There must be a kind of system I was unaware of over there in Deadsville. God, I hated this.

Finally, Logan said, "While I have no need to explain my actions to you, I will answer you. She carries Indian blood."

After a moment of shocked silence, my mother's laughter rang through the house. "She has absolutely no Indian blood!" she crowed.

Shaking his head sadly, he said, "Nell, you think only your bloodline runs through her veins?"

She stopped laughing. "You can't mean her worthless father had Indian genes in him? He was full-blooded Irish."

His watchful gaze never left her face. Their eyes locked once more as he said, "Full-blooded Irish, except for one Indian woman in his heritage. It is enough."

Eyes narrowing, Mom said, "I never heard about this. What tribe?"

"Cherokee," Logan calmly answered.

My mother's breath caught. That one lady in my genetic pool must be important. Who knew?

"Who?" was all she was able to choke out.

"The information is none of your concern," Logan answered. Holy cow, he was as cool as a cucumber.

Fists clenched and her face a fury, Mother faded. When she was gone, I turned to Logan.

"My ancestor was an important person?"

"While she may have been important to the Cherokee, she was not historically known. You would not recognize her name. Your mother wanted knowledge she is not entitled to have." He shrugged. "I told her the tribe because she would recognize the spiritual importance."

He didn't bother to explain, so I raised a questioning eyebrow.

"This particular Cherokee woman had great spiritual powers, not as strong as mine but strong enough," he said in response to my unspoken question.

"Am I allowed to ask questions?"

He nodded, smile in place.

"Why was Mom so afraid when she realized I'm under your protection?" I had a million others, but I figured this was a good start.

He thought for a moment before answering, "Your mother realized she cannot interfere as much as she had obviously counted on doing. That limits her ability to stop the investigation. She must need to prevent these murders from being solved." I could see the concern on his face, which did nothing to make me feel safe, secure, or happy.

"So this is a problem?"

He nodded. "Most likely."

"Then help me solve these murders!" My frustration was at an all-time high.

He shook his head. "I have told you: that is your mission. Mine is to protect. Yours is to solve."

"This is getting out of hand! Why am I attracting so much attention?"

"Excellent question. I would advise you to solve the murders as soon as possible."

"Really? That's your advice?" I snapped.

He smiled. "I have faith in your abilities."

"Oh, that makes all the difference in the world," I sneered. "Thanks."

Fading, he continued to smile.

My head was pounding.

Chapter 13

I glanced at the clock once my kitchen was free from the dead and was shocked to see it was almost lunchtime. Could these entities form a time warp of some sort? I'd had no idea hours had passed—creepy. Or had I blacked out somehow and was finally waking up? God only knew, and he wasn't helping my situation either. Maybe this was a type of test—you know, to see how much turmoil I could handle. Or, my personal favorite, I was in a coma, and none of this was real. Until I could decide on one of those scenarios, I would continue as though the dilemma was real.

Sighing, I made a decision to accomplish an act of normalcy, namely, wash a load of clothes. That was tangible and mundane. Maybe it would help my headache. As I sorted the colors from the whites, my mind wouldn't quit running overtime. So what was the deal with my small drop of Indian heritage? Why had my mother been so freaked out? How did a murder from the nineties play into the spiritual world? Why was it so important for me to cease investigating? Even I noticed these were all questions with no answers coming to light.

Loading the washer, I heard a commotion in the kitchen. I froze. The dead gang didn't make noise, and Andy was at work. I looked frantically around for some type of weapon and grabbed a container of bleach. The sucker was new and heavy as hell. I always bought the two-gallon jugs because they were cheaper, and this baby could carry a wallop. I should know; I'd dropped it on my foot a month back and thought I had broken every bone. The bruise was still fading, even though it was a sick yellow at this point.

I cautiously made my way to the kitchen. The laundry room was on the other side of the house, so whoever was in the kitchen was noisy. The closer I got to the sounds, the more confused I became. It sounded as though whoever was in there was looking for something specific. What did they think I had hidden in my kitchen? Secret million-dollar recipes?

I paused before the last corner, my stomach reacting to the tension that was freely flowing through my system. I finally got enough nerve to peek my head around the corner for a quick look. My grip on the bleach jug was white- knuckled. When I saw who was standing in the kitchen, I dropped the bleach on my foot. Damn.

"Shit! Damn it to hell!"

Owen looked up, surprised. "Hey, Mrs. S. You okay?"

Hopping around on one foot, I screamed, "What the hell are you doing in here?"

He flashed his famous 200-watt smile, answering, "Your front door was open. You know that isn't safe, right?"

"What do you mean the door was open? Open, open? Or just unlocked?"

"Open. I thought I'd better check it out. Heard you in the laundry room and realized everything was fine."

I hopped over to the table and sat down, slipping my shoe off to inspect any damage to my foot. Glancing at the pie Owen held in his right hand, obviously scrounged from the fridge, I raised my eyebrows, both of them.

His eyes followed my glance, and he looked back at me with a sheepish grin. "It's okay, right? You never minded when we were in high school."

I sighed. "Owen, high school was a long time ago."

"You changed your hiding place," he said. "You always kept pie in the cabinet with the health food. Guess you figured no one would ever look there. Want some?" he asked innocently.

"No thanks," I said wearily. "What were you doing in here?"

"The chief asked me to check in on you during patrols. When I saw the door ajar, I figured I better make sure you were okay. You *are* okay, right?" he asked, watching me rub my foot.

"I was until I dropped the bleach bottle on my foot."

"Gosh, I didn't mean to scare you."

"Hearing someone snooping around the house is frightening," I snapped. From his face, it was clear this was news to him. Obviously, he was as comfortable prowling around my kitchen as he had been as a teenager. I sighed, pushing my anger away. Waving a hand, I said, "It's fine. But while you're here, think you can walk through the house? I'm not sure why the door was wide open. Also, check around the perimeter, just in case?"

"Yep, right after I eat this pie." He nodded.

"Fine. I'd better get back to the laundry. Let me know before you leave." I slipped my shoe back on and stood, testing weight on my foot before heading back to laundry. The last thing I needed was a broken foot.

"Sure thing. Thanks, Mrs. S." He threw a smile at me again as he turned to his plate. Unlike Jack, he was using an actual plate. He better damn well wash it himself.

I paused and turned back to Owen. "Do you remember Alex Hayes?"

Owen frowned. "Sure, why?"

I hesitated for a moment, then asked, "Was he trouble?"

Owen slowly shook his head. "I don't want to cause the guy any problems."

I sighed. "Owen, was he honestly a bad kid?"

Owen searched my face for a clue to why I was asking, but I kept my expression as blank as possible.

"Alex started dabbling around with minor activities when we were in junior high school. You know, little stuff like swiping pens off a teacher's desk. Over the next few years his antics became more serious." He shook his head. "I tried to help steer the guy in the right direction, but I have to be honest: he was headed for trouble."

I nodded as Owen spoke. "What kind of trouble?"

Owen studied the floor a few moments before saying, "He was playing around with drugs." He held up his hands. "Not sure how deep he got, but I know he was smoking pot. At some point in high school he became really unstable." He shrugged. "I have kept in touch a little through the years but not enough to tell you anything more."

"I appreciate your honesty. Thanks."

He nodded. "No problem. Oh, and don't worry; I'll wash the plate before I leave."

For Pete's sake, who knew letting my kids' friends have free reign of the house would turn into this? Shaking my head at the situation, I limped back to dirty clothes. Owen must be a fast eater, because a few minutes later I heard him go out the back door to fill my request. He was a good kid, and I appreciated the precaution Jack was taking concerning my safety. Knowing the front door had been open sent shivers down my spine. Hell, through my entire body. Shaking off the fear, I promised myself to be more cautious about locking doors.

Owen also seemed to be a fast walker, because it wasn't long before I heard him start his patrol car, followed by the crunching of the gravel on our driveway. I frowned, wondering why he hadn't remembered to check with me before leaving. After a second of thought, I realized he must have been called out to a scene. I wondered if someone else had found their front door wide open; wouldn't surprise me. We didn't have much crime here, if you ignored the occasional murder; breaking and entering seemed to be the norm and usually the height of our crime sprees. Probably a bunch of teenagers.

Finally finished loading the washer, I spun the dial to start it and decided to get a little investigative work done. Grabbing my laptop, I limped back to the kitchen table. Once I got comfortable, I stared at the screen, wondering where to start work. Inspiration finally hit, and I typed in Alex Hayes's name. It's a little amazing, and a lot scary, how much information about people exists on the Internet. If you don't believe me, try searching your name, and see what pops up. Thought your life was private? Ha!

I skipped through most of the information showing up but stopped and clicked on the entry about his current residence. It would be nice to know where the little creep was living these days. My eyes popped open when I realized his address was right here in Bath. Since when did he live in the township? I knew his dad still resided in Akron; he was the mayor after all. I hadn't heard any news about Alex living out here, however. That would be news, since most of the township's population despised his father. Maybe he was living with someone and no one knew he was here. That information wasn't available, but I noted the address and typed it into the search. Hot damn! The property was in his dad's name! Why hadn't I heard something about this through the gossip mill?

I sat thinking about the fact his dad owned property in Bath. I was surprised it wasn't a well-known fact. Grabbing a pad of paper I used for grocery lists, I jotted down a reminder to ask Jack if he was aware of this golden information. Tapping the pen against my lips, I wondered if it was one of the many secrets a chief of police had to keep to himself. It wouldn't surprise me. I didn't think Jack knew Alex Hayes was living in Bath, though. He wouldn't hold back that tidbit, would he? I made another note on the pad to ask Jack about Alex also.

The shrill of the phone made me jump. To be honest, I almost peed my pants. Apparently my stress level was higher than I'd realized. For some strange reason, I didn't want to answer it and considered letting the machine take a message. Figuring this was the coward's way out, I was reaching over to pick up the receiver when it suddenly stopped ringing. Thankfully, the decision was out of my hands. Andy and I had contemplated getting rid of the landline and using our cell phones as our children had advised, but we were used to it and liked having it as a backup in case one of the cell phones wasn't charged. At our age, or maybe because of it, we believed in backup plans. It made us feel safer. What could I say? We didn't like change. Andy loved technology, but he was the most adamant about keeping a "real" phone. I think he believed his cell phone was a toy, and why not? He played enough games on the darn thing.

I returned to the task at hand but came up empty. Couldn't think of another line of research. I was absolutely not cut out to be a detective. Sighing, I turned my gaze to the woods. The kitchen and den windows both faced the woods, which was one of the reasons Andy and I had fallen in love with the old farmhouse. Woods surrounded our house on three sides, with the front being open to a quiet road. It was beautiful year-round. The view alone had driven us to buy the house as newlyweds. We'd ignored the many faults of the century home and taken the plunge. We had never once regretted our decision. I found myself searching for signs of the watchful Indians but saw nothing. It made me wonder if they, unlike Bob, had long ago figured out how to be invisible. I hoped so; it would give me a sense of security to know they were there, whether I could see them or not.

Tearing my eyes away from the empty woods, I glanced at the computer again. Opening the drawer nearest to me, I grabbed a map of the township. Why we had one was a mystery, but had one we did. I checked the screen to confirm Alex's address was on Revere Road. Which part of Revere was the question. Whoever had named the roads way back when had decided it would be cool to have that named road cut across the entire township. Problem was it wasn't a straight cut. Revere Road had more than one dead end but would pick up a block or two farther down another named road. Drove me nuts, but no one asked what I thought.

Checking the house number, I realized he lived on North Revere near the high school. Our high school football team was the Minutemen. Hope you made the connection, because if you didn't, then our education system concerning American history is in more trouble than I want to contemplate.

Drumming my fingers on the table, I pondered driving past his house. Not the smartest move, but neither was digging up an old murder possibly involving the mayor's son. I had almost talked myself into the foolish move when the air changed and my arm hairs curled. Guess who. Turning, I saw Elaine's sour face glaring at me.

"Don't you ever work?" she asked, acid dripping from her voice.

My eyes narrowed. "What makes you think I'm not working?"

She waved a hand around. "Every time I visit, you are either shopping or woefully gazing out that dirty window. I don't consider it working." Eyeing the window, she added, "Do you ever wash your windows?"

I ignored the window remark; I had no idea when I'd washed windows last. Ten years ago maybe?

"Thinking *is* working," I said, icicles dripping from my words. If she could use hot, I'd use cold. You know, just to balance it out a bit.

Ignoring my tone, she fluttered her hand dismissively. "You are being lazy. I told you who murdered us. Now prove it!"

I would have flattened her sorry butt right then and there, but I was pretty sure contact couldn't be made. Maybe Logan had specialized abilities, but my guess was few on this side of life did. If what Logan had told me was true, his capabilities were pretty darn rare. I didn't think that was a bad thing. Couldn't have millions of dead folks wandering around being able to grab us living ones—talk about mass hysteria.

I studied Elaine's sharp features. She could have been a real beauty if her disposition hadn't been so nasty. It had pinched her mouth into a bitter line, and her eyes didn't have laugh lines. The wrinkles she did have reminded me of rivers that caused deep ravines, sort of like the Grand Canyon. Her bottle-blonde hair was shoulder length and thick. I would have paid good money to have hair like hers. She looked younger than Bob, much younger. A thought hit my brain.

"Elaine, I understand your appearance to the living is your choice. What age do you choose to appear?"

My question caught her off guard. She joined everyone else's habit and looked out the window. I told you there must be a magnetic force connected to the darn thing. Wonder if it was the grime and dirt on it? Her lips clamped together tighter than a drum. I almost laughed; even dead, age was a touchy subject with her. Talk about ego.

"I'm asking because Bob looks much older than you, but I remember reading you guys met in college. I'm guessing you are close to his age." I paused, noticing she looked totally self-satisfied. "Not that you look *better*, mind you, just younger." So shoot me. I couldn't pass up the chance of slapping that smug look off her nasty face. The payoff was worth it; I thought she was going to self-combust. I was pretty sure we didn't have blood pressure when we were dead, but Elaine turned so purple I would have sworn hers was rising to epic proportions.

When she turned her eyes back to mine, I was a tad alarmed at how black with rage they had become. Creepy. She and my mother must be headed for the same afterlife prison camp. I mean, surely these people couldn't roam around causing problems forever.

"Don't push me too far," she warned.

I somehow held my ground. Not being known for bravery, I was out of my comfort zone with these crazies. Knowing Logan was more than likely nearby had given me a little more confidence. I realized I had pushed Elaine, but hells bells, she deserved every bit she got.

I had to laugh. I mean, really? "You came to *me*, remember? I'm working on your case, so bug off."

"We were *sent* to you! I would never have chosen you!"

My own anger rising, I stood to face her. "Look, bitch! Back off! Get out of my house!"

Even fuming, Elaine had to leave once I ordered her to go. Thank God!

I continued to stand there, chest heaving with outrage and maybe a teeny bit of fear. Elaine was a horrible person, but something told me she was becoming worse since I had first met her. What was going on here?

A figure stepped out of the shadow in the one corner that allowed for any type of shelter—if you were dead, that is. I almost peed my pants until I recognized the face. Dad. I sat down with a thump.

"My God, you people have to stop scaring the crap out of me!"

He smiled. "Didn't mean to startle you, but I saw her slip over here and thought she needed to be watched."

This was news. "You can see when someone comes here? How?"

He cocked his head, thinking. "It's a bit like looking through a thick glass. We can see you, but most people can't see us." He stopped, thinking again, before continuing, "Think of Jell-O. That's the closest I can come to explaining."

"You have to walk through this Jell-O stuff? But you can watch anyone here?" That wasn't comforting. Face it: knowing millions of the deceased could

sit on the other side (I'd quit thinking of it as heaven; that train had left the station) and watch us slogging along life was creepy. We weren't a damn movie to entertain them. It might be all warm and fuzzy to some but not me. I was a private person and didn't want to be on some universal stage, like an actor in a play.

I laid my head on the table. "This is getting too metaphysical."

He threw back his head and laughed. "Babe, it isn't all bad." Watching me pout, he smiled. "You haven't changed much through the years."

I raised my head. "What?"

Shrugging, he continued to grin. "You always did like situations to be simple. Life is rarely simple."

"From what I've seen, death isn't all that straightforward either." I plopped my head back on the table.

He shrugged again and moved around the kitchen. I watched him from the corner of my eye. A thought raced across my brain, and I sat straight up in the chair. "Dad?"

"Hmm?" he answered as he looked at the wallpaper. What was it with the damn wallpaper that he and Nana couldn't keep their eyes off the stuff? Jeez.

"Dad!"

He turned to face me.

"Do you know who killed Bob and Elaine?" Figured I might as well ask; you never knew, he might actually have the answer to the puzzle.

Shaking his head, he said, "Even if I did, I'm not sure I could tell you. We have rules."

I could feel my anger slowly building. "Rules? I have an Indian that is dead but able to massage my neck. I have Mom popping in and out, threatening me. There are dead people watching us. And you tell me there are rules?" I had allowed the anger to take shape. "Screw the rules!" I immediately clapped my hand over my mouth as he raised an eyebrow, oh so slightly, at my speech. Had I just screamed at my dad?

Slowly, the grin I remembered so vividly spread to a full-fledged smile. "You still have a temper."

Shaking my head, I got up and walked to the sink. "That's all you can say?" I had to do something, so cleaning came to mind. Since scrubbing wasn't my usual go-to when stressed, the action was curious. Go figure.

His eyes never leaving me, he shook his head sadly. "I can't break them, not high enough up on the food chain."

Food chain? There's a corporate ladder over there? I thought. Arching an eyebrow, I asked, "Really? Are you dodging from helping me?"

"Nope. Just the way it is."

"Then why is Logan able to help?" I asked.

Shrugging, Dad said, "Simple. Higher up."

I slammed the water off and stomped back to the chair. Sitting down, I pulled paper and pen over to me. I wrote down the address of Alex's house. Looking up at Dad, I asked, "You know where this is?"

He glanced down at the paper, nodded, and looked at me. "What about it? You aren't thinking of going over there, are you?"

My reliable eyebrow rose. "You know who lives here?" I asked.

"Sure, old man Hayes."

"The mayor lives in this house?" I was shocked.

Shaking his head, Dad said, "Nope. *His* dad. Bought it after the war. Korean, not Second."

"The mayor of Akron was raised out here in Bath?"

"No. The old man bought it for his parents, but he and his family lived in West Akron before moving to Cuyahoga Falls."

The Falls was a lovely city a tad north of Akron. It had its problems, but the majority of the city was nice.

"By the time the old man's kids were grown, his parents had died, so after a few years, he moved into that house. Lived there till he died."

"Well, I'm driving past the house. Wanna go with me?"

Sighing, he said, "Twinkle toes, I'm always with you."

That statement immediately brought tears to my eyes. Blinking them back as quickly as I could, I nodded. "Let's go."

As I opened the front door, a cop car drove up and stopped at the house. I frowned. What could be the problem now?

A uniformed policeman exited the car, glancing quickly around the yard. Turning to me, he asked, "Mrs. Shaw?"

I nodded. "How can I help you?"

Smiling, he said, "The chief sent me over to check on you. Any problems?"

Frowning, I shook my head. "Wow, Jack really must be worried about me! But two cops here in one afternoon is overdoing it a bit, don't you think?"

"Ma'am, I do as I'm told. Orders given were to keep a close eye on the house and yard. The chief wants random surveillance during all shifts."

His extreme professionalism irritated me. I must have become comfortable with the easygoing nature of the officers I knew in the department.

I held my hand out. "I'm Peg Shaw. And you are?" I hoped my friendlier demeanor would thaw his civic commitment a degree or two.

"Officer Thompson, ma'am." He didn't look thrilled to shake my hand but followed through with the ritual in spite of himself.

I smiled. "Nice to meet you, Officer Thompson. Thank you for checking on me."

"You mind if I take a few minutes and walk through your house?"

Sighing, I stepped back, allowing him to enter the house. He made quick work of his inspection, nodding as he returned to the living room. "I'll take a quick look around back. Then I'm out of your hair." He smiled and looked as though it pained him. Looking down at the purse I was holding, he said, "I see you were on your way out."

I nodded. "Yep. Tell Jack I appreciate his concern. If you're done in the house, I need to get going."

"Yes, ma'am," he said as I walked past him to my car.

Once in the car, I turned to Dad. "Jack is taking this seriously."

"He should," Dad said. He turned, watching the cop make his way to the backyard. "That guy new?"

I shook my head. "Have no idea. I don't know all the guys at the department."

"A little too stiff," Dad said.

Laughing, I said, "Jack likes to run a tight ship. I do feel safer knowing he's having the house watched. But two guys in one day? Isn't that a little overboard?"

"Nope," Dad said.

Chapter 14

I have to admit that driving around town with my dad was awesome. He hadn't been there to teach me to drive or at my wedding or at the birth of my children. But here I was, cruising through the winding roads of Bath with my dad sitting next to me. Sorta.

The township was home to hills and valleys, twists and turns. Any road you chose was scenery at its best.

"Drive down Ira Road," Dad said. "I want to see the Firestone Estate. Always loved that property."

Ah, yes. The Firestone property—the tire company Firestone. Raymond Firestone, Harvey's son, had bought fifteen hundred acres of land on Ira Road. He and his first wife, Laura, had named it Lauray Farms, a combination of both their names. Most of the land had been sold in 1987 to Ohio State University, but Bath had bought over four hundred acres, which had become Bath Nature Reserve. Anyone could hike or stroll along the main paths and enjoy nature. There was also a horse trail, marshy areas, and general outdoor loveliness. Akron University, the last time I'd paid attention, had been using the property to conduct a study of wetlands. Even though it was quite popular with dog walkers, it was never jam-packed with people.

I shook my head. "Dad, they sold it off, and now it is a subdivision of homes, along with Bab's Orchards up in Richfield." I'd grown up eating those wonderful apples and had cried when the old couple had shut the orchard down. I understood they were older and tired, but I missed the crisp, sweet taste no other orchard in the area could match.

In my peripheral vision, I could see the shock on his face. "You've got to be kidding me!"

I chanced a quick glance at him. "I thought you were up to date on the area," I said. "You know, keeping up with the news."

Shaking his head, he said, "Anything that affects you, yes. I don't bother with the rest, too much happening too quickly."

I thought about that for a minute before answering, "Yeah, I know what you mean. Seems as though even the living can't keep up with world events."

"World events?" he asked. "I'm not talking about the world; I mean here in Bath. People leaving, people moving in, being born, dying. It's busy."

I shot him a quick look of surprise. "Really? I had no idea."

He snorted. "Babe, you need to keep up with the excitement!"

"I don't have the energy to keep up with the social news."

Nodding, he said, "That's why you love living on that hill."

Yeah, my dad knew me pretty well for not having been alive since I was a kid. Amazing. "How much do you know about me?"

"Pretty much everything there is to know. I was there when you graduated, got married, had your babies, when your mom died. Hell, I was even waiting for your mother on the other side."

"How'd that go?"

He laughed the belly laugh I had missed for so long before saying, "She was not happy to see me. I didn't expect her to be, but it was the right thing to do." He shrugged. "So I was there."

I didn't remember much of my dad; I had been so young when he'd died. But I did remember that he had been a kind, honorable man. Nana had loved him more than she had her own daughter. She'd always spoken highly of him, even though it had irritated Mom.

"Did Nana know you were around me all these years?"

He shook his head. "Not sure. Probably not. She's been rather busy since she arrived. I stayed in the background as much as possible. Easier that way."

I turned off Ira Road onto Revere Road, slowing down to a crawl so I wouldn't miss the house. "What's the number?" I asked Dad.

Glancing down at the paper on the seat, he said, "6522. It will be on the right. But keep going slow. It's an old farmhouse, sits back quite a ways from the road."

Nodding, I kept crawling forward. "There's the mailbox," I said. There was no traffic, so I pulled over to the side and put the car in park. Grabbing my cell phone from my purse, I aimed the camera down the long drive.

Once I was able to figure out how to zoom in, I took four quick shots of the house. Just as I was ready to put the phone down, the front door opened. I zoomed in tighter on the face standing on the porch and sucked in breath as I recognized the mayor's mug. Holy smokes!

I snapped a quick picture, threw the phone on the seat, and pulled the car forward before he could recognize me. I drove about a mile down the road before I could breathe again. Sweat was trickling down my back.

When Revere Road finally made a dead end into Wheatly Road, I took a left and pulled into the nearest parking lot, which happened to belong to a McDonald's. Fine by me; I needed to pee anyway. Once I'd parked and turned off the car, I looked over at Dad. He'd been quiet since we'd seen the mayor.

"I have questions, so don't go anywhere. I'll be right back."

He remained quiet but nodded.

My hands were shaking so hard I didn't think the door handle would respond, but I finally got it open and ran for the bathroom. Once done there, I decided coffee and a couple of slices of apple pie sounded in order, so stood in line to get them. Coffee might not have been my wisest move, since my hands hadn't calmed down, but the pie sounded great. Maybe it would offset the shakes; wouldn't know until I tried.

Heading back for the car, I was worried Dad would have faded away, but he was still patiently sitting in the front seat waiting for my return. Relief flooded my body, and I could feel tears threatening. Hormones must be at work again.

Once I got myself settled back in the driver's seat, I held the coffee cup for the warmth, not bothering to open and drink it. It wasn't a cold day at all, but I was suddenly freezing. Dad remained silent, watching me struggle for control. After about five minutes, the shakes started to subside, but I was still chilly.

"Try drinking a few sips; it will help warm you up," he said gently. He continued to keep an eye on me as I dutifully sipped the hot drink.

A few more minutes and I was within normal temperature range. I sighed. Looking over at Dad, I said, "That scared the poop out of me."

Nodding, he merely said, "I noticed."

We sat in companionable silence a few minutes more. It was comforting, having him next to me as I pulled myself together.

"Was I wrong to be so frightened?" I asked.

"Not necessarily. You aren't sure how the family fits into the scheme of things, so being seen could be a problem."

"Well, word is the mayor isn't someone to screw around with much. His possible involvement has even Jack worried."

"Then be careful," he said. "People can be pretty stupid if they're threatened. This guy sounds as though he would make decisions without much thought."

"I'm not so sure. His political future hinges on being smarter than the average guy."

"Wrong," Dad said. "It depends on how well he can clean up mistakes."

Oh crap. Dad was 100 percent correct. "There have been rumors he is quite tight with the mob, at least what's left of the Ohio mob." The Mafia used to be very busy in northeast Ohio. It was a pretty open secret Youngstown had once been a hotbed of mob activity, which had leached out to surrounding areas. The old dudes were dying off, leaving less capable offspring to run their empires. Gangs had moved in to take up the void, leaving the mob flapping in the breeze for the most part.

One thought had been nagging me since I'd seen Bennet Hayes on that front porch: What exactly had he been doing there? Visiting his son didn't have the ring of truth, but why else would he have been at his father's old house?

Dad must have read my thoughts, because he said, "There are a dozen good reasons he could have been there. His family still owns the property. Maybe he was checking the plumbing."

"For God's sake, Dad. The guy tried to intimidate me at my own house! I don't trust him as far as I could throw his sorry ass."

"Watch your language."

"I'm old enough to be a grandmother, and you worry about my language?" I asked, one eyebrow in a nice arch.

He grinned. "It isn't ladylike."

I laughed. Unwrapping the pie, I asked, "What now? Do I keep digging into that family or see what other trouble I can manage to find?"

"I'd put the mayor's family on hold for now; dig around a little more. Aren't there other people you can pester about the murder? Someone around here must remember information from the time."

Munching happily through the pie, I thought about the people who had lived near Bob and Elaine.

"Oh my God!" I exclaimed, apple bits spewing over my dash. I dug through my purse, looking for a note card I'd written information on for quick reference. Finding it smashed at the bottom of my purse, I retrieved it, holding it up in triumph. "Yes!"

"Okay, I'll bite. What's that?" Dad asked.

"Bob and Elaine's address. They also lived on Revere Road! Here's the number: 5526. Right down the road from the mayor's property." I dropped the pie remains on the seat next to me, stowed the coffee in the cupholder, and started the car. How had I forgotten their address?

"I take it we are going to drive past their house?" Dad asked. Was there a bit of sarcasm there? Maybe explained where my own came from.

"Yep," I answered. "Let's see how close they lived—could be a clue."

I headed out of the parking lot and made a beeline for Revere Road. "The numbers here are too high, so we need to get closer to where we started," I said. Dad nodded. I drove slowly, looking for mailbox numbers. We passed the mayor's property and finally the stop sign. "Damn. Must be on the other side of Ira," I said.

I turned, drove about half a mile or so, and found another piece of Revere Road, turning onto it with irritation. "Why in the hell they have this road stopping and starting is beyond me!"

Dad found this humorous and told me, "It's the great mystery of township politics."

I saw the familiar sight of a police cruiser coming toward me. Habit made me sneak a quick peak at my speedometer to check I was firmly within the speed limit. I could sense Dad grinning next to me. "Never hurts to check," I said. As the cruiser came closer, I realized one my favorite cops sat behind the wheel. I threw Owen a quick wave and was rewarded with one of his lovely smiles. As we passed one another, he nodded my direction. Once the acknowledgements were over, I returned to the task at hand.

Finally, finding ourselves nearing Bob's old house, I slowed to a snail's pace. Dad nodded toward a mailbox. "There it is."

I parked close to the driveway and peered through the bushes to see the house. My view sucked, so I grabbed my phone and started to open the car door .

"Whoa, sweetie," Dad said. "Where do you think you're going?"

"I want a picture! I can't see much from here, but if I get closer to that big lilac bush, I think I can focus the camera and get the shot."

Scrunching his eyes at me, he said, "That the only way?"

"Pretty sure," I answered as I opened the car door. Creeping up to the bush, I held my phone in front of me to see what type of shot I was able to make. Zooming in, I could clearly make out the entire front of the house. "Eureka!" I took the shot and scooted back to the car. Once inside, I showed the picture to Dad. "Pretty good, huh?"

He looked at the phone, then at me. "That's a phone? With a camera?"

"Yep. You saw me take the picture at the mayor's."

Sighing, he said, "I was more concerned about you rather than the device you were using." Eyeing the phone again, he said, "I missed out on so much."

"Dad, you'd have been playing games on the darn thing as much as Andy does."

"Games? It's a camera, and you play games on it?"

"Yep, and more," I said. To prove my point, the phone chirped, letting me know I had a text message. Since I was parked, I read it and laughed.

Dad's eyes were huge as he asked, "What happened?"

Flipping the phone around for him to see, I said, "Andy sent me a message. Wonders what is for dinner."

"You can send notes through the thing too?" Clearly, he hadn't been paying much attention as he'd watched me through the years. Andy and I texted throughout most days, usually him asking about dinner and me telling him. I turned the phone back my direction and texted back to Andy. Hitting the send button, I flipped it back toward Dad. "See, I just answered him."

Shaking his head in wonder, he said, "I really did miss out."

"I'm thankful you are here for me. You've been able to watch out for me more dead than alive. I only wish I had known all those years. I missed you so much." Tears were not far off, so I stopped talking.

Dad, apparently noticing the crack in my voice, said, "I agree. If we had been able to communicate while you were growing up, it would have helped, especially where your mother was concerned. That's why I urged your grandmother to be such a huge part of your life."

Thank God I hadn't started driving yet; I'd have wrecked the damn car. "Nana could see you? And she never told me? I thought she didn't know you were around!"

"She didn't. There are more ways than direct contact to deliver messages."

"Such as?" My anger built at the thought that Nana had known he was near but hadn't shared the information with me.

"Dreams are the easiest but iffy. People forget their dreams easily. I didn't think it was wise to contact you."

"Dad! It would have helped!"

He sat silent for a moment. "Sweetie, it would have been harder unless you could see me yourself. Trust me."

"But Mom was so ..." I couldn't think of words to finish the sentence, but he understood.

"I know. Exactly why I wanted your grandmother to protect you. Your mother hasn't changed, and I'm beginning to believe she is quite dangerous. Be careful when you are dealing with her."

I snorted. "That much I know."

"Maybe. But she's on my side now and has resources she didn't have while alive."

His words sent chills down my spine. "Can you keep an eye on her?"

"Somewhat but not entirely. I don't run in the same circles she does."

"You don't run in *any* circles from what you've told me." I thought a minute before saying, "Maybe Logan can help us where Mom is concerned. She is deathly afraid of him."

Dad smiled. "Logan is a major power, but I'm pretty sure she's hanging out with her own sources who have equal capabilities. I'll do what I can."

"Dad, this is getting ridiculous. I'm worried about the mayor and his mob friends here and extreme powers there. I have no control over anything."

"I'll talk to Logan. Maybe he knows how to control your mother. I'll gladly hand the responsibility over to him."

I thought about Logan's discussion with Mom. "I'm pretty sure Mom is scared of him enough to watch her p's and q's. There's something about my Cherokee blood that shook her up quite a bit."

Dad nodded but didn't reply. That raised my suspicions, but I kept them to myself. No sense arguing with a dead man who could fade away if the conversation became uncomfortable for him.

For a few minutes, no noise filled the car except the sound of the tires moving along the pavement. Dad asked, "What now?"

"I've got to figure out the connection between Bob and Elaine and the mayor's son. There must be one."

"How are you going to do that?" he asked.

"No damn idea," I said. "I'm not a detective. I talk to dead people."

He laughed. "You'll figure it out eventually."

"Maybe." I drummed my fingers on the steering wheel as I thought about the situation.

"Logan told me one of the Indians would be with me whenever I left the house. Do you see anyone riding along in the backseat that I'm not aware of?" I asked.

Dad looked out the window, totally silent.

I sighed. "You are my protector." It wasn't a question. "Why didn't you tell me?"

Dad tore his eyes from the scenery and looked my direction. "I didn't want you to think that was the only reason I was riding along." He shrugged. "If I couldn't be here for some reason, Logan would have assigned someone to be with you; actually, he probably has them lined up already."

My fingers resumed their drumming; they had a mind of their own. Something wasn't adding up, but I had no idea what it was and was pretty sure I didn't want to know.

I turned onto Cleveland-Massillon Road, heading home. Surprisingly, *this* particular road's name had a *purpose*. The road ran between the two cities of Cleveland and Massillon. Pretty smart, huh? It ran pretty much parallel to the Ohio and Erie Canal. The canal had been built in the early 1800s to make a waterway from Cleveland to the Ohio River, which was the border between Ohio and Kentucky. At one time Ohio had been a hopping place, and the canal had allowed goods, along with people, to travel statewide quicker than a horse and buggy. Of course, once trains had come along, the canal had no longer been able to brag about speed. So while the canals hadn't lasted long, they had played an important part in the commerce of the state.

Dragging my thoughts back to the issue at hand, I asked Dad, "So you will be with me everywhere I go?"

He nodded, saying, "Yep."

"If I find myself in a real pickle, is there actually anything you can do to save me from myself?"

"Very little."

Then why tag along? Jeez. Logan running around town with me made more sense. He could make substantial physical contact with the living; he'd proved that to me. I wasn't being nasty about Dad's presence, but let's face it: he couldn't do much to help.

He must have read my mind—I wish these dead people would stop doing that—because he said, "I'd get help. It isn't as though I'd have to track Logan down. I have a direct line of communication with him."

Well, why the hell hadn't he mentioned this little tidbit before? I felt an eyebrow rise but kept my mouth firmly shut. After all these years missing him like mad, I wasn't going to waste time arguing with him. I gave a quick nod of affirmation. "That works."

But of course he knew the thoughts flying through my mind and said, "There's some constrictions regarding information given to you." He shrugged. "I don't necessarily agree with the rules, but I follow them—mostly."

I sighed, nodding. "Okay." I had a feeling Logan was running this show, and I hoped to hell he knew what he was doing.

Chapter 15

Dad and I were sitting happily at my kitchen table, safe and sound. Dad looked over at me, saying, "I'm going to leave you alone for a while. I've got a couple of errands to run."

Errands? For God's sake, the man was *dead*. What type of errands did dead people literally *do*? My face tightened at the thought of being alone. You know how the pit of your stomach feels when instinct finally sets in and you realize there might be danger around the next corner? Yeah, pretty much how I felt. I couldn't put my finger on it, just an icky feeling.

Reading my expression, Dad said, "You are protected as long as you stay home. Sorry, babe, but I wouldn't leave you if I didn't trust the guys in the woods."

I glanced out the window but still could not see the Indians. I knew they were there; Logan had promised. It would have been more reassuring if I could *see* them for myself. Logan must have had some type of veil covering them since I had been able to see them once before.

"Where exactly are you going?" I asked. Figured a blunt question might induce a straightforward answer. I should have known better.

Smiling, Dad said, "Can't say, but trust it's important."

"Mom?" I asked, wondering if he was concerned about her role in this mess. If so, then my worry level would increase dramatically. Her involvement was questionable, especially considering I was pretty damn sure my best interests weren't on her radar. Not to say she had never been what you could call nurturing when she'd been alive. Dead, she might be a little on the dangerous side. Since everyone, except Logan, was quiet about powers people had on the other side, I had no idea if Mom had acquired skills harmful to my health—or life for that matter.

"Stay on the property" were Dad's parting words as he faded. Great. Until I heard from him, I was stuck at home. Figuring, since I was cemented here, I might as well do something useful, I looked around the kitchen. I knew performing a job having substance to the murder might sound like the logical movement, but I was tired of the burden. Shrugging, I decided picking up around the house would fit the bill as useful. Hell, with all the visitors I'd been entertaining, dead and alive, cleaning might not be a bad idea. It was shocking how the days had flown by, and I had been totally unaware of the dust piling up, along with actual grime. Jeez.

A few minutes later, armed with dust rags (the ones in those little blue bags that have become impossible to find), vacuum cleaner, and elbow grease, I got busy. Starting in the den seemed the right choice, since there had been more activity in that room since the dead had shown up than in the previous five years. Once the kids had left the nest, we'd had a significant drop in household traffic. Thank God. During their teenage years, the kids had had so many friends over it had been worse than Grand Central Station. Explained why Owen was comfortable enough earlier to find the newest hiding place for pie. He had been here continuously during his high school years, discussing football strategy with our son Brian and making spreadsheets for all the weekly games on TV. I smiled at the memory but didn't miss how hectic life had been back then. I liked peace and quiet—boring.

Shaking off the stroll down memory lane, I stepped back and surveyed the room. Dust bunnies gone, furniture gleaming, spiderwebs out of the corners of the ceiling—ah, felt good. A quick glance at my watch informed me, surprisingly, it was time to start cooking dinner. Then the shock set in; I hadn't hit the grocery store in recent memory and had no idea what to cook. Well, hell, we'd go out to dinner. Then my head dropped in frustration as I realized that if Dad wasn't back, I couldn't leave the damn house.

Since he was off doing some "errand" I assumed was important to my long-range safety, I resigned myself to cooking. My mind had been preoccupied with the dead, so nothing was thawed. Wondering if eggs and bacon were a reasonable choice, I headed for the kitchen to check the fridge.

I hadn't gone ten steps when the doorbell rang. My stomach immediately turned into a huge knot. Who could be here? I peered through the living room curtain that was closed due to my fears the mayor would show up again and saw an old Jeep sitting in the driveway. I had no idea who it belonged to. Honestly, I was actually thinking about not answering when the darn bell rang again. Sighing, I went to the door. Taking a deep breath, I cautiously opened it about an inch. My mouth dropped when I recognized Alex Hayes standing there, looking drained. It only took a moment for me to realize the kid standing at my door, tall and slender with the same dirty-blond hair I remembered, was filled with a melancholy that broke my heart.

Not opening the door any further, I asked, "Yes?" Not my best opening line, but I had no idea what the correct procedure was in this case. He was my number one suspect, and allowing him to enter my house would probably fall under the heading of "Stupid Ideas."

"Hi, Mrs. Shaw. You remember me?" he mumbled, looking at my face but not meeting my eyes.

"Speak clearly; you know better than to mumble," I responded instinctively. For Pete's sake! This was probably not the best time to have mom mode enter the scene. But damn if it didn't work.

He stood up straight, looked me in the eye, and said, "I'm Alex Hayes. Do you remember me by any chance?"

I found myself opening the door a little wider, which showed how stupid I was sometimes. He didn't bust in as his dad probably would have but stood there respectfully. It was sheer dumb luck, given the chance, that he didn't force his way into the house.

I studied his face before answering, "Yes, Alex. I remember you. Is there something I can help you with?"

He shifted his stance, which of course made me tense up from head to toe. But thankfully, he was just moving his feet. He looked so miserable that I did the unthinkable: I invited him in the house.

Relief seemed to flood his body. "Thanks. I appreciate you taking time to talk with me."

I quickly glanced around to see if any Indians had popped into view but no such luck.

"Come on back to the kitchen. I think there is a slice of pie with your name on it," I said, leading the way, which, of course, was more than likely another bad idea. I should probably have walked behind him for my safety, but my brain didn't seem to be in total working condition.

"I don't think I could eat, but thank you," he replied. He didn't sound dangerous.

"Of course you can. Want some coffee to go along with it? Or tea?" This kid needed some type of help; that much was clear. Pie was apparently not the answer, but it would relax him. Maybe.

121

Not willing to argue with me, he shrugged. "Okay, sure. Coffee's good."

Nodding, I pointed to a chair for him to sit in, which he did. Puttering around the kitchen, getting out a plate and fork, I asked, "What have you been up to since graduation?"

His face filled with shame. "Not much really. You know, working."

"That's nice. Where are you working?" As I said before, I didn't interrogate well.

"For my dad, mostly. His campaigns."

I nodded. So the kid had no direction and no career. Working for a jackass couldn't be easy.

"I'm sure he appreciates your help," I said, watching his expression. Bingo. The statement paid off. He winced as though I had smacked him full in the face. My conclusion was his dad treated him like hell, which made sense. The man was a total jerk. Alex answered with only a quick shrug of his shoulders. He wasn't the best conversationalist I'd ever met, but he was here for a reason, and I needed to figure out what it was.

Setting his pie and coffee in front of him, I said, "There, sweetie. Eat up."

He automatically picked up the fork but hesitated before taking a bite.

"Alex, is there something wrong?" I asked.

He used his fork to push the pie around on the plate. Finally looking up at me, he asked, "Are you trying to reopen the murder case from the nineties?"

The bluntness of the question took me by surprise. Didn't think he had it in him, to be honest. I hesitated before answering, watching his face closely. "Which murder are you referring to?" I asked with all innocence—well, not really, but I tried to make it sound angelic. Nothing like a bit of virtue thrown in to make it interesting. Plus I was stalling since I had no idea how I should answer his question. Since he was my main suspect, I didn't think tipping him off to the investigation would help. How could I explain Bob and Elaine? Or Jack? My headache was decidedly returning.

He looked hopeful for a split second. Then his face clouded. "I'm serious, Mrs. Shaw. Are you nosing around?"

"Does it matter?" Still stalling. He stared at me quietly. "Eat your pie, Alex." I was running out of ideas in the stonewalling department.

I had to hand it to him: as bad as he looked, his brain was working just fine. He recognized my maneuvers for what they were—beating around the bush. He was staring me down and, sad to say, was winning the contest.

Fork still in hand, Alex said, "It's important, Mrs. S. You could get hurt."

"Is that a threat?" I asked while my stomach decided to start performing jumping jacks.

Shaking his head emphatically, he said sincerely, "No, ma'am. Not at all. But the case was closed, and it's better for everyone, including you, if it stays closed."

I realized he was sincerely concerned for me. The concept not only surprised me but also made the knot in my stomach relax enough for me to have a cup of coffee, as I now knew the coffee would stay put and not bounce right back. Throwing up was at the bottom of my bucket list.

"Eat," I said. Encouraging him was not my attempt at kindness, not really. I needed a few moments to think. Dad was nowhere to be seen, and I was alone in the house with Alex, my number one suspect, and the poor kid was worried about my safety. Not adding up in my estimation. Watching him, I began to have a nagging sense that something was definitely off and that I was on the wrong path concerning Alex Hayes. If not Alex, then who? Elaine was so confident he was the murderer; it was the sticking point. She must have seen his face in those final moments. Realizing my fingers were tapping the coffee cup, I set it down with a thud. No point in allowing Alex to have the impression I was analyzing the situation.

He sat quietly as he slowly ate his pie. I watched as he took each bite, his expression pained, as if chewing was agonizing. What was wrong with this kid?

"Alex?"

As his eyes met mine, it hit me how tortured his face seemed, as though he had harbored some deep torment that refused to be ignored or forgotten. What the hell had happened to this kid? I decided on a softer approach. His dad might be a jackass, but this kid certainly wasn't a chip off the old block. Not as far as I could see, anyway.

"Is there a piece of information I should know?" I asked. "Some little tidbit that would help me?"

He held my stare for a moment before looking away. His eyes meandered around my kitchen, occasionally pausing as they found an article of interest, then continuing on their journey. Finally settling on the window with its view, he stayed silent a moment longer. Making a decision, he turned back to face me.

"Mrs. Shaw, I honestly wish I could give you the information." He paused, returning his gaze to the window. See? Everyone was drawn to staring at the damn woods. Maybe some primal instinct pulled their subconscious to the area. Who knew? But as far as I was aware, no one else knew about the dead Indians out there. Even my mother had been shocked when she'd realized the protection residing in my own backyard. His attention still held by the magnetism of the wooded area, he continued, "I just can't."

I had a quick retort on the tip of my tongue but thankfully didn't let it pass my lips. Better to allow him to follow his own instincts in this arena. There was obviously knowledge stuck in that brain of his that, for some reason, he believed he couldn't share. At least with me. Watching his inner torture was painful. The poor kid obviously knew vital clues about the murder, but even after all these years, he couldn't bring himself to share them.

Sighing, I reached over and patted his back. "It's okay, Alex. I won't push the matter. You look as though this is tough enough without my interference."

Sure enough, hearing my words, he relaxed his shoulders and gave me a quick nod. So I could make a decent decision once in a while. No telling what Jack's standpoint would be if I decided to tell him about the encounter. I'd worry about Jack's temper later; now I needed to focus on Alex.

Glancing down at his half-eaten pie and lukewarm coffee, I asked, "Need a refill on those?" I decided if I made the conversation normal, he might open up a bit more. I was wrong.

Turning to me, he said, "Thanks, Mrs. Shaw, but I should be getting home." He rose from the chair and gave me a tight smile. "I appreciate you listening." Listening to what? His warning? He hadn't said much else. In fact, he'd given me absolutely no information? I could feel sarcasm fighting to escape my mouth, but once again, I refused to allow its departure from my firmly closed lips. Smiling and nodding, I stood up as he began walking to the front door.

"I appreciate your coming by, Alex. Feel free to drop in anytime." Giving him an open invitation might make him more willing to stop by again and just possibly tell me what the hell he knew. Figured it wouldn't hurt.

He nodded at the invite, turning to the front door. As he grabbed the doorknob, he faced me again. "Honestly, Mrs. Shaw, please drop whatever snooping you may be doing. It could be dangerous." His sadness returned as he spoke.

Taking pity on the kid, I patted his back. "Alex, don't worry about me. Take care of yourself."

Realizing I wasn't backing down, he slumped his shoulders as he made his way out of the house. I watched him until he got in his old Jeep. I leaned against the closed door and slid to the floor. Damnation, the episode had led nowhere at all. I sat there for a few minutes, reviewing the visit. Not finding any holes concerning my handling of it, I struggled to my feet. No holes except for the major flaw of not securing one bit of useful information he undoubtedly knew.

Walking back into the kitchen, I stopped suddenly, seeing Logan sitting at the table. Now he showed up? Jeez.

"That went well," he said. No sarcasm in his voice, so I guess he meant it.

"Really? He didn't give up what he knows," I said as I reached for my coffee cup. Might as well have another shot of caffeine to distract my mind from the fact dead people were sneaky little bastards.

Smiling patiently, he said, "You made a connection with the boy. Quite important. The information you need will come eventually."

"How long have you been here?" I asked, my eyes smushed up into a good squint. I wanted him to know I was irritated.

"Long enough," he calmly replied. "You were in no danger."

"Well, I didn't know that, did I?" I snapped. Maybe more caffeine wasn't the answer, but what the hell, I needed something hot in my system.

His smile turned into a grin as he said, "But you followed your instinct and allowed the boy into the house."

"A stupid move on my part! He could have easily killed me!"

"But somewhere, deep inside, you *knew* he wasn't an immediate threat. It was worth the risk; he might have told you what you need to know." Shrugging, he continued, "Life is full of uncertainty. You measure risk by instinct. You did well."

Shaking my head, I said, "I disagree. He could be suffering from depression dating back to the murders and might have snapped while he was here. Plus, my instinct isn't all that great. I've never picked the correct lotto numbers!"

He laughed. Hard. I mean, really? It wasn't funny in my opinion, and his response infuriated me. I grabbed my coffee cup and took a huge sip. It burned my mouth, but there was no way I was letting Logan see pain on my face. "Now what?" I asked once the scorching sensation had receded.

"You were never in a moment's danger, I assure you. Alex's visit was a very important step in the right direction." He looked around the kitchen. "Your father will be returning from his task soon."

"About that," I asked, "what is the deal with Dad running off to do errands? I thought he was protecting me?"

"He is only a small component of your security. While his presence is not entirely necessary, we recognize your emotional need of him."

"A small component? I have a huge security detail? Like the president? And what's the deal with errands? You people are dead!" Questions poured out of me like a damn waterfall. I'd hit my limit with the secrecy about the other side. It had gotten old, and I was emotionally drained.

He sat silently, allowing my spewing to come to a halt. Aware that my expression was way beyond angry, I tried to rein it in a bit, but it was a losing battle. Damn it, I was pissed. His quiet countenance was enough to make me want to smack the calm look right off his face. I was pretty sure my hand would glide straight through him, so I restrained my actions, barely. Logic finally began to override emotion, and I took deep breaths to control myself. Trust me: it was a struggle.

After a few moments of his calm demeanor, he said, "Peg, you have received a large amount of information in a relatively small time frame. Your life has been disturbed greatly. Trust we will continue to protect you and keep careful watch."

As he spoke these final words, he began to fade.

Chapter 16

Cleaning up after Alex left calmed my frayed nerves. Standing at the sink washing his pie plate and coffee cup, I decided this bizarre case was knotty, and it was obviously up to me to undo the knots, one by one, if necessary. No, brave genes didn't suddenly appear, but disgusted genes surfaced. Let's face it: Nana had told me she was in a bit of a pickle and had dumped her problems in my lap. Why did I have to be the one cleaning up her dilemmas?

I looked down at my hands and realized I had been washing Alex's cup for the last five minutes. I was pretty confident his cup didn't need the extreme scrubbing, so I rinsed it with hot water and set it on the drying rack that had lived next to the sink for over twenty years. I had tried finding a newer one to replace the poor thing but was always surprised how small they made them now. Mine was huge, big enough to dry dishes, pots and pans, and cups from an entire meal. The dinky ones in stores today were so small you'd think no one washed dishes by hand anymore. Since we lived in a semirural area, most residents had water wells and septic systems. That alone made me hesitate to install a dish washer. Wasn't that why I had kids? The boys hadn't especially loved dish duty, but they'd usually managed to clean them enough to pass inspection. Of course, they'd also had to mop the floor every night to sop up the water that always mysteriously jumped out of the sink. I smiled at the memories while wringing out the dishrag.

A noise to my left made me jump. Turning, I saw Bob watching me. Startled that I hadn't felt his presence, I felt an eyebrow travel north.

"What do you need?" I asked, tired of all the dead visitors I was receiving.

Clearing his throat, he hesitated before saying, "We may have a problem."

Sighing, I said, "What's new?" I decided I probably needed to be sitting to hear what was on his mind, so I made my way over to the kitchen table.

"Um," he started, then stopped.

I turned to face him. "Damn it, Bob! It's been a lousy day, so out with it!"

His face turned red, but he finally blurted, "I don't think Alex Hayes murdered us."

I sat down in the chair with a thump. "What?"

"Yeah, at least I'm pretty sure."

"Start at the beginning," I said wearily. My headache was creeping back.

He rubbed his hands together nervously as he organized his thoughts. "Well, you know how I've been spying?" I nodded, and he continued, "I heard Alex and his dad talking earlier today. His dad told him he didn't have anything to worry about because there was no proof he was guilty."

I waited for Bob to continue, but he stood there silently. "That's it? That one piece of a conversation makes you think Alex is innocent?"

Bob was surprised at my reaction. "He must be innocent. Why else would his dad tell him there was no proof?"

I held the anger that was rising at bay. "Bob, seriously? His dad could have made sure any existing proof disappeared. Files are missing from the police station. Plus his dad has connections to unsavory people. Honestly!"

"Well, I was watching your conversation with him. He didn't look guilty of murder."

That bit of news stunned me. Bob had been here, and I hadn't felt him at all? I narrowed my eyes, saying, "You were here? I didn't sense you."

A look of pride appeared on his face. "Neat, huh? I figured if I stayed invisible and out of range, you couldn't tell I was here!"

Oh, great! Just what I needed: Bob learning stealthy spying crap. He watched me anxiously, obviously not wanting to endure my anger. Considering the hell Elaine had put him through, alive and dead, I wearily relented.

"How'd you find out about this new ability?" I asked.

"I got to thinking if you can tell when I'm around, there might be others that could too. So I did experiments at the mall. You'd be surprised how many people actually have the ability but ignore it. Fascinating!"

"What type of experiments?" I asked, intrigued. Bob was learning new tricks almost every day, and I wasn't sure it was healthy for either of us. But I could be wrong on that count; any evasion of Elaine he discovered probably made his existence easier.

"The food court seemed the best place to start, so I would sit next to them while they were eating. I found people could tell something had changed, so I would back off, then approach them slowly. The closer I got, the more they reacted, so I realized if I kept a certain distance, they couldn't feel me." He stopped a moment, then said, "It took me an entire lunch hour to test my theory, but it was worth it."

I stared at him. He was conducting public experiments now? I realized my fingers were drumming on the kitchen table and pulled my hand into my lap. No sense making Bob more nervous than necessary.

"Good information to know," I finally said.

He nodded happily. "Yep."

A thought struck me. "Logan was here. Why didn't he feel you? He's damn powerful from what I've been told."

A nervous looked crossed his face. Shaking his head, he said, "I spotted him here and backed off immediately. That guy gives me the creeps!"

Logan gave Bob the creeps? That was not good news. "Bob, you're dead. How can another dead person give you the creeps?"

Cocking his head, he said, "You really don't understand how things work over here, do you?"

"Enlighten me," I said, maybe just a bit nastily.

"I never paid much attention until recently," he said before stopping suddenly. Turning red again, he looked at me squarely. "You know how Elaine is sometimes?" I nodded, and he continued, "Dealing with her took up all my energy, so I didn't have time to get the hang of things on our side." He shrugged. "Guess my thoughts were taken up with Elaine; my awareness of our surroundings wasn't too involved. You know what I mean?"

Nodding again, I motioned for him to continue.

He smiled. "Then you came along, and I was interested in helping solve our murder. Let me tell you, I've had more fun in the past few days than I have in years!" He beamed at me.

"That's nice, but you haven't explained how Logan gives you the creeps." I needed to know if Logan could possibly not be exactly what I thought. Shivers ran down my spine. What if Logan was a bad guy?

"Oh, that. Well, he is superpowerful—something about his spiritual abilities when he was alive." Bob waved a hand around. "I don't really understand that part. Elaine and I weren't what you'd call churchy." He glanced quickly at me, as if apologizing for his lack of religious knowledge.

I acknowledged his statement with a quick nod. Satisfied that I wasn't judging his shortage of religion, he continued, "I'm still trying to piece together why those powers transferred to our side of life. But he is extremely capable over here and has privileges most of us won't ever have available." He thought for a moment, then said, "He's a pretty cool guy most of the time, but I'm not going to step on his toes."

"So you don't necessarily mistrust the guy, but his power is enough to make you cautious?" I asked.

Bob thought about my question before saying, "Yeah, sounds about right." Seeing my relief, he asked in a surprised voice, "You were thinking he was a baddy? Just because I'm nervous around the guy? Gosh, I'm sorry."

His sincerity made me wince. I didn't want to be mean to Bob, but he could get on my last nerve. Sighing, I forced a smile. Suddenly, the air changed. Damn! Now what? I turned to see my dad standing by the sink. Sagging with relief, I said, "Hey, Dad, glad you're back."

Bob's head snapped around. Seeing my dad, his face lit up. "Dave! What are you doing here?" He looked back at me. "You know this guy?"

I looked over at my dad. Hadn't Bob heard me call him Dad? Shaking his head, Dad smiled tightly and gave a quick shrug.

"Hi, Bob. How's it going? Peg's my daughter. Thought you knew."

Bob's shocked expression gave way to sheer delight. "I had no idea she was your daughter! That's awesome."

"I gather you two know each other?" I asked. Well, hell. The fun never stopped around here.

Dad nodded. "We were in high school together. Haven't seen Bob in years." Dad didn't appear overly impressed to see Bob hanging around my kitchen. Bob, however, was thrilled—no surprise there.

Turning to face me, Bob said excitedly, "Gosh, this is so fantastic! I can't believe you're his daughter. You see, I was in the band, and your dad was on the football team. We saw each other at every game!"

I chanced a quick glance at my dad and spotted his quick expression of frustration. So Bob irritated everyone, *and* he was a band geek. Don't take it the wrong way; I admired anyone who could play a musical instrument. They weren't easy to learn; it took a lot of hard work and practice. I should know; my boys had all played in the high school band, and the hours of listening to them practice had been enough to make a sane person drink. But I also knew the band kids usually fell into a certain personality group: good students, good grades, but not necessary voted most popular.

Dad, on the other hand, had probably been great at football, had had fabulous social skills, and hadn't been too concerned about his GPA or an Ivy League education. He *had* been voted most popular his senior year of high school but hadn't necessarily ended up with a wonderful post–high school education. Something was poking at the back of my mind, but I couldn't quite get hold of the complete thought. I knew from experience it would drive me nuts until I figured out what my brain had already realized. Jeez, another thing to push me closer to the edge.

Dad directed his attention to Bob. "I understand you've been doing a bit of undercover work for Peg. Find anything worthwhile?"

Bob's head got busy nodding as he enthusiastically said, "Oh man, Dave! You wouldn't believe how great this being dead stuff is working out for me!" Seeing Dad's sardonic smile, he added, "Well, maybe *you* understand, but I know Peg doesn't."

I jumped in my seat hearing Bob use my name. Pretty sure it was the first time he had ever uttered it out loud, and it was obvious it hadn't registered with him that he had used it. He kept going at a rapid speed. I wondered if it was excitement or his nerves acting up since he'd realized he knew my dad.

"I was just telling Peg about Alex. I don't think he murdered us, but Peg doesn't agree. She thinks I don't have enough proof," he told my dad. "Yet."

I was startled at the defiance clearly on his face but had to grin to myself at his attitude. If he tried this new approach with Elaine, she'd eat him for lunch. Not my problem, but I had to admit there was a small section of my heart that wanted him to be able to deal with her better. Eternity with Elaine couldn't be easy.

Dad nodded and beckoned Bob to keep at his reasoning. Bob said, "I know just hearing his dad tell him there was no proof isn't necessarily validation that Alex is innocent, but it got me to thinking." He stopped talking dead in his tracks. After a moment, Dad and I looked at one another questioningly. Had he come to the end of his rationale? Bob stood next to the kitchen table, a faraway expression on his face. After what seemed like hours, he turned to us, shock clearly visible. "My God!"

"What?" I demanded.

Bob looked at us, startled by my question. "I'm almost positive Alex had no part in the murders." He paused, reliving the experience. "I remember seeing his face," Bob began, then stopped again, screwing up his face in thought. "But there was someone else with him. I'm sure of it."

I stopped breathing at this revelation. Elaine had never mentioned anyone else being involved. I looked over at Dad, who was studying Bob.

"You sure?" Dad asked.

Slowly nodding, Bob said, "Yeah, pretty sure." He continued thinking, his expression confused, as if logical thought processing was a new concept for him. Since he had been a successful businessman, surely he knew how to think through problems. But this one seemed to be challenging his brain cells. Maybe his success had been pure dumb luck, but that idea didn't seem sensible. Had Elaine actually been the success? Who the hell knew, with these two? She might have handled the business side while he dealt with customers—not Elaine's strong suit. Their relationship took on a whole new dimension in my mind. Holy cow, they might have actually been the perfect couple. I shivered at the thought.

Dad continued watching Bob as he relived that night. Finally, Bob looked at us with wide eyes. "There were two guys in our bedroom. I don't have a clue who the second person was, but I'm pretty sure he was the culprit."

"So Alex could be innocent?" I asked pointedly. "How convinced of his innocence are you?"

That faraway expression returned before Bob answered, "Pretty convinced. I can see him standing in the corner, his face filled with shock." Shaking his head, as if clearing away a fog, he continued, "Alex wasn't anywhere near our bodies during the murders. He must have yelled at the guy, which would have made us look over at him." He snapped his fingers. "That's why Elaine remembers him so clearly."

My eyes narrowed. Sounded as though Bob was remembering new details, even to him. I straight up believed him. For Pete's sake. This was becoming more tangled the deeper we investigated. I started to ask a question, but Dad held up his hand to stop me. My mouth snapped shut immediately.

"Bob," Dad asked, "would Elaine agree with your memories of the murders?"

Bob sadly shook his head. "Don't count on it. Once she makes up her mind about something, it stays stuck. No matter how much proof you put before her, she is blind to anything that would alter her decisions. She believes with all her heart it was Alex."

Elaine had a heart? News to me. I refrained from commenting.

Dad sighed. "That's what I was afraid of." Looking over at me, he said, "You've got to find out who Alex was hanging out with back then."

"Easier said than done, Dad."

Nodding in agreement, he continued, "That could be the key. But I must caution you: this is a new wrinkle in the mix. Bob's information could put you in greater danger. As long as Alex was the focus of everyone, including the mayor, the real culprit felt safe. If you poke around in the wrong arenas, you could alert him."

Oh great. As if I wasn't in enough deep poop, now the murderer would know if I asked one too many questions.

Sighing, I said, "Maybe Jack Monroe would know more about Alex. Think I can trust him?"

Bob chimed in, "I hope so! I really like him!"

Dad remained thoughtful. Finally he said, "Peg, let me check in with Logan. He has a sense about people. Don't contact anyone until you hear back from me. Okay?"

I nodded. Damn it, I could feel tears threatening. I needed to be able to trust Jack of all people. Next to Andy, he was the only other living person who knew the possible danger I found myself in, and I needed him helping me.

"Your dad has a good point. And it shouldn't take long for him to track down Logan. I mean, that Indian is freaking everywhere, so he shouldn't be too hard to locate. Right, Dave?" He sounded too hopeful to be confident.

Dad smiled, shaking his head at Bob's eagerness. "I'll be as quick as possible. Logan knows you are in a certain amount of danger already, so my guess is he hasn't wandered too far away." Giving me a quick grin, he said, "You'll be fine. Don't go anywhere without Andy. Got it?"

I nodded, afraid words wouldn't make it out of my mouth without tears flowing. Damn, I hated dropping hormones—too many of them, and you cried, not enough of the darn things, and you cried. This sucked.

I watched Dad fade away and turned back to Bob. "You did a really good job."

He looked startled at the praise, then broke into a huge grin. "Thanks."

It broke my heart to see his surprise at any type of positive encouragement, so I continued, "I mean it. You really worked hard conjuring up the memory and came up with a fantastic clue."

Shaking his head, he said, "I think I've relied on Elaine's memory all this time. Had no idea I could relive that moment. You know what I mean?"

"Yeah, I get it." What other memories had Elaine erased from his mind by the sheer strength of her personality? Millions, probably.

"Okay, Bob. We're on the right track now. But it doesn't let Alex off the hook entirely. He never came forward with the information."

"I don't blame him. He would have been included in the charges just for being there."

Wow, Bob understood Alex's dilemma and felt sorry for him. I didn't. If he had gone to the authorities at the time, he might have been able to strike a deal with the district attorney. But I'd bet money his dad knew the whole damn story.

Chapter 17

Somehow, even though my nerves were in tatters, I managed to throw together dinner before Andy walked in the door from work. Don't be too impressed: it was leftover roast with frozen veggies on the side. Added in a little garlic bread, and we had a decent meal. I didn't cook fancily, but it was tasty. A few years ago I had been addicted to a cooking channel. Andy had endured many new recipes that had required a great deal of thought and a ton of spices I'd never known existed. I was a garlic salt, pepper, and basil kind of gal. Who knew saffron cost a million bucks an ounce?

A flood of relief coursed through my system when I spotted Andy's car zipping up the driveway. Tears once again brimmed, but I was able to maintain control as he walked in the kitchen door. No sense in scaring the daylights out of him by falling apart the instant he entered the house.

"Hey, babe, what's for dinner?" He had asked that question almost every night since our honeymoon. Funny how those insignificant words brought a huge sense of normalcy to any situation. They reminded me that my life hadn't completely derailed and that dinner was next on the agenda. I liked routine, and Andy provided a steady-Eddy type of existence for me. Nana had been the only other person able to maintain a constant comfort level in my life; Mom certainly had never given it a try.

"Leftovers," I answered. There must have been the slightest quiver to my voice, because Andy's head snapped around to face me. After studying my face for a few moments, he crossed the kitchen and wrapped his arms around me in a cocoon embrace. Well, hell. I lost it, sobbing into his chest, snot flying. I was a mess, but bless his heart, he didn't ask any questions until I reached for a tissue to blow my nose.

"What's going on now?" he asked once I'd finished draining my nose.

I took a deep breath before answering, "Well, it's not really horrible, but a monkey wrench has been thrown into the mix."

He arched an eyebrow but remained quiet, waiting for me to continue. He was good about allowing me time to gather my thoughts.

I plopped down on my chair at the table and rested my head on my hand before recounting Bob's memories. When I had finished filling him in on the latest developments, he stood quietly, thinking through the information. He leaned against the counter, hands in his pants pocket, head tilted to one side. I had to admit I was relieved he understood the increased danger to me. Now I had no idea who had murdered Bob and Elaine, so I could unintentionally ask the culprit questions, alerting him or her I was digging around the old case. Could be very unhealthy for me.

"When do you expect your dad to come back with news?" Andy finally asked.

I shrugged. "Have no idea. Nana has been suspiciously out of the picture for a good bit now. Can't figure that piece out, unless Logan has something to do with it."

"Why would Logan not want Nana around?"

I cocked an eyebrow at him. "You think Logan shares any type of information with me? Give me a break."

I could feel a tad of anger mounting, which I figured was a good thing. At least I didn't feel helpless and weak when I was angry.

The air suddenly sparkled with energy. The sensation was so heavy you could almost hold it in your hand. I sat up straight in anticipation. Andy noticed my expression and quickly scanned the room for any signs of danger. I waved my hand to let him know it was the dead, not the living, making an entrance. Logan was suddenly standing in the middle of the kitchen. I blinked at the golden aura surrounding his frame; I had only ever seen that once previously. Before I could finish the thought, another figure emerged from the blinding brilliance. My spirit guide smiled at me, saying, "Hello, Peg. Nice to see you again."

"Not trying to be rude, but why are you here?" In lightning speed, I had made the connection that both she and Logan appearing together probably spelled trouble for me. I had never considered myself necessarily a quick thinker, but with ghosts dropping in and out of my life, I was beginning to develop certain skills. I guess you could say it was keeping me on my toes. I didn't like it.

Her smile was beginning to annoy me. I remembered how easily she'd kept it in place at our last meeting. She probably smiled so much because she knew a darn sight more about my current situation than I did and was enjoying the fact. Irritating.

She looked around the kitchen, inspecting it, looking for hints of my personality hidden in the peeling wallpaper. Bite me, it was *my* kitchen, and I *liked* the damn wallpaper.

She turned back to me and said, "Peg, you have now entered the more dangerous aspect of your mission."

Mission? I was on a mission? I thought I was getting Nana out of a spot of trouble.

Shaking my head, I said, "I'm not on a mission. You lot are and are dragging me along. I don't appreciate you involving me in circumstances that are none of my business and then telling me the situation is dangerous! Hell, I've known from the beginning it was dicey."

Her smile still firmly in place, she said, "I understand your anger, but you are involved. You must tread carefully from this point on."

"Really? Like I hadn't realized that, especially once Bob remembered Alex Hayes was basically innocent!" I snapped.

She tilted her head. "Alex isn't completely innocent. He will eventually answer for his lack of action concerning the incident."

"Incident! Not only did he witness a murder, but he could also be charged with accessory! Probably why the idiot father covered up the whole thing!"

I glanced at Logan. He was obviously enjoying the scene I was making, and I had no idea why. Maybe my spirit guide had driven him nuts over the years; she was certainly irritating the heck out of me.

Andy could only surmise the conversation based on my comments, but he interrupted at this point. "Peg, if the mayor knows Alex didn't commit the murders, he probably knows who did. Alex would have told him, don't you think?"

Andy's logic stopped me cold. Let's face it: I didn't like the mayor, but he could now be in danger. Glancing at my annoying spirit guide, whose name I still did not know, I was deeply satisfied to see the smile gone. Take that, bitch! My enjoyment must have shown on my face, because Logan burst out laughing.

"Have you factored the new information into our present dilemma?" he asked my guide.

She remained silent. So they weren't all-knowing, after all. As rewarding as the thought might be, it was also bothersome. There was a certain amount of emotional safety I enjoyed believing they knew all aspects of the situation. Realizing they could be surprised made me uneasy.

Logan looked at Andy, studying him, weighing his worth. I could feel the intensity of his search as clearly as touching a solid object. The magnitude of Logan's power was making my stomach flip to the point of wanting to throw up. I was glad I was sitting down; I would have fallen otherwise. Finally, satisfied with his inspection, he turned back to me.

"Your father informed me of the new development. Surprisingly, Bob has proven to be a valuable asset in this endeavor."

Nice to know I wasn't the only one who had underestimated Bob.

He continued, "Recalling the memory must have been a difficult undertaking, considering Elaine's insistence that Alex was their murderer." He paused, choosing his next words. "To complicate matters—"

"My God, Peg!" Bob suddenly interrupted, bursting into my kitchen, not realizing we weren't alone. "You won't believe who Elaine's hanging out with!"

Logan frowned; my guide looked on with obvious interest.

"Bob!" I said, trying to make Bob focus on the fact there were others present. The poor guy was so agitated he was oblivious. I sighed.

"Peg, this could be serious! I'm not kidding. Where's your dad?" He stopped talking to look around the room for Dad. Immediately, his face lost color. I still didn't understand how that happened to ghosts, considering they didn't have blood. Maybe What's-Her-Name could answer that question if she *ever* decided to give a direct answer to any question. Okay, I was being nasty, but my guide was no longer in my favorites column. She didn't seem interested in *guiding* as much as appearing superior. Bite me.

"Bob, calm down. Dad found Logan, obviously," I said.

Bob swallowed, hard. He turned to me, nodding. "Yeah," he said, barely audible.

I had to feel sorry for the idiot. His eyes involuntarily turned back toward Logan. Gosh, Bob was scared stiff of the guy. Go figure.

"Bob!" I snapped.

Bob's eyes swiveled, meeting mine.

"What were you trying to tell me?" I asked him.

Bob swallowed again. He opened his mouth, but not one word made it out of there. He closed it again with a jerk of his head aimed in Logan's direction. I didn't think Bob's mind had even registered What's-Her-Name was also in the room. He was too focused on Logan's presence.

"It's fine. You can talk in front of him," I said, trying to encourage Bob.

Logan raised an eyebrow at my comment. Tough. He might as well get used to the fact I had become a tad overcautious—not my fault. Dead people were running through my house like a frat party on a college campus, and Logan should know I couldn't trust all of them, dead or not.

"Bob, you need to focus on me right now. Who is Elaine friends with?" The thought of Elaine being friends with *anyone* was unsettling. She had avoided mingling with others over on the other side for well over a decade, so the fact she had even one friend now was worth our attention.

"Your mom," he choked out.

Well, this *was* news and not necessarily *good* news.

Logan frowned. Not a good sign at all. What's-Her-Name looked mildly surprised. I slumped back in my chair. Mom was probably not the best person Elaine could have chosen as her first friend in the afterlife. I was pretty sure Mom's intentions were rotten.

Logan spoke to Bob directly, which almost gave the poor guy a heart attack—if dead people could have heart attacks. These thoughts were too confusing for me.

"Bob, what led you to believe your wife is now friends with Nell?" Logan quietly asked. You had to hand it to Logan: he knew how to work with people like Bob—calmly, quietly.

Bob swallowed before managing to choke out an answer. "I saw them." Not exactly a comprehensive reply but enough information to get the ball rolling.

Logan nodded before asking, "Any other reason you believe they are now friends?"

Bob thought a moment. "They were really into a deep discussion. Not just passing comments but really animated."

Logan again nodded and glanced over at my guide. "We were aware of their acquaintance." Turning to me, he said, "I was informing you of this situation before we were interrupted." He glanced at Bob. "However, now Bob has given us a clearer picture of the situation."

Andy cleared his throat and said, "Um, Peg?"

We all looked at Andy. "Yeah?" I asked. "Why am I able to see Logan now?"

I stared at Andy, shocked. Bob's mouth dropped open. What's-Her-Name narrowed her eyes as she turned to Logan.

Logan nodded, saying to me, "Your husband is an important piece of this investigation. He offered a sound piece of logic. I determined he had earned the ability, so I made it possible for him to see as much as his mind would allow."

"Can you hear him?" I asked Andy.

Shaking his head, he said, "Not clearly. Sounds muffled, like he's talking with a towel over his mouth."

I looked back at Logan, who shrugged. "It's the best I am able to do for him, but he deserves to be involved."

"It's against the rules!" What's-Her-Name said, clearly not happy with this new development.

Logan glanced at her before saying, "No, it is not. I do not apply the ability often, but in this case I deemed it necessary. My choice, as you well know."

Wow, an argument between two powerful spirits. Who knew there were pissing contests over there? My guide merely turned her head and looked out the window. That window was getting a lot of use lately.

"Will Andy be able to see everyone I do?" I asked.

Logan shook his head. "No. He will be able to see anyone assigned to protect you; that is all. At this time."

Ah, so there was a chance Andy could earn the right to see all of them. Noticing my guide's shoulders twitch at Logan's ending statement, I decided Logan could have been trying to irritate her. Her attitude was surprising, considering how kind she had been at the library. I was having a hard time figuring out these people. They didn't play by the same rules as living folks did, or did they? I'd have to put some real thought into human relationships. As I sat there, mulling over the weird rules of afterlife, a more crucial thought hit me.

Turning to Logan, I asked, "What about Jack Monroe? Is he friend or foe?"

Logan smiled at my question. "Friend."

I slumped back into the chair as relief flooded through my body. I needed Jack's help with the investigation. If he had turned out to be rotten, I would have been not only stuck but also in danger. Couldn't allow the bad guys to obtain any information if I could help it, and I had told Jack everything right from the get-go.

Watching me, Logan must have taken pity on my situation. He actually praised me. "You have done quite well to this point." It would have been nice had he stopped while he was ahead, but he put the fear of God in me, saying, "However, I must warn you: the next few steps are critical. Do not trust *anyone* that I have not vetted. No one."

My arm began tingling, and I looked around the room. Logan's eyes never left my face, but he said, "Dave, your timing is perfect."

Dad stepped from the corner shadows. Seeing him, I burst into tears. Jeez.

"It's okay, twinkle toes. Hang in there." Dad glanced over at Logan. "Thanks for coming so quickly."

Logan nodded but remained silent.

"Peg, I can see your dad," Andy said calmly.

"He is another protector of your wife," Logan told him. "If you care to look out the window toward the woods, you will detect more." Andy started to scan our backyard, so his ability to hear Logan must have improved. Andy's eyes became huge saucers as he spotted the group of Indians scattered throughout our woods. "Wow."

Even though I had told him about the guys out back, it was different when you could actually witness their presence. A bit like watching a reenactment down at Hale Farm and Village, which was our local historical site. The historical society had moved eighteenth-century buildings to the property, so you had a feel for a small village in the early history of Ohio. There was a glassblower, which was my personal favorite, a church, a few houses, a barn, and a schoolroom. They had a pottery guy there, and in the gift shop, you could buy items actually made on site. Our kids had loved going there during the summers and for the few winter activities also. Not as big as Williamsburg, but they gave you a real feel for that era. But to see actual Indians hanging out in your backyard was quite a sight. I knew exactly how Andy felt as he watched them.

"You will be able to detect anyone protecting Peg," Logan informed Andy.

"Dead or alive?" I asked hopefully.

Logan gave me a look indicating how stupid my question was before asking, "Can you detect a person's intention, dead or alive?"

My shoulders sagged as I answered, "Nope."

"Neither will Andy. But the positive element is Andy will be able to detect *only* spirits that are *protecting you in some way.*"

I thought about that tidbit for a moment before the light dawned. "Ah. So when a dead person shows up, if Andy can't see them, there is a good chance they aren't here to help."

Logan turned to Andy. "Sir, are you able to make out spirits other than Dave and me in this room?"

Andy looked around carefully. "Well, I can see Peg's dad." Well, hell, we knew that! I began tapping my foot, waiting for him to scan the room.

"There is someone by the window, but very faint," Andy said as he spotted my guide. His gaze continued moving until he hit the area Bob where was standing. "Something by the table, but it's extremely faint."

Logan nodded. "They are what I consider fringe helpers. Bob's involvement is more on the investigative side of the situation, not necessarily protection, but his information will fold into her protection."

Bob beamed with pride at Logan's words. He certainly was enjoying his new position as a spy rather than Elaine's whipping post. I didn't blame him.

"What about her?" I asked, jerking my thumb in What's-Her-Name's direction.

Logan smiled, saying, "She is a minor protector."

My spirit guide stiffened at Logan's positioning her as "minor." I grinned; she wasn't my favorite at this point.

Seeing my grin, Logan cautioned, "She is important, but this is not her area of expertise." Well, hell. So much for Logan taking her down a notch. He was merely explaining her part of the drama in which I found myself stuck. Logan continued, "Your husband can barely see them because they are in what you could call the outer circle of your security."

"So what's my next move?" I asked Logan.

"That is your decision," Logan told me as he began fading, along with my spirit guide. "I need your help!" I yelled at his faint outline. Logan faded completely.

Damn.

"Wow," Bob said. "That was so awesome!" He was almost jumping with glee.

Andy looked at me. "What's the game plan?"

"Hell if I know," I answered with my head in my hands. "Hell if I know."

Chapter 18

Bright and early the next morning I bounded out of bed, energized. Well, maybe that was a slight exaggeration. It wasn't *too* early, and I didn't actually *bound* out of the bed. I dragged myself from beneath the blankets to hit the bathroom before Andy took it over for his morning routine. I was merely trying to stay positive under the circumstances, which were becoming worse, in my opinion.

Staring into my cup of high-octane coffee, I urged my brain to kick into at least low gear. I wasn't the greatest morning person, but I did manage to become functional after coffee. If left totally alone for those crucial first couple of cups of coffee, I operated at a decent level.

Slowly but steadily, I woke up, one section at a time. Drumming my fingers on the kitchen table, I attempted to form a plan of action. There had been a time I'd had good organizational skills, but then the kids had come along, and any organizing had gone out the window. Kids did that to a person.

I heard Andy in the bathroom, going through his own routine—shaving, showering, getting ready for work. Glancing at the kitchen clock, I wondered what time Jack made it to his office. I decided probably around eight, which gave me a timetable for getting my act together. Brewing another cup of coffee, I contemplated breakfast, which usually consisted of peanut butter on toast. Not a bad way to start the day.

Hearing Andy make his way to the kitchen, I reached into the cabinet for his mug. We had picked it up in Niagara Falls one vacation a few years back, and he had faithfully used it every morning since.

"Hey, babe," he said, kissing me on the cheek. Glancing at my own coffee cup, he added, "Where we at?"

I held up three fingers, informing him I had started my third cup of coffee. He nodded, saying, "Good, we're on safe ground."

Grinning at me, he filled his mug and walked over to sit at the table. Andy didn't eat breakfast most work mornings. He was convinced it slowed his brain activity. He relied on a hearty lunch to get him through his day. I had decided years ago he was full of baloney and probably didn't like breakfast food.

"Have you decided your next move?" he asked, sipping his coffee.

I threw him a warning glance, but he wasn't buying it. "Peg, now that you aren't working to put Alex behind bars, you need to find out exactly who he was with the night of Bob's and Elaine's murders." He took a healthy swig of coffee, wincing at the burning sensation as the hot liquid slid down his throat. "Why don't you ask Alex?"

"If the kid hasn't told anyone for over a decade, he isn't about to tell me," I snapped.

Andy shrugged. "You never know."

"I'm not sure what my next move is, but it isn't talking to Alex. Not yet." An idea was trying to form, but I couldn't quite grab hold as it floated around in my brain.

Draining, his mug, Andy said, "Give Jack a call. Just be careful."

I watched as he rinsed his mug out with hot water, and nodded. "I'm waiting until he's in the office." Glancing at the clock again, I said, "Probably in about an hour."

Andy nodded. "Sounds about right. But tell him everything, and watch your back. I feel better knowing your dad travels around with you."

His comment brought a smile to my face. I enjoyed Dad hanging out with me. But let's be honest: as great as it was to be with him, ghosts couldn't knock out a bad guy for you. Well, maybe Logan could, but so far my dad hadn't shown any ability to make physical contact.

Seeing my smile, Andy grinned. "I know it's ridiculous, but it makes me feel better."

I nodded. I understood what he was saying. A dead bodyguard was better than no bodyguard at all. Andy kissed me good-bye and was off to work. Sighing, I contemplated another cup of coffee but settled on a promise to myself to have one with Jack. Too much coffee, with too few hormones, did not make for a good day. Maybe hormones ate the caffeine. I had no idea. I could honestly say that caffeine could become a gal's worst enemy once the hormones decided to begin a disappearing act.

I rinsed my cup and was making for the bedroom to get dressed when the phone rang. I frowned, looking at the clock again. Who the hell was calling this early in the morning? Fear soared through my body as I worried something was wrong with one of the boys. I grabbed the phone and was relieved to hear the mayor's voice. Go figure.

"Mrs. Shaw? This is Mayor Hayes. Too early for you?"

Of course it was too damn early! There was no way I was going to admit that to him, however. "It's fine," I answered shortly.

He was silent for a moment, digesting my answer. "We need to talk," he said.

"Really?"

My short responses were obviously making him uneasy, because I received another dose of quiet. Worked for me.

Clearing his throat, he asked, "Would you please meet me at Jack Monroe's office around nine this morning?"

I was stunned—not that he wanted a meeting but that he'd *asked* rather than ordered and said *please*. This investigation must be pushing buttons in his life for me to be receiving this type of treatment.

I let him wait a moment before answering, "I don't think it's necessary." The last thing I needed was his butt mucking up the situation any more than he had over the past decade.

More silence. "I think it would be beneficial if we met," he eventually said.

"For who—you, Alex, or me?" I could feel the shock he felt at my question, but I had to hand it to the guy: he rallied pretty well.

"Maybe for all of us," he said with a sigh.

A chill ran through my body, and I glanced around, looking for one of my dead associates. Spotting Dad by the oven, I relaxed. He nodded at the phone and then whispered, "Go to the meeting." I wondered why he'd whispered; it wasn't as though the mayor could hear him. I frowned at his comment but followed directions.

"Fine. Nine o'clock. Don't be late, please."

I could sense his relief before I hung up the phone. Turning to Dad, I asked, "Why the hushed tone? He couldn't have heard you if he was sitting right here."

Shaking his head, Dad said, "You never know who's around."

His statement was a bit unnerving, but I continued my line of questioning. "So why should I be going to this meeting with him?"

Dad tilted his head and said, "You need information; that guy has information. Find out what he is trying *not* to tell you by hearing what he *is* willing to share. And you may get lucky; maybe he'll flat out divulge what he does know. A long shot maybe, but it would help lead you in the right direction."

I thought a moment about Dad's advice, then nodded and started back toward the bedroom to get ready for the meeting. "You'd better be there with me!" I called over my shoulder. He chuckled, which warmed my heart.

Walking into my bedroom, I got another surprise. My mother was standing there, along with Elaine. My heart jumped into my throat, but I now realized why Dad had been whispering.

"God, Mom. You scared the crap out of me," I said once I got over the shock of seeing them both. Together.

I ignored Elaine, but it wasn't a good sign she was here with my mother. Jeez, what now?

"So, when did your dad decide to get involved?" my mom asked. Nothing like getting down to business and ignoring the niceties of polite society. "Seriously, Peg. How long has Dave been hanging around?" she demanded.

"Go ask him yourself," I said, walking over to the closet to get a clean blouse. Face it: I had to keep myself busy doing something, and getting dressed seemed like the best way to go. Mom made me a nervous wreck, but she didn't need to know it.

She snorted. "Just like your grandmother! Never answering a simple question."

"Not necessarily any of your business, though," I said. Grabbing a blouse, I made my way to the dresser for a clean pair of jeans. I had to remind myself to go through the motions, keep moving, and not tell her anything important.

"Have you seen Bob lately?" Elaine asked. I wasn't thrilled with her tone of voice either. So I continued to ignore her.

"I have errands to do, so you need to leave," I said. Sweat was beginning to form on my upper lip, but I refused to acknowledge the fact in front of either of them. "Don't follow me into the bathroom, please. I want to get dressed in private."

Mom laughed. "I don't have to *follow* you anywhere."

I almost stopped in my tracks at her remark but forced myself to continue through the bathroom door. Once shut, I leaned against the door and let myself slide slowly down until my butt landed on the cold tile floor. Well aware of the nasty fact Mom could reappear in front of me as I dressed, I tried to calm myself with deep breathing. I rested my head against the door and analyzed current events. Why exactly was my mother interjecting herself into a murder investigation that had happened years ago? Elaine's cozy friendship could spell trouble, but I couldn't decide precisely what sort of trouble. Dragging my emotionally weary butt off the floor, I pulled my jeans on, followed by the slightly crumpled blouse. No way I was going back out there just to iron a damn blouse. Surveying myself in the mirror, I decided I could look a lot worse and grabbed my makeup bag. Seven minutes later, makeup on, hair combed, and teeth brushed, I took inventory of myself in the mirror. Eh, not good, not bad, sorta medium.

Cautiously opening the bathroom door, I peered around the bedroom. Relief coursed through my body as I realized no one was there. I would have yelled for joy, but I heard voices in the other room. Andy had already left for work, so the talking I heard could only mean one thing: dead folks in my living room. Damn it.

Walking down the hall, I discovered where Mom had gone after leaving me. She and Dad were unhappily surviving one another's company in my living room. I didn't remember much of their married life, but I did remember the monumental arguments. Sneaking a quick peek around the doorjamb, I saw a familiar sight. It was interesting to note that while Mom still screeched at him, Dad obviously had the upper hand, which only increased the volume of Mom's anger.

"Why are *you* here? Get out!" Mom yelled.

Dad smiled at her, quietly enduring her anger. He was facing my direction and noticed me watching the scene. When she had finished stomping her foot, he said, "The big question, Nell, is *why* are *you* here? I am trying to help Peg, but since that was never your strong suit, I'm assuming you are here to hinder."

Mom's mouth snapped shut, and she quickly faded. I frowned, unsure what her disappearing meant. Had Dad cornered her with his question?

"Dad?" I asked.

He winked at me, grinning. "That was easier than I thought it would be."

"Getting rid of her?" I asked.

"Nah, that's always easy; just have to piss her off enough. I'm referring to tricking her into giving information."

"I didn't hear her tell you anything at all," I said.

Still grinning, he said, "It's what she *isn't* saying I find most important."

"Okay, what *didn't* I hear her tell you?"

"Exactly what she is doing here! Plus, the fact she didn't try to evade the question with misdirects."

"Why didn't she lie? That's always a quick, easy solution to a tricky question."

Dad's grin became wider. "She can't." He laughed—I mean a real belly laugh. "Your mother relied on lies her whole life. On this side? Nope, no can do."

I stood there, stunned. Well, hell! No one had bothered to inform me the dead weren't allowed to lie!

"You weren't aware of that?" he asked, surprised.

"Nope. Kinda important, don't ya think?" I asked. I had to admit there was a little bite to my tone, but some of the rules of the afterlife would be nice to know.

"Well, consider yourself apprised of that particular procedure for us dead folks." He grinned again. I nodded as I met his grin.

He rubbed his hands together, asking, "Weren't you planning on meeting with Jack?"

I sighed. "Yeah, let's get moving. The quicker we clue him into Bob's discovery, the better."

I grabbed my keys, and we headed for the police station.

As we drove up, Owen was making his way across the parking lot. I beeped the car horn and waved. He smiled and returned my wave. He waited for me to park and walked me into the station. Dad remained quiet, which helped me to maintain the illusion I was alone. I had a bad habit of responding to comments made by all my deceased buddies, and Dad refraining from any remark helped me not appear crazy.

"What's up, Mrs. S?" Owen asked, holding the door open for me. Manners were a dying custom, and I appreciated the gesture.

"Nothing much," I said. "Need to check in with Jack about a few things. What about you?"

He shrugged. "Same ol', same ol'."

I grinned up at him. "I like boring!"

He laughed and left me to find my way down to Jack's office. There wasn't anyone to stop me as I made my way down the hall, so the new rule about township nonemployee's wandering the halls must have already been forgotten.

Jack's office door was open, so I stuck my head in, saying, "Hey there. Busy?"

He looked up from a mound of paperwork and smiled when he saw me. "Hey, Peg. Thank God you've come to rescue me from this crap." He waved a hand over the pile that sat on his desk. "Paperwork will drown us all one day. Coffee?"

"No thanks," I said, making myself comfortable in the chair opposite his desk. I decided not to take a chance on caffeine overload. "Got some news for you."

He looked at me a moment, then got up and closed his office door. "What type of news?"

"Bob is convinced that Alex didn't murder them." Might as well throw it out there right off the bat. No use building suspense; it was a simple fact.

Jack stared at me a moment before asking, "How sure is he?" Yeah, he was aware of Bob's personality and probably didn't consider Bob the most reliable source of information. Jack sat back in his chair, studying my face. Finally, he sighed, asking, "Do you believe him?"

I nodded. "Yep. I questioned him thoroughly. Dad was there with me, listening and thinking. Hell, Dad's here now."

I watched with amusement as Jack swiveled his head around, searching his office for signs of Dad. "Jack, you can't see them, remember?"

He sighed again. "I know, but I keep hoping just once I'll get a glimpse." I thought of telling him about Andy's new abilities but figured it would depress him, so I kept the news to myself.

He returned to his thoughts, finally asking, "Your dad trusts Bob? I mean, this *is* Bob we're talking about."

I smiled as I turned to Dad, who had made himself comfortable leaning his frame against the outside wall of Jack's office. Other than riding with me in the car, I'd never noticed him physically leaning or touching a single solid thing since he'd first arrived back in my life, so it startled me a bit to see he had the ability to lean against a wall. He noticed my surprise and grinned. I decided to ignore his skill, asking, "Dad? You sure Bob is remembering the events correctly?"

Dad thought a moment before nodding. "Yep. He was reliving the moment vividly." He stopped, thinking, then added, "Almost too vividly."

"Meaning?" I asked.

"I thought the poor guy was going to faint," Dad said with a sad smile. "There are some memories that should stay in the past. But he did provide important evidence."

I turned back to Jack. "Dad's comfortable with Bob's memory."

Jack nodded. "Exactly what did Bob tell you?"

I recounted the entire episode, with special emphasis on Alex standing in the corner. Jack listened intently, grabbing a pad and pen to jot a few notes down. When I finished Bob's shocking evidence, Jack threw the pen on his desk, muttering, "Damn. We had such a neat and tidy package, just needed evidence. Now we have nothing except the fact Alex witnessed a murder."

"And the fact we now need to convince Alex to tell us who he was with that night," I added.

Jack frowned. "Fat chance."

There was a knock at the door, and Jack yelled, "Yeah?"

Owen stuck his head through the opening and said, "Chief, the mayor is here. Something about a meeting with you and Mrs. S?"

I had totally forgotten about the meeting. Jack checked his watch and nodded. "Thanks, Owen. Show His Highness in, will you?"

Owen grinned and disappeared, returning a moment later with the mayor in tow. I had to admit, the guy looked as if a truck had hit him, but his appearance didn't make me like him.

Jack motioned toward a chair and said, "Please take a seat. As you can see, Mrs. Shaw arrived a few minutes ago."

Once Mayor Hayes had gotten settled in the chair next to mine, Jack asked, "Why did you need to see both of us?"

The mayor squirmed around that chair as though it had ants on it, then looked at Jack. "I understand you are still investigating a cold case from the nineties?"

Jack raised an eyebrow but remained mute.

Still squirming, the mayor said, "I'm not trying to hinder any official investigation, but this isn't really official. Could you give me a reason for digging up old news?"

I could tell he was trying to bully us, but his heart wasn't in it.

Jack continued observing the mayor, not inclined to divulge any information unless forced. "This has nothing to do with Akron," he said. "Why exactly are you interested in what our township may or may not be investigating?"

More squirming from the chair next to me. Finally, the mayor cleared his throat. He took a deep breath and said, "I may be able to help."

Jack looked at me, I looked at Dad, and Dad looked at the mayor.

"Without knowing what the investigation entails?" Jack asked, fake innocence dripping from each word.

"Yeah," the big guy next to me said as he looked down at his Italian loafers. "Yeah."

Chapter 19

My eyebrows crept northward, ending somewhere around my hairline. I hadn't realize I had been holding my breath until it rushed from my mouth with force. Wow, here was the head honcho from Akron inspecting his handmade Italian shoes and offering information a few days ago he had denied even possessing. I glanced at Jack, wondering what his next move would entail. His eyes had narrowed, which was interesting. He must not trust the weasel sitting next to me any more than I did.

"Your help would be appreciated, if there is, of course, any ongoing investigation," Jack said. "You obviously have something to share, so why don't we start there?"

The mayor looked up and studied Jack's face. "I believe you are nosing around an old murder case that was never solved." He shook his head sadly. My eyes were drawn to his hands as they began shaking. I frowned, wondering what would fall out of his mouth next. Whatever he was prepared to share had his gut in a twist.

Jack nodded, keeping his mouth firmly closed. He glanced grimly at me, then back at the mayor. I had no idea if Jack was sending me a message or not, but I decided to take the bull by the horns.

"Okay, Mayor. Let's cut to the chase and get this over with. You seem pretty upset, so treat the situation like a bandage and just let 'er rip. Less painful in the long run."

I had to admit diplomacy was never my strong suit. Watching the man squirm, I could feel the motherly side of my personality rising to the top, and I didn't want to end up feeling sorry for him.

He turned his gaze my direction, then back at Jack. "Alex had nothing to do with this; I swear to God."

"Who said Alex was involved?" Jack asked. "Why don't you start at the beginning?"

Nodding, the mayor said, "The night the murders occurred, Alex came home late." He stopped talking and closed his eyes. Memories were nasty little buggers, and this particular memory must sting like a son of a bitch. His eyes remained shut as he continued, "It was quite late and past his curfew, so I was more than prepared to ground him for the remainder of the semester." Opening his eyes, he said, "For no apparent reason, his grades had been slipping. My wife and I were worried he was hanging around kids who were unhealthy for him."

Jack nodded his understanding of parents everywhere; good kids could go horribly wrong during those volatile teen years. We all sweated through it, some more than others. I glanced at Dad, who was watching this exchange with great interest. He had missed all the fun of parenting a teenager; being dead did that to a person. He saw me watching him and winked. Okay, maybe he *had* been near me, but *I* hadn't been aware of his presence. My eyes misted at the thought; it would have been great if I'd had the ability to see him back then. Living with my mother had been no picnic.

"He came in the house that night white as a sheet, shaking from head to toe. We thought there must have been an accident of some sort," the mayor continued. "It took us almost an hour to pull any information from him. He was scared to death."

I remained still, afraid any movement on my part would stop the flow of words. Jack was frozen as well, apparently having the same idea. Taking a deep breath, the mayor said, "He told us a couple had been murdered. He had witnessed it, but he wouldn't tell us who did the actual killing." He suddenly stopped, his eyes pleading with Jack to believe his story.

Jack met his gaze but said nothing. Every ounce of my parental instinct rushed to the surface, damn it. I knew the guy was telling the truth, but I still didn't like him.

Sighing, the mayor said, "I'm not proud of my next move." He watched for Jack's reaction but was disappointed, since there wasn't one at all. No movement, no sound, just Jack's watchful eyes. It was unnerving but probably what made him such a good cop.

"What exactly was your next move?" I asked. I couldn't keep myself from asking the question. Jack might have nerves of steel, but I sure as hell didn't.

Turning to face me, he said, "I took advantage of my position and pulled any evidence that proved Alex had been in the house." Well, hell. The man was being more honest in that moment than his entire political life.

"Why didn't you let the chips fall and get him a good defense lawyer?" I asked.

The mayor snorted in disbelief. "Are you kidding? My political enemies would have had a field day with that! Good God, woman, it would have been the end of my career."

In one sentence, he swept away all sympathy I had felt toward him as he'd recounted that night. Good to know he really was the creep I thought.

"Nice," I responded, sarcasm firmly in place.

"But that was minor compared to the horror Alex was enduring. Whoever killed that couple threatened Alex. He was smart, though. He said if Alex ever told anyone the truth, he would kill our entire family but leave Alex alive."

Jack finally spoke. "So it was a male that killed them?"

The mayor looked confused for a moment. "I told you: I have no idea."

"You said 'he' was smart," Jack said.

"I guess I did," the mayor said, frowning. "Never realized, but Alex kept referring to the person as 'him.' Didn't think twice about it, to be honest."

"You didn't think about anything," I said angrily. "By trying to protect your son, you have allowed him to live all these years miserable. No wonder he is a wreck!" I visualized Alex sitting at my kitchen table, eating pie, his face pale. Poor kid.

Surprised, the mayor said, "I never meant for this mess to ruin him. I was honestly trying to keep him safe."

"And protect your own career!" I snapped. "God."

"I was trying to do both; I don't apologize."

I shook my head, disgusted.

"What would you have done?" my dad asked from his corner of the room.

My head snapped in his direction, but I was savvy enough not to answer in front of the mayor. I frowned.

"He did what some parents would have done; not how I would have handled it, but some would," my dad said. "He was trying to save the entire situation. Don't be so arrogant to think you would have made wiser decisions."

My eyes stung at his rebuke. His expression softened, and he said, "Peg, sweetie, we screw up. It's part of life."

I gave him a quick nod and turned back to the man next to me. "Why now?" I asked him.

Mayor Hayes gave me a surprised look. "What do you mean?"

"Why tell us the truth now?"

He shrugged. "Alex told me the investigation had reopened. I tried talking to you at your house, but you wouldn't listen."

I could feel myself turning a light shade of pink. He was right. I hadn't given him a chance.

Looking back at Jack, the mayor asked, "Do you believe me? That Alex is innocent?"

"Yep" was all Jack said.

Shocked but relieved, the mayor asked, "Why?"

Jack's eyes slid to meet mine. I shook my head. Sharing the fact I had an eyewitness wasn't on my agenda. It didn't help that my eyewitness was deader than a doornail. Jack got the message.

"Let's just say we have a person of interest shedding new light on the old case."

Hope sprang into the mayor's eyes. "A witness?"

"I wouldn't exactly put it quite that way," I said evasively. "Enough to make Alex's involvement clear."

The mayor looked back and forth between Jack and me. "How so?"

Jack wagged a finger at the man. "Look, Alex was there. Unlawfully. He could still be indicted on accessory charges. He isn't totally cleared of responsibility."

"Did Alex explain what they were doing in the house?" I asked.

Sighing, the mayor said, "They thought the couple were out of town. It was a lark; they were going to steal a few things just for the hell of it."

Ah, that explained a lot. "Someone his own age?" I asked. Teenagers could dream up pretty stupid stunts in their spare time.

Shaking his head, he said, "Never could get much information out of him, but I did have the feeling it was another teenager."

Nodding, Jack said, "Makes sense. Two teenage boys, bored with being teenagers, out goofing around." He thought for a moment before asking, "You think the other boy was from Bath or Akron?"

"I have no idea. Even though Alex grew up in Akron, he spent most of his summer vacations at his grandfather's house here in Bath. I've given this a lot thought through the years but never could come up with an answer to that question."

"We still don't know who killed us?" Bob asked from behind me. I jumped in my chair and almost peed my pants. Clamping my lips tight so I wouldn't yell, I glared at Dad. He could have warned me Bob was in the room. But one look at Dad's surprised face told me he hadn't felt Bob's presence either. Bob was becoming a bit too capable at spying, in my opinion. Jack, seeing my reaction, understood another visitor was in the room. He gave me a slight nod and said to the mayor, "I can't help Alex until I talk to him. Do you think you could arrange a meeting?"

Frowning, the mayor said, "I doubt it, but I'll try." Looking around the office, he said, "Not here—he wouldn't feel safe. Anyone could witness him coming to the station. Maybe at his house?"

Jack nodded. "That works. Call me when you have it set up." He rose from his chair, ending the meeting. He stuck out his hand and said, "Thanks, Mayor, for coming in and talking with us."

Surprised at the dismissal, the mayor stood, saying, "I do appreciate you two sitting down with me. But understand, I want Alex's name to stay out of this completely."

"No promises, but I'll do my best," Jack said. He ushered the mayor to the door.

Pausing before he left, Mayor Hayes turned to Jack and said, "Thank you for your time."

Jack patted his back, saying, "No problem. Just set up the meeting."

With a quick nod, Alex's father left us alone in Jack's office.

I waited until I was sure the man had cleared the hall before turning to Bob, asking, "What the hell? You scared the crap out of me!"

"What do you mean?" he asked innocently.

I watched him a moment before believing he actually had no idea he had startled me. "I didn't realize you were here."

Surprise spread over his face and then was replaced with glee. "Really?" he asked. Rubbing his hands together, he said, "That is so cool! I'm getting pretty good at this spying stuff, aren't I?"

I closed my eyes and slowly counted to ten. When I opened them, I spotted Dad in the corner trying to hide his laughter. "Not funny," I said through tightly clenched teeth. "At all." Dad's amusement didn't fade one bit. Choosing to ignore Dad for the time being, I turned to Bob. "We need to have some sort of agreement concerning your appearances. I almost blew it with the mayor when you showed up."

"Gosh, Peg, I'm not sure I would know how to do that." He frowned, thinking over my demand. "I'll nose around and see if anyone on my side can give me some pointers."

Sighing, I looked over at Dad. "Well? Any ideas?"

Shaking his head, he said, "It works differently for everyone. Can't help you, sorry."

Studying him a moment, I wondered if he was being totally honest. I knew he couldn't lie outright, but I bet he could get by with a little fudging. I could easily imagine Dad withholding information from Bob that might make my life easier. He seemed to be enjoying the situation, even though it was at my expense. *I guess when you're dead, you take entertainment where you can get it,* I thought.

Bob said, "I'll work on it; I promise."

I nodded at his obvious sincerity.

Jack cleared his throat, reminding me of his presence. "Well, what do you think of our little meeting with the big guy of Akron?"

I thought a moment before answering, "Interesting. He plainly wants to protect his son. I hate to admit it, but I don't blame him." I glanced quickly at Dad. I knew he was absolutely correct with his analysis of the mayor's decisions years ago. I merely disagreed with those decisions. "Especially if the guy responsible for these murders threatened the entire family."

Nodding his agreement, Jack said, "Tough situation for a kid to handle. My problem is Alex isn't a kid anymore. And you called it correctly: if they had come to us at the time, we probably could have struck a deal with the district attorney."

"Absolutely! The mayor should have known better than to hide evidence, even if it would have damaged his political career."

Agreeing with my analysis, Jack said, "He's made it a bigger mess by evading the issue." Sighing, he added, "You think we can clean up this botched chaos?"

Before I could answer, the hairs on my arm flew up at attention. Oh God, now who? Before I could turn to see her, Elaine screeched, "There you are! I've been looking everywhere for you!"

Bob cowered at the sound of her voice. I didn't blame him one bit. Dad was no longer leaning against the wall but was standing straight, watching Elaine carefully. Jack had realized there must be some sort of commotion by my reaction to Elaine's howling at Bob and asked, "Now who?"

Sighing, I answered, "Elaine's yelling at Bob. It's getting a tad crowded in here."

Jack shook his head. "This is becoming a three-ring circus with your dead friends."

"Not actually friends!" I snapped.

"What are you doing here?" Elaine demanded. Poor Bob.

"Still working on our murders," he said quietly.

"Huh! These idiots won't ever figure it out! They should quit while they're ahead," Elaine snarled.

I frowned at her remark. Not the idiot part—that attitude was normal for Elaine. Hell, it was normal for me. But when had she decided we should stop investigating the murder? This was a new development and not necessarily good news. Had my mother influenced Elaine for some reason? I glanced at Dad. He was continuing to watch Elaine very carefully. My stomach churned with the realization Mom could be affecting this investigation.

"We need to get out of here!" Elaine commanded.

Bob's mouth dropped open in total shock. "After all the years I listened to you complain about our murders, you want me to stop looking now?" he asked.

Gosh. So I wasn't the only one surprised by Elaine's decision.

"No way!" Bob continued. "They might be on to something, and I'm not leaving!" I had to hand it to him: he was actually challenging Elaine's authority.

Elaine's eyes narrowed as she glared at Bob. "I'm not kidding! Come with me right this second!"

Bob shook his head stubbornly. "Nope."

Wow. I wasn't sure exactly what type of revenge Elaine could take out on Bob, but knowing her, it could be nasty. I looked toward the corner where Dad had been and was startled to see him gone. Quickly glancing around the room, I realized he was nowhere to be seen. My stomach twisted. As long as he was here, I felt safe, but now … Just as panic started to set in, a thought flew into my head.

I turned to Bob. "Um, Bob?" He turned to face me, and I said, "Maybe you should go with Elaine. It might be better." I tried boring my eyes into his, hoping he'd get my message.

His face fell at my words, but bless his heart, he actually took time to study my face. Thankfully, after a few seconds of silence, his eyes lit up, and he nodded.

"Are you sure?" he asked. But I could tell by his expression that my message had gotten through.

"Yep. Be careful, though."

Nodding, he said, "Okeydokey. See ya later." He was gone in an instant, pulling Elaine along with him, thank God.

Jack had stayed quiet, hoping to figure out the drama unfolding in his office by listening to my reactions. After a few moments of silence, he asked, "The coast clear?"

"Yep. They're all gone. Even Dad."

"What was that about?" he asked. I could read the concern on his face a mile away.

"Elaine wants Bob to stop helping us with this case," I said. "But I sent him to spy on Elaine and Mom. I am positive she is involved somehow."

"Uh-oh. Doesn't sound good," he said.

"It isn't," my dad said. I whirled around, surprised he had come back. He wasn't alone either; Logan was with him. In a split second I realized where Dad had gone—to get reinforcements.

"Now who?" Jack asked.

"Dad and Logan," I answered.

"Quick thinking, having Bob go with Elaine to check out what exactly they are up to," Dad said.

I glanced at Logan. What would he think of my plan? It had been an idea on the fly, no thought involved really. Maybe it was the wrong plan.

He nodded as he said, "Smart. There is a chance Bob will discover an indication of their motives."

My stomach relaxed at his words. I was surprised to realize how important his opinion was to me. If Logan thought it was a good idea, then it was a good idea. Nice to know I could think in a pinch.

Owen stuck his head in the door. "Uh, Chief?"

Jack looked over at him. "Yeah?"

"I'm supposed to remind you of the meeting with the trustees. It starts in a few minutes."

"Damn! Thanks, Owen," Jack said. Turning to me, he said, "Peg, gotta go. Sorry."

He left me alone in his office. I hoped the trustees didn't find out he had left nonpolice personnel in his office. There'd be hell to pay.

Chapter 20

I grabbed my purse and was standing to follow Jack's exit when Logan asked, "Who was the young man?"

"What? Oh, Owen. He's a cop here," I answered. "Why?"

"I believe it is important to know who is around you at all times," he said. "Precautions."

I laughed. "I've known that kid forever."

He nodded but said, "I realize you may know him well, but I do not."

I recognized the protective mode and appreciated his concern. "He grew up here in the township, went to school with my kids, and after college came home to the local police department," I said, waving my arm to indicate the building we were inhabiting.

Logan nodded again. "Thank you for the information." Turning to Dad, Logan said, "Elaine's demands have piqued my interest. The fact she also, along with your wife, wants to hinder the search for her murderer raises questions. We must examine our realm for possible problems." He sighed before adding, "I had hoped to avoid this dilemma."

Well, he wasn't making me feel all warm and cozy. I had felt secure knowing Logan was involved, but if he could be taken by surprise by events, then I wasn't so sure my safety net of Indians was a solid shield. I glanced at Dad, wondering what his next move would entail. I didn't have to wait long.

"We need to increase her security detail. Our limitations force us to use physical means." Dad's face was serious as hell, and my stomach twisted into new knots.

Logan thought a moment before responding, "I agree. It could be problematic, however. Who do you suggest?"

"The mayor."

Well, hell. I just about fell over from sheer shock. Was Dad out of his mind? "What?" I screeched. I was starting to sound like Elaine, which didn't help my self-image one bit.

Dad held up a hand to silence me before I could get a good head of furious steam started. "Peg, he has connections. We need those contacts for your safety."

"They are thugs!" I said, teeth gritted so hard I thought for a second I'd break them to bits.

"Yep, precisely why they are perfect."

"I don't trust him; he's sleazy."

Dad laughed. "Exactly. The only living person, other than Jack and Andy, who we can trust at this point is someone who obviously is not involved. It comes down to the mayor and his acquaintances."

Sighing, I said, "Dad, I think he has friends in the mob."

Dad nodded. "Good. His connections will come in handy."

Exasperated, I looked over at Logan. "Well?" I demanded. "The mob?" he asked.

"Bad guys. They are involved in all types of illegal activity," I snapped.

Logan took a moment to think through this new information before nodding. "I agree with your father. There are many types of warriors. We are in need of relentless dedication."

"Jack will have a heart attack if we involve the mob," I said.

Dad thought for a moment before saying, "I disagree with you. He's a cop, and he will recognize the necessity of bringing in some big guns." His expression softened. "Twinkle toes, listen to me. Logan and I will be surveying our side of this problem, but I need to know your safety is secure. Go talk to the mayor."

I opened my mouth to respond but was interrupted.

"Mrs. S? You okay?"

I turned to see Owen's concerned face in the doorway. Damn it, caught talking to myself again! When would I learn to close the damn doors!

"I'm fine. This purse is so big I can't seem to find my car keys," I said, gesturing toward the piece of luggage I called a purse.

His million-watt smile appeared as he said, "Okay, just checking. Thought I heard you talking with someone."

"You did. I was bitching to myself about the darn keys." I laughed and hoped he believed me.

His face cleared of concern, and he said, "Hope you find the keys. Gotta get back to work." He turned and walked down the hall.

I grabbed my purse, motioned for Dad and Logan to stay close, and headed for the car. No sense remaining in Jack's office talking to dead people. I could get caught again but by someone convinced I was nuts.

Heading out to my car with my duo following along, I waved to Owen as he prepared to go out on patrol. I noticed he was using a new SUV the township had recently purchased. There had been a big discussion last year concerning the department's vehicles and the need for an upgrade. It was good to see the budget had allowed for sturdier transportation. Winter roads could be brutal around here until Lake Erie froze. Lake-effect snow piled up pretty fast and made driving treacherous. Owen smiled, returning my wave.

Once in my car, I turned to the front passenger seat, where Logan was sitting. Dad had taken the backseat, which pretty much defined their relationship. Logan was definitely in charge, with Dad taking the role of second banana.

"Well, I have to ask," I said. "Are you both sure this is a good idea?"

"Yep, sweetie. Positive," Dad said.

Sighing, I started my car and made my way to downtown Akron. I couldn't stand driving downtown anywhere; all those one-way streets confused me. I long ago had found a solution to the problem by parking in the garage on Main Street and walking to whatever building I needed. I found parking a bit farther down Main Street, near the Akron Civic Theatre. I had always loved that place since my first date with Andy, a showing of the classic movie *Casablanca*. What wasn't there to love about Humphrey Bogart?

My companions remained quiet throughout the drive downtown. I figured Dad knew how nerve-racking downtown driving was for me and had wisely decided silence was my best friend.

Once the car was safely parked, I turned to Logan. "You guys coming with me?" I asked hopefully.

"Absolutely," Dad answered as Logan silently looked around the garage. Was he marveling at how far we'd come transportation wise or merely irritated with so much concrete? No way to know since he remained poker-faced.

"Good," I said, relieved I wouldn't be facing the big man alone.

It was a few blocks over to the mayor's office. As I was walking, I realized I should have called ahead. It had never dawned on me to ensure the mayor would be in his office.

"No worries," Dad said next to me with a grin.

"What are you talking about?" I asked.

"Just checked; he's in his office. Don't let his secretary tell you he's in a meeting either," he said as we reached the entrance to the municipal building.

"Why would she tell me he was in a meeting?" I asked him as I entered the building. I reminded myself to stop talking a split second before I noticed the horde of people milling around inside. Didn't they have jobs they should be doing? Hard-earned tax dollars at work.

I asked the guard for directions to the office in question, and after giving me a startled look, he pointed me in the right direction. Dad resumed his spiel concerning my upcoming encounter with the secretary.

"She'll tell you he's in a meeting; trust me." He sounded confident in his analysis of the situation. I shrugged but agreed with a quick nod of my head.

Entering the office, I did a quick glance around the place. Not too impressive, which was a little disappointing. Plain white walls, a few chairs, and a couple of magazines placed on ordinary side tables. I wasn't sure what I'd expected, but this wasn't what I had pictured in my mind. Obviously, television programs made official offices more impressive than real life.

The secretary looked up from her paperwork—no inviting smile, merely a short acknowledgement of my entry. "Yes?"

Maybe she had zero people skills, or maybe she was an old hand at handling the public and not impressed with what she had witnessed through the years.

"I'm here to see the mayor," I announced quickly. She glanced at her computer screen, then looked back at me.

"No appointment?"

She really had a way with words. I shook my head.

"Sorry, but he's in a meeting."

"Ha! Told you so," Dad said. I didn't dare chance a quick glare at him, so I ignored his remark.

"I don't believe he actually is in a meeting. Do us both a favor and let him know Peg Shaw is here and would like a minute of his time." I could be aggressive when push came to shove, and I wanted this encounter over as soon as possible.

Her expression changed from bored to irritated. I didn't care; I wasn't backing down. I stood there quietly but resolutely. She must have recognized stubbornness when she saw it, because she picked up her phone and buzzed the boss. Her smugness was quickly replaced with a look of surprise as she answered in the affirmative. Glancing at me with new interest, she got up and showed me into the big office behind her desk.

Giving credit where it was due, I had to admit I was impressed that Bennet Hayes got off his fat butt and came around his desk to shake my hand, welcoming me to his domain. My skinned crawled a bit as I took his hand, but at least the handshake was firm. That surprised me; I had expected squishy. Probably another reason he won votes.

"To what do I owe this visit? I saw you less than an hour ago," he said as he sat back in his oversized chair. He motioned for me to take the seat in front of the desk, which I did thankfully. My feet hurt from walking two blocks from the parking gaarage; I really needed to get a little exercise.

Now that I was actually here, sitting across from a man I despised, I had no idea where to start. I looked around for Dad and Logan. I needed some sort of guidance. I decided since this was their idea, they could help me out a bit. Both were standing behind the mayor, Logan looking out the window. What was it with windows lately?

"I'm not quite sure how to begin," I said, more to Dad and Logan than the mayor.

The mayor leaned back in his chair, folded his arms across his massive midsection, and said, "I was given a piece of advice recently: treat it like a Band-Aid and let 'er rip." He grinned.

I clenched my teeth and narrowed my eyes as he threw my own words back at me. How in the world had I gotten myself into this mess?

"Tell him who your witness is; should start the ball rolling," Dad advised.

"Great," I said to the air over the mayor's right shoulder.

Looking into the mayor's eyes, I said, "This is going to sound ridiculous, but hear me out before you jump to conclusions."

He nodded, his face as still as stone, and motioned with his hand for me to continue.

"We do have an eyewitness to the murders," I began.

"I knew it!" he exclaimed.

I held up a hand, then continued, "There is a slight snag to this particular witness."

The mayor's eyebrows rose, questioning.

"He's no longer alive and was one of the victims." I sat back in my chair and waited for that tidbit to sink in a moment.

Frowning, he remained silent for a whole minute before saying, "I'm not sure I understand."

"Two people were murdered that night, right?" I asked him.

Nodding, he said, "Yes."

"Bob and Elaine Bradley, correct?"

The frown deepened as he tried to grasp the meaning of my questions.

"Bob is our eyewitness. Elaine only saw your son so is convinced Alex murdered them. Bob only recently allowed himself to remember the night of their murders. He realized there was a second person in the room."

"This isn't funny! I don't appreciate your wasting my time with this drivel!"

"Do you honestly believe I would drive all the way downtown, park blocks away, and sashay my butt in here to tell you something this ridiculous if I wasn't telling you the truth?" I snapped.

I looked over at Logan, who had now moved closer to the paperwork on the mayor's desk. Glancing over at me, he said, "Tell the mayor papers on his desk will move at the count of five."

"Mayor, your paperwork will move when I count to five. Ready?" I counted off the numbers. The split second I said *five*, the paperwork flew off the desk. Even I was surprised, since I had expected Logan to move them rather than shove the whole lot onto the floor.

The mayor's face turned white. After a moment, he passed his hand over his face, then looked at me. "You're serious."

"Yep."

I had to feel sorry for him; I knew exactly how he felt. The disbelief, the fear, and, most of all, the worry your mind had happily taken a field trip and might not come home. I continued watching him, hoping like hell Logan's little trick wouldn't give the guy a heart attack. Maybe I should have asked the mayor about any health conditions before pulling the paper stunt. Oh well, live and learn.

He looked around the room, searching for clues of invisible visitors, but could detect nothing. I glanced at Logan, who was still standing next to the mayor's desk, quiet but watching the man's expressions. Sensing my stare, he turned to me and nodded. "He believes you. I advise continuing with your story."

Sighing, dreading the need to tell him Bob's version of events, I said, "I'm not nuts, and neither are you." I decided he needed a little encouragement, even from someone who couldn't stand the sight of him. It was better than nothing.

He didn't seem able to meet my eyes, but I continued my tale in spite of his reaction. "Bob and Elaine showed up in my life a few weeks back. Until that point I hadn't given their murders a second's thought in years." I paused, then added, "Bob's a little squirrelly, but Elaine's a nightmare."

That got his attention. His head snapped up, and his eyes met mine. "Did you know them before?" he asked.

I shook my head. "Nope. I don't know everyone in the township. I had never met them before they showed up and demanded I figure out who killed them." I stopped, thinking about that day, and realized Bob had not demanded anything from me. *Figures*, I thought.

"I ask because your description of their personalities may not have been in depth, but it's one hundred percent correct. That woman was a pain in the ass!"

Well, he'd recovered from the shock pretty darn fast. The mere thought of Elaine overrode any other emotion, obviously. It was nice to know I wasn't the only one carrying around that particular opinion of her. Dad's face spread into a wide grin at the mayor's assessment of my troublesome couple, and I grinned back.

The mayor saw my expression and instinctively turned to see who was receiving my smile. Seeing nothing, he shook his head. "This is an unusual situation."

I shrugged, saying, "At this point, I've gotten pretty used to them. I have a herd of dead people I'm dealing with here, so count yourself lucky you only have to put up with me."

Nodding, he stared down at the mess of papers that still decorated his carpet. "I suppose your friend doesn't clean up after himself?"

Logan laughed at the mayor's comment.

"Well, you got him to laugh," I informed the mayor.

Sighing, he leaned over and started picking up the wreckage. I kept my butt firmly in the chair; they were his papers, so he could do the cleanup just fine without any assistance from me. Once the chaos was back on his desk, he rifled through the papers, putting them in neat piles. I watched, fascinated, as he placed the paperwork carefully in order, straightening each pile. Though not a perfectionist myself, I recognized one when I saw one. He finally satisfied himself all was back to normal.

Looking at me, he asked, "Could you tell me exactly what Bob told you? It would help me understand why you are positive Alex didn't commit those murders." He winced as he said the final few words.

Nodding, I repeated what Bob had told me, making sure the mayor understood how intense Bob's concentration had been as he'd relived those final moments of his life.

Listening closely, the mayor never took his eyes off my face. He remained stock-still until I finished the tale. "He saw Alex in the corner? He's confident his memory was accurate?"

"Yep," I said. "He was absolutely positive he was recalling the night correctly."

Closing his eyes, he leaned his head back against his chair. I suddenly understood that all these years he had not quite believed Alex's side of the story. There had been doubt, even if just a smidgen. It had been enough to weigh on his mind and probably his heart. I hated to admit it, but I felt a wee bit sorry for him at that moment. I respectfully kept my mouth shut, letting him work through this new information at his own pace. Might as well be nice for the time being, since I needed any evidence he had so conveniently hidden away as well as his protection.

My cell phone rang, which was unusual. I grabbed my purse and dug around trying to find the damn thing. Peering down at the noisy object, I saw Jack was calling. Uh-oh. I hadn't told him I was meeting with the mayor, and he might not agree this was the smartest move I could have made. I hit the "ignore" button and tossed the phone back down the cavern where it lived.

"Why did you decide to come talk to me?" the mayor finally asked.

I took a deep breath and answered, "Because I may need to use some of your …" I stopped. Well, hell, I couldn't very well tell him I needed the mob to protect me.

He frowned at my sudden silence. "Yes? My what?"

"Protectors." I couldn't think of a better word. I hoped he would figure it out on his own.

He did. "Ah. Why?"

"Well, my dead friends can only help me to a certain extent." I nodded toward the paperwork on his desk. "That is about as physical as I can hope for in a pinch." Remembering the neck massage Logan had given me, I wondered how far he could push his abilities, but I decided living people would make me feel better anyway.

"Since we have no idea who actually did the murders, at least until Alex tells us, I have to be extremely careful. My dad wants me to have a bodyguard, and you are rumored to know a few." I stared him square in the eyes as I finished speaking.

He returned my stare but remained quiet. Damn it.

"Look, if I get killed trying to solve this mess, I'm going to be pissed! Not to mention the fact I'm the only one in contact with Bob and Elaine. If either one of those idiots actually remembers who did the deed, it won't help if I'm dead and buried."

Watching me carefully, he finally said, "I'll make a few calls and see what I can do for you."

Standing, I said, "Call me when you have a plan of action. I'm in the phone book." He could damn well call the house; I wasn't about to give him my cell phone number.

I turned to leave but stopped as he said, "Mrs. Shaw?"

I swiveled my head to face him but didn't utter a word.

"Thank you." I gave him a short nod, then left his office. I needed to breathe fresh air.

Chapter 21

I made the trek back to my car, cursing my aching feet. Why did aging have to include aches and pains? There was a time nothing in my body had a mind of its own and worked perfectly. Now, hormones disappeared, feet ached, and basically my entire body had started a revolution I was pretty sure would not lead to any type of victory for me. Maybe I really should consider exercising.

Once safely in my car and away from prying eyes and ears, Dad said, "Well, that went well. Frankly, better than I expected."

I turned to face Logan. "Are you satisfied with the meeting?"

"It was adequate," he answered.

"Adequate? How could it have been better? He didn't throw me out or tell me I was nuts!" My teeth were so clenched as I spoke that I was surprised the words made it out of my mouth.

Logan turned to face me. "There is nothing wrong with adequate. He took the news surprising well, considering his attitude toward the spiritual realm."

I cocked my head, asking, "How do you know what his religious views are?"

Logan shook his head side to side. "Not religious views. The spiritual arena. He's gone to mass faithfully most of his life, but his objective was to score political points." He smiled. "I've watched politicians for decades, and they all seem to follow particular patterns."

Nodding, I said, "Yep. Make your voters think you're one of them by going to church, PTA meetings, and office picnics."

"PTA?" he asked.

I sighed. How to explain parent involvement at school? Shaking my head, I said, "Parents help at their children's schools."

He thought about my explanation for a moment, then nodded. "Politicians can be untrustworthy, but in this matter I believe we have good reason to believe the mayor will keep his word." He paused, then added, "However, it does not indicate we should trust him completely."

I laughed. "I don't trust the sucker at all! But I do agree he will keep his mouth shut about this situation. He wants to protect Alex."

I paused and then asked Logan, "What's our next move?"

He looked out the window, saying, "I believe exiting this area would be refreshing. It is uncomfortable, and sunshine would be welcome."

I grinned as I started the car. Once I had maneuvered the car out of the tight parking space, I said, "I think a call to Jack is probably in order. He tried calling while I was with the mayor. I'm fairly positive he isn't going to be thrilled I informed the mayor of my new abilities without his blessing."

Dad chuckled. "Pretty sure he'll understand. He's a reasonable guy and will see the advantages. He is unable to give you the type of protection you need. But until we have all the facts and players in this case, he should keep quiet. No sharing information with anyone, even people at the station."

I glanced at Dad in the rearview mirror, nodding. "I agree. We can't be too careful at this point. Those walls have ears, and gossip is rampant at every office."

The car became quiet as I swung onto Main Street and remained so until I turned left onto Market Street. I wondered if every city had a Market Street— sure seemed common. I navigated traffic, trying to remember which lane was necessary for upcoming lights. Some became turn-only lanes, and if a person waited too long, he or she would be forced into taking complicated routes home. Once I had gotten closer to home ground, the conversation picked back up with Logan.

"There are many buildings here," he said.

"We are still in the city. That's one reason we live in Bath—trees!" I answered, laughing.

He nodded but continued surveying the surroundings.

"This area has built up quite a bit," Dad said. Like Logan, he was intrigued by the changes that had occurred since he was living around here. Well, living at all actually.

"Treeline! It's been here forever!" Dad said. "God, I miss their hamburgers. It used to be one of the few buildings this far out of town."

"Dad! Some of this area was built up when you lived here!" I caught his eye in the rearview mirror.

"There are plenty of new ones since my time, sweetie."

As I turned onto Ghent Road, Logan stirred beside me. Pointing, he asked, "What is that building?"

I chanced allowing my eyes to leave the road, answering him before returning to watch the traffic. "Summit Mall? It was built over fifty years ago!"

"After my time" was all he said.

I glanced quickly his direction before asking, "Is that land important?"

A quick shrug of his shoulders was all I received. Wondering if this was an important parcel of land to his Indian tribe, I decided to do a little research later. Couldn't hurt.

The silence was stifling. Finally, for no other reason than to have some type of noise in the car, I reminded them both, "I'm calling Jack when we get home."

"Yep, good idea," Dad said. "Watch the car in front of you."

"No backseat driving!" I laughed. I had taken my eyes off the road for a split second and found myself needing to sit on the brakes. "Damn," I muttered. "I hate when people don't use turn signals!"

Logan waved his hand, and the car in front of us turned faster than its driver had intended. We sailed past with no problem. Once my breathing returned to normal, I said, "Thanks, Logan."

A quick nod was all he was willing to impart. His continued silence was making the hair on the back of my neck stand up—never a good sign.

"Logan? Are you okay?" I asked.

"Yes. Thank you for asking." Turning to face my profile, he said, "You no longer need my assistance today. I will keep in touch." Suddenly, the seat next to me was empty.

After a moment, I glanced at Dad in the mirror. "He's a bit creepy sometimes."

Dad chuckled. "He has a lot on his mind. I was glad he was with us today. Remember, sweetie, Logan's only around when you absolutely need his help."

Nodding, I said, "Fine. But why all the silence?"

"Not much of a talker to begin with, but I get the feeling he is worried about things over on our side."

"Well, hell. Doesn't make me feel better! Gosh, Dad. What could be so bad in heaven it has Logan upset?"

"Sweetie, haven't you figured out yet that this isn't heaven as you think of it? We merely live in the spiritual realm, which has problems of its own to handle," Dad answered quietly.

I allowed his words to soak in a bit before saying, "Not necessarily a warm and fuzzy feeling, you know."

He laughed. "You'll get used to it eventually."

Turning into my long driveway, I spotted Jack's car sitting in front of the house. "What's he doing here?" I wondered aloud.

"Good timing. You needed to call him; now he's saved you the trouble."

Parking the car next to Jack's, I sighed once I saw the expression he wore. "Bloody hell. Now what?"

He strode purposefully toward me, anger obvious on his face.

"Uh-oh," I said. "

Yep. Bet he got a phone call from downtown," Dad said.

I opened the car door slowly and swung my legs around, settling my feet on the gravel driveway.

"Peg! What the hell is going on?" Jack shouted.

Wincing, I stalled for time. "Jack. What are you doing here?"

"You know damn well why I'm here!"

Sighing, I asked, "The mayor?"

Jack looked startled, then frowned. "What's the mayor got to do with this?" he demanded.

It was my turn to be surprised. "Um, what are you talking about?"

"Alex Hayes called. The poor kid is scared out of his mind. What have you been doing to stir him up?"

I frowned. Alex had called Jack?

"I haven't been stirring anything!" I retorted hotly. It was one thing to be yelled at for something I'd done, but when innocent, my advice was to fight back.

Jack's face fell. "Damn. I took it for granted you were the culprit."

"Come on in and tell me what he said to you. In extreme detail," I said as I unlocked the front door. I frowned as I put the key in the lock. How had those scratch marks gotten on the door? Andy would have a fit; this door was his pride and joy. We'd had to replace the original years ago, and he had searched all over the state for a door that would fit comfortably with the style of the house. He had finally found an old farm in southern Ohio being torn down for another housing development. It had taken him over two weeks to convince the owner he wanted only the door, and they had settled on a reasonable price. He had been so proud of his discovery and purchase he had treated the door with loving care ever since. The scratches would break his heart, even after all these years.

My thoughts were interrupted when Jack asked, "Everything okay?"

I glanced back at him. "Yep," I said, then paused. "Except that I don't remember these marks on the door. They look fresh."

Jack moved around me to investigate. He leaned down to study the marks, standing straight after a few moments. "Yeah, they do look fresh. Let me go in first."

I gladly moved to the side once the door was unlocked and allowed Jack to take the lead, following closely behind. He turned to motion me to stay put, but there was no way I was leaving his side. If there was someone around, I had no guarantee they had stayed in the house. Hell, with my luck, they were outside waiting for me to be alone while Jack was inside checking out the situation. My stomach was clenched into a million knots, and I had a terrible urge to puke. I glanced around the yard quickly, hoping I wouldn't see someone behind a tree. Sensing there wasn't an immediate threat outside, I turned my attention inside. Where were the dead guys when you needed them? Jeez.

Jack quietly made his way through the living room and turned to inspect the den. A quick glance told us it was empty, and he moved toward the bedrooms. I peeked into the main bathroom, and it was obviously empty, thank God. Following closely on Jack's heels, I noticed my breathing—or lack of breathing. I seemed to be holding my breath and tried to force a little air into my lungs, figuring it was better than passing out in my own house. It was difficult, but I finally managed to get enough oxygen in my system to ward off fainting.

Once Jack had determined the bedrooms were empty, we headed toward the kitchen. I had an icky feeling the moment we stepped onto the tile floor. There was no one in sight, but I swear it felt as though someone had been in there. He must have picked up on my discomfort, because he turned to face me.

"Well? Anything out of place?"

I took a quick survey of the kitchen. Nothing seemed out of order. Pots and pans where they belonged, dishes exactly as I had left them, which meant piled in the sink from breakfast. I walked over to the table and caught my breath.

"What?"

"Something's wrong. I can't put my finger on it exactly, but the papers seem moved." I studied the mess of papers I'd piled on the table so I wouldn't forget to file them away at some point in time. The pile seemed to grow daily. They were neatly stacked, which was not how I had left them.

"They look fine to me," Jack said as he joined me at the table.

"Yeah, but I don't do the neat thing very well. Someone has looked through them but didn't make sure they replaced them correctly. I remember last night thinking the mess needed to be dealt with, but I was just so damn tired I decided to file today."

"Not good," Jack answered.

"Nope." "Anything pertaining to our investigation?" he asked.

I shook my head. "No way. I wouldn't have left anything out, since I never know who's showing up next to drive me nuts."

We looked at each other, then back at the paperwork. The knot in my stomach was growing, and my headache was back. Great.

"I think you had better call Andy and let him know someone broke into the house," Jack said finally.

Sighing, I nodded as I grabbed the house phone and began dialing. Sending a text message would not work for this news. He answered after the third ring.

"Hey there. I'm pretty sure someone broke into the house today while I was out running a few errands." I quickly informed him of the events.

"The door has scratches on it?" he asked. "How bad is it?"

While not totally surprised the front door took the major portion of his attention, it did irk me he wasn't focusing on the real problem.

"Andy, someone broke into our house. Nothing is stolen or destroyed, but the paperwork on the kitchen table has been inspected for some reason."

He must have heard the agitation in my voice, since the next words out of his mouth were "Sorry, babe. You okay?"

"Yeah, Jack is here with me. He was waiting for me when I got home."

"Where's your dad?" Andy asked.

Dad! I had totally forgotten him. Where the hell was he? Looking frantically around, I finally spotted him in the woods talking with some Indians, whom, for some strange reason, I could now plainly see. By the looks of their expressions, they were informing him of the intruder.

"Talking with the Indian guys out back in the woods," I answered.

Andy sighed deeply, then said, "Find out if they noticed the intruder. Call me back." He must have been quite upset, since he forgot to tell me good-bye. I looked down at the phone in surprise before putting the receiver back on the base. When I glanced up, Jack was studying my face.

"You okay? Maybe you should sit down. Your face is decidedly pale."

I waved off his concern as I headed for the back door. "I'm finding out if my protection squad bothered to notice anything important. Why have the troops out back if they can't stop my house getting broken into!"

I stomped through the yard and reached the ongoing conference in time to hear my dad ask, "Are you sure you didn't see his face?"

I could hear the frustration clearly as I approached the gathering. Dad glanced in my direction but quickly returned his attention to his conversation with his dead pals.

"Explain again exactly how the person entered the home," Dad said.

The tallest of the group answered, "He opened the back door and walked into the house. There was little we could do, but he seemed confident about entering the home. Logan came by, but the man had already left the property." Ah, so this was why Logan had disappeared from my car earlier.

"Can you see them? What are they saying? Is your dad mad?" Jack's voice startled me, and a short, shrill noise escaped my throat. Jack had peppered the questions so quickly I couldn't respond to any of them. It didn't help he had startled me to the point my heart was racing at top speed. It took a few moments to calm myself enough to continue listening in on my dad's queries.

"Did the man leave with anything in his hand?" As Dad continued to pry information from the bunch, I noticed one of the men was looking toward the house, frowning.

"Hey, Dad!" I called over to him. Irritated at my interruption, Dad barely turned his head in my direction. Ignoring his bad attitude, I continued, "The guy toward the back may have something to say. The one with the scar on his forehead."

Dad fully turned toward me, not used to anyone horning in on his existence, his face scrunched in a frown. I paid no attention to his bad manners but jerked my head toward the man in question. After a moment, Dad allowed himself to focus on the face I had described. He must have seen in the man's face what I had, namely, confusion at the situation.

"Peg! Tell me what's going on! The suspense is killing me!" Jack said. I had ignored him earlier, and he wasn't pleased.

"Tell you in a second. Hang on," I muttered.

"This is ridiculous! I'm the cop!" he stammered impatiently.

I waved my hand at him for silence. Couldn't he see I was busy?

Dad had begun questioning the Indian I had indicated. The poor guy looked surprised he was being addressed for an opinion. These men must have a hierarchy that I was unfamiliar with. Watching his face, I decided he must be at the low end of the totem pole. Made me wonder if he had done something in life making his existence unimportant.

The original guy Dad had been questioning clearly did not appreciate being sidestepped for anyone else and threw Dad a deep glare, which my dad ignored completely. Attitude obviously ran in the family, and I realized I'd inherited mine from both parents. Go figure.

I watched Dad's face as he listened closely to the information from the man with the scar. His anxiety grew the more information he gathered, and his posture changed as the conversation continued. The news definitely was

173

a shock to Dad; he shook his head in disbelief before turning to me. "Not good news. They've seen the man here before, so they weren't sure quite what to do about the situation. That's why they called in Logan."

"What do you mean he's been here before?" I asked, frowning.

"They saw him enter the house once while you were home. Not wanting to raise an alarm if he was your friend, they had to discuss the situation among themselves first. Finally, they made the decision to call Logan, but he arrived too late to see who entered."

"Who could it have been?" I asked.

Dad shook his head. "I have had to leave a few times. Who's been here while you were alone?"

I thought frantically, trying to remember. Then it hit me: Alex had come by, and I had invited him in the house! But why in the hell would he have broken in? "

Alex? He stopped by that day. But he isn't the killer."

"Well, someone else damn well has been here!" Dad said.

"What the hell in going on!" Jack demanded.

Turning to him, I said, "They have seen the intruder here before. But I have no idea other than Alex who it could have been."

"Shit," Jack said.

Chapter 22

I felt myself lowered gently to the grassy ground beneath my feet. Everything had gone black for a few moments, and once my butt hit the ground, my body sagged completely. Jack was crouched beside me, talking in gentle tones. "It's okay, Peg. Just breathe through your nose and out your mouth. Don't allow yourself to think—just breathe."

I listened to his voice more than the words, but eventually Jack's composure allowed me to take a deep breath. Opening my eyes, I saw my dad's concerned face peering down at me. Jack's face was so close it appeared his body had two heads. I decided closing my eyes was for the best.

"Dad, I'm okay," I said when I could find my voice. My lips appeared to be a bit numb, but I ignored the sensation. I heard Jack fumbling with his cell phone, then hitting buttons.

"You better damn well not be calling 911!" I snapped.

"Nope, you'd kill me. I'm trying to call Andy," he replied.

I opened my eyes enough to see him through the slits of my eyelids. "I'm fine. Just give me a damn minute, will ya?"

He sighed as he put his phone away. "You're a terrible patient."

"I'm not a patient. Just went a little light-headed. Jeez."

"Peg, you sure?" Dad asked.

"Yeah. At least Jack didn't merely watch as I hit the ground with a thud." I grinned up at both of them. "I can feel my feet again, so help me up off the damp grass."

Jack reached down and pulled me up. Back on my feet, I wobbled just a little but was under control quickly. "See? Everything is A-okay."

Dad's expression hadn't changed, but Jack was clearly relieved.

"Has there been an accident?" came a voice from my left side.

Dad and I glanced over to see Logan standing quietly.

Jack sighed, asking, "Now who?"

Ignoring the question, I glared at Logan. "What the hell good are my Indians out here if they can't actually protect me?"

He stayed irritatingly calm, answering, "You are who they are protecting. Not the house. Not the property. You. Since you were not here, they had a dilemma, and I solved it."

"Really? You know who was here?" I asked.

He paused before answering, "Not exactly. I only know who *was not* here."

That stopped me in my tracks. I had expected one of his all-knowing answers. Was it my imagination, or was he slightly embarrassed he had no idea the identity of my intruder? I would probably never know for sure.

"Okay, smarty-pants. Who *wasn't* here?"

"Alex Hayes."

Believe it or not, I was relieved. So I hadn't misread the kid after all. Thank God.

Nodding, I said, "Good news. How can you be so sure?"

"Mr. Alex Hayes was attacked earlier today. He is in a hospital. Something called ICU."

The world come dangerously close to fading out again, so I took a deep breath and allowed myself to lean against Jack for support. It only took a moment for the yard to stop spinning as I felt anger mounting. Who had attacked Alex? Turning to Jack, I said, "Call the mayor. Right this minute. Alex has been attacked and is in the hospital. Ask him for information." I loved anger; it allowed me to function under stress.

Jack grabbed his phone and started dialing.

Glancing at Dad, I asked, "How much can Mom actually do physically?"

Shaking his head, he said, "Not this much." He nodded toward Logan. "It takes years of experience to achieve his level of capabilities. Even then, certain abilities you had to have while living. That's why Logan is so damn powerful. No way your mother even comes close to having the strength to physically harm. Her danger lies in that mouth of hers. She can manipulate people with words."

I thought about this new information a moment. His assessment of Mom made sense. She had always used her words to make anyone feel like crap but had never used physical means to harm someone. Why would she bother when she was so damn good at emotional abuse?

"I agree. So it must have been a living person that hurt Alex?"

Logan gave me a short nod. A few steps away Jack was talking earnestly into his phone. I didn't try to listen in, knowing he would inform me when he ended the call. I wasn't wrong. As soon as he hung up, he turned to me.

"The mayor actually answered his cell phone. He's at the hospital with his wife and told me Alex was found less than an hour ago in the driveway. Someone had beaten him within an inch of his life. He's in surgery as we speak."

My heart broke at the news. The kid had been through so much, and now he was fighting for his life.

"I need to get back to the station," Jack said. "This happened in the township, so our department is in charge of the investigation."

"Who took the call?" I asked.

Jack grabbed his phone again and answered an incoming call. After asking a few questions, he told the person on the other end that he was on his way.

Turning to me, he said, "Officer Jones. He's an excellent cop and our lead investigator. I'm heading to the station. Then I'll head over to the crime scene." He turned to go, then paused and looked me in the eye.

"Peg, call Andy. He should probably stay home for a day or two until I can get a solid handle on this case. It's getting too dangerous for you to be here alone."

I opened my mouth to argue; I wasn't home alone. Jack must have read my face, because the next words out of his mouth almost made me laugh. "Your dad doesn't count as someone here to protect you!" He glanced around our surroundings, then added, "Sorry, sir, but you have to admit you have limited capabilities."

I chanced a quick glance to see how Dad took Jack's assessment of the situation. Instead of the irritation I expected, he was nodding his approval.

"Tell him I totally agree," Dad told me.

I relayed the message to Jack, who gave me a quick nod. "Call Andy." Then he left me surrounded by ghosts.

Sighing, I started toward the house to make the call. I knew I would feel much better once Andy was home and I had a living person with me. Dad was great, and I did appreciate my band of Indians. But let's be honest: when it came right down to it, I needed a warm body to hold my hand.

The hairs on my neck stirred. Someone new had joined the party. I glanced around quickly and spotted Bob by the back door. My face tightened, and my eyes narrowed as I approached him.

"Well, you missed the fun. Where have you been?" I asked him as I reached the door.

He gave me a sad smile before saying, "Dodging Elaine. She keeps hanging out with your mom. I'm sorry, Peg, but your mom scares me spitless."

"I don't blame you. I've got to make a call, but after I'm done, you are bringing me up to date with any news."

As I reached for the phone, it began ringing. I hated when that happened; made me feel squishy inside.

Thankfully, the voice I heard on the other end was Andy's. Relief flooded through my body.

"Peg, what the hell is going on at home?" he asked.

"I'll explain everything later, but can you just come home now?" Silence answered my question. In all the years we had been married, I had asked him to leave work early only a handful of times, usually because of some catastrophe with the kids—broken arms, calls from the school spelling trouble—things with a certain level of importance. I never bothered him with minor issues, so he knew if I wanted him home now, it spelled trouble.

"I'm out the door as we speak," he said. "You okay?"

"Yep, but I'll be a hell of a lot better once you get here," I answered.

"It'll take me about twenty minutes. Anyone there with you?"

I looked around the room. Dad, Logan, and Bob stood watching me. Outside the window, my band of protectors were watching the property carefully. It dawned on me I could see them consistently now; I'd have to ask Logan why I hadn't been able to see them before this event.

"No one with a heartbeat," I said. Dad grinned at my answer, but Bob seemed to feel ashamed he couldn't be more help. Logan stood quietly watching me.

Andy sighed. "Keep the damn doors locked. Okay?"

"Yep." Obviously, locked doors were not going to help much, but I kept the thought to myself.

I hung up the phone and sat down, wondering what my next move should be. One thing was clear: our little investigation had stirred up a hornet's nest. Glancing up at Bob, I asked, "Were you here to tell me anything important?"

He looked at me, then down at the floor. Not a good sign of things to come.

"Just spill it, Bob," I told him.

Bob gave Dad a quick glance but ignored Logan. He was still uncomfortable around the powerful Indian, and I couldn't blame him.

"I'm pretty sure your mom is cooking up something really bad. She and Elaine have been glued together since I left you earlier."

I frowned, wondering if Bob would ever have more useful information other than the fact those two bitches were together.

178

"That's not exactly news. You've already informed me they're together much of the time." Did they have "time" on their side of life? Did they even think of time as we did on this side of the equation? I doubted it.

Bob looked around the kitchen, obviously avoiding my observation of his lack of new information. I narrowed my eyes but remained quiet. I knew that my silence had a tendency to drive Bob nuts, so I used his discomfort to my advantage. After a few more moments of mute treatment, he folded. Bingo!

"Okay, here's the deal," he began nervously. "They both scare me to pieces. I don't mind following them around, sneaky like, you know. But I'm not kidding, Peg; they are creepy."

I shook my head in disgust. Of course I was more than aware both of these women were scary. Hell, I'd been raised by one of the shrews. But Bob was as dead as they were for Pete's sake. What harm could they actually do to him? Jeez.

I eyed him a moment longer, then said, "Bob, are you getting close enough to hear any of their conversations? Or merely trailing along after them?"

He looked down at the floor. "They speak very hush-hush. I know they are up to no good but have no idea what they are planning."

I finally took pity on the poor guy. I couldn't stand the look of shame covering his face. Sighing, I said, "It's okay, Bob. We'll eventually figure out what they are up to. Why don't we change your assignment for a few days? Elaine and Mom go on the back burner for now. How's that sound?"

He perked up immediately. "You mean it? Wow, thanks!" His goofy smile returned, and I could sense his relief at my suggestion. "What do you need me to do?"

I looked over at Dad for ideas. He had been watching my exchange with Bob and grinned over at me. Logan stood quietly, but from his expression I knew something was wrong.

"What's with the serious face?" I asked him. It was a stupid question, as I had seldom seen him with anything but a serious expression.

His eyes slid over to meet mine. "I'm not happy with Elaine's newfound interest in your mother's activities."

A familiar knot in my stomach began to form again. Logan didn't waste time on matters unimportant. If he was increasingly worried about Elaine and Mom, it could mean stormy times ahead for me. Not a happy thought.

"I don't think Bob is going to find out anything useful. What errand could we send him on that would keep him busy?" I asked.

Logan thought a moment before answering, "Bob, I would appreciate if you would agree to act as our security agent for Alex. He is still in great danger. Your abilities would be perfect for the job. I would rest easier knowing we had you guarding him in his time of need."

I thought Bob was going to faint when Logan began speaking directly to him. If the situation wasn't so serious, it would have been fun to watch him squirm. He had opened his mouth to reply, but no words came out, which was fine by me. His constant chatter drove me nuts. Finally, he decided to merely nod. Logan acknowledged Bob's silent agreement with a nod of his own. Bob faded quickly, probably thrilled to be out of Logan's company.

I heard the key in the front door and was amazed at how fast Andy had made it home. Dad and Logan had turned toward the door at the sound. Deciding it would be wise to check exactly who was entering, I called out, "Andy?"

"Peg? You okay?"

I slumped back into my chair, surprised as relief flooded my body. When he turned into the kitchen, I felt tears threaten. Fighting them back, I smiled up at my husband. He came over to me, lifting me off the chair into a bear hug. I had to admit, it was nice to know I wasn't the only one scared by the most recent event.

Andy eventually released his hold on me. He gripped my hand as he pulled a chair next to mine, and we both sat down with a plop. Staring directly into my eyes, he asked, "You sure you're all right?"

I took a deep breath and nodded. "I feel better now that you are home. My security detail has definite limitations." I looked over at Dad and Logan, smiling. "No offense, guys, but you have to admit it's a fact."

They had both been carefully watching as Andy and I battled our emotions. Nodding his approval, Logan said, "Sadly, you are correct." He paused before continuing, "I am confident you will be fully secured once the mayor's friends are involved."

Hells bells! I had absolutely forgotten about those thugs with all the new excitement.

"Don't expect much from him," I said. "He's probably forgotten about his promise now that Alex is in the hospital."

Logan shook his head. "I do not think that is true. More than likely, the attack on his son has made him realize how much protection you actually need."

I cocked my head at his words. "I'm pretty sure the guy has more important issues right now."

The phone rang. I gave Andy a startled glance before answering it. "Yes?" I was surprised at the level of fear I felt. Honestly, it was just a phone call.

"Mrs. Shaw?" I recognized the mayor's voice and threw Logan a quick nod. You had to give the guy credit for reading people so well.

"I heard about Alex. I'm so sorry. Is he out of surgery?" I felt like an idiot, but now I knew how Bob felt when he was nervous. Words kept flowing out of the mouth whether they were a good idea or not.

He sighed, and my stomach knotted. "He's stable, for now. The docs think he has a good chance of surviving but aren't sure about brain damage." He paused before adding, "The blows to the head were extensive."

I gripped Andy's hand tighter. "Is there anything I can do to help?"

"Other than finding out who the hell did this to Alex? Pretty sure there isn't much anyone can do," he said angrily. I could tell some of that anger was directed at me. If I hadn't started this mess, Alex would not be fighting for his life right now.

"I can't undo what has happened, but I am sorry," I said. Shaking my head at the inadequacy of the statement, I continued to dig myself deeper into a pit. "I know it doesn't help, but this wasn't my idea. It must be extremely important on some level to solve those damn murders."

This comment was met with silence. Not knowing if I had deepened his anger or shocked him with my stupidity, I remained quiet—a small miracle considering my habit of babbling when nervous. I would have to remind myself not to get so irritated with Bob next time his nerves got the best of his mouth.

Finally, he sighed. "I'm not angry with you. I'm disgusted with my own actions years ago. Had I insisted Alex explain the situation then, we wouldn't be here today."

Well, let's face it: that was the bald truth, maybe one of the few times the guy had been honest with himself throughout his entire political career. I wasn't going to spoil the moment with some nasty remark. I tightened my lips and kept my big fat mouth firmly closed.

"But I called about the matter we discussed earlier. Some acquaintances of mine will be at your door anytime now. They may not be up to your standards of polite society, but they will protect you. Completely."

How had Logan known the mayor had already accomplished our request? The guy was spooky.

"Thanks for the information. Any idea when they will show up here?" I asked.

"Should be arriving shortly. Standard procedure is to meet the family so they know who's allowed on the property."

I nodded as he spoke and then said, "I do appreciate the help. The house was broken into today, so our nerves are on edge."

This news was met with another silence. "I can promise it won't happen again. These guys are good at what they do, so rest assured your property will be guarded."

"Thank you."

"Um, Mrs. Shaw? I have a small request." Ah, here it came, some sort of favor he wanted in return for providing armed guards.

"Please don't let them know about … your friends," he said. "It could complicate matters."

Complicate matters? Who was he kidding? News the mayor had dealings with dead people would ruin his career. But, hey, I absolutely understood his request.

A small laugh escaped as I said, "I don't advertise my situation. Won't be an issue."

I could feel his relief through the phone line. "Good." The line went dead, with no warning, which wasn't a huge shocker to me.

Hanging up, I looked around at the men in the kitchen. "Thug detail should be here soon."

"Thugs?" Andy asked.

Oh, damn. I had forgotten Andy had no idea the mob was now protecting us. "Um, yeah. New development. The mayor has friends that are helping us."

"Friends? The mayor's friends? From Youngstown?" Andy stammered.

"Uh, sort of."

Dad sighed. "Tell him it was my idea." I nodded without turning to face my dad.

"Dad wants you to know it was his idea and backed by Logan." Might as well throw him under the bus along with Dad. Out of the corner of my eye, I noticed the tiniest smile on Logan's face. So he did have a sense of humor after all.

Andy's free hand was now supporting his weary head. "Yeah, I heard him. God, Peg. What's next?"

It felt good to laugh. "I have no idea."

Chapter 23

The doorbell rang while I made Andy a cup of coffee. Logan had left moments earlier, but Dad remained. Andy needed a shot of caffeine, so I brewed the coffee as strong as I could. I was thankful Dad trailed after Andy as he went to answer the door.

I could hear muffled talking, then the door closing. I frowned, wondering who had been at the door.

Andy rounded the corner into the kitchen, saying, "Well, your thugs have arrived. After they walk the property, they want to have a chat. Any pie left?" Dad had not returned with Andy, and I assumed he was out with the thugs.

"Nope, but I have frozen cookie dough." I turned the oven on the correct temperature, then dug around the freezer looking for the package of dough I had thrown in there the last time I'd stirred up a batch of cookies. I'd learned years ago that the best way to have fresh cookies when a horde of teenagers came tromping through your house was to freeze balls of dough each time you mix a batch. The hardest part had been keeping the kids from eating the frozen dough, which they had decided was fabulous. I wouldn't know, since the thought of raw dough made me gag.

It didn't take our security detail long to walk around our backyard. I saw them approach the area filled with Indians but could barely make out the shapes that only a few hours back had been crystal clear. Logan had clearly warned the Indians about the security team, because they didn't seem agitated with the new visitors inspecting their domain—no fluttering of arms or gestures of any kind. They seemed interested in these new faces but not overly impressed.

Less than fifteen minutes passed, and then the security detail approached the house just as the buzzer on the oven rang. Good timing on their part.

Andy opened the back door and allowed three of the biggest guys I'd ever seen into our house. My first thought was the cookies would never satisfy this group. Oh well.

As they got themselves settled at the kitchen table, I set a steaming cup of coffee in front of each man. I pushed the cream and sugar over, but they ignored the gesture.

"Let's get down to business," the biggest of the men said.

"Why don't we start with introductions? I'm Peg, and this is my husband, Andy." My kitchen, my rules.

He frowned, then gave me a short nod. "Antonio." Dark hair with matching eyes, strong jaw, and a no-nonsense attitude, Antonio was a born leader.

The guy next to him, though smaller, was still big enough. He seem surprised by the fact that I'd taken control of the conversation but said, "Santino." Again, dark eyes and hair, nice looking, but a twinkle in those eyes warned me this one had a wicked sense of humor.

I turned to face the third man. He smiled and said, "Bill." Different from his friends, Bill had dirty-blond hair and blue eyes. Reminded me of Robert Redford's gorgeous pair of peepers. His face was kind, but there was evidence alerting me he wasn't anyone to cross.

Noticing the surprise on my face, he shrugged, explaining, "My mom liked William Holden. You know, the actor?"

I nodded. Two Italian names and one actor. Okay by me.

"Here's the deal," Antonio began. "We follow you everywhere. One of us will be in the house at all times—two in the yard. Front and back. We will switch off every few hours."

"Is there a second crew?" I asked.

Antonio apparently didn't like questions and frowned at me. "No."

"When do you sleep?" "We don't. Not until the job is finished."

I frowned. How could they stay alert with no sleep? Seeing my expression, Bill said, "We are all ex-military, highly trained. We can go for days without sleep. Don't worry."

Nodding, Antonio said, "Stay out of our way, and we'll stay out of yours."

I could feel my temper rise a bit. He seemed irritated at his new assignment and a little too nasty for my taste. Andy, seeing my face, quickly said, "That works. Is there anything you need from us?"

For the first time, Santino spoke up. "A list of who's allowed in and who's not. It's pretty simple."

"The list is short for who usually comes here. Mainly the police chief," Andy told them.

Antonio's expression was priceless and made my day. The shock on his face was worth a ton of gold. "The police chief?" he asked quietly.

"Yep. Any problem?" I asked. I was enjoying his discomfort.

His eyes met mine, and I had to admit that a shiver ran down my spine. This was not a guy I wanted after me for any reason. I was able to meet his eyes and not look away, but it took every bit of strength I possessed to accomplish the feat. My hands were sweating by the time he looked back down at his paperwork.

"Any kids?" Bill asked.

Shaking my head, I said, "All grown and living all over the country. They only make it back for holidays."

He nodded and smiled. "Good. Makes our job easier."

"Anyone else allowed?" Santino asked.

I thought a moment before saying, "Not really. We lead pretty boring lives."

"Obviously not too boring, or we wouldn't be here," Bill said with a smile. I paused before saying, "It's complicated."

He nodded. "Yep. That's what we heard." He held his hands up. "Don't bother trying to explain. I don't want to know."

I decided silence was my friend so kept quiet. Andy looked at me, then back at our new friends. "What exactly do you expect?"

"Nothing. Everything. We come prepared, and that's all you need to know," Antonio said.

His social skills were minimal, but I had a feeling his professional skills were pretty damn impressive. I could deal with his lack of warmth, knowing he had huge amounts of expertise in his field. That thought alone would normally give me nightmares. But not now. Now, I was relieved to have him on my side.

I got up from the table and grabbed the plate of still-warm cookies. Placing them on the table, I said, "Help yourselves."

Bill and Santino each took one, but Antonio ignored the goodies. All business, all the time.

The shrill of the phone ringing made all us stop in our movements. Andy and I looked at each other, then back at the phone.

I reached over to answer, but Antonio grabbed my hand, shaking his head. Santino picked up the receiver, saying, "Shaw residence." He paused a moment and then said, "Yes, sir, she's right here." He handed me the phone, shrugging as he looked at his friends.

"Peg? Who the hell answered the phone?" Jack asked.

Oh damn! I had totally forgotten in the flurry of activity to explain to Jack about the mayor's thugs.

"Friends of the mayor's. They are here to help."

The information was met with silence. I noticed the frown on Antonio's face and realized he probably didn't want everyone aware of their involvement. I ignored him, knowing Jack would feel pretty much the same way. It wouldn't be good PR if the population got wind of the fact the mayor's mob friends were alive and well, active in our little township.

I quietly waited for Jack to digest this bit of news. After a few moments, he asked, "Since when?"

"Since now. I'll explain later. Why don't you come over in a few hours? I'll fill you in on events." He had a right to know how we'd arrived at this point, but mentioning Dad and Logan in front of these guys was not an option. It could make more problems than was necessary. No need for them to know about all the dead people milling around; my two security details wouldn't bump into each other. I glanced out the window and noticed I couldn't see my Indians at all now. Must be a need thing. When I needed them, I could see them. When I didn't, they were invisible to me. Good to know that was how it worked. I figured if I could start to see them all, I was in deep trouble. At least I had a barometer of sorts regarding my danger level. The bumped-up security obviously allowed the Indians to relax for now.

Another long pause. "I'll be there in an hour. We're finishing up at the crime scene."

Damn, I had gotten so caught up in my own drama I had momentarily forgotten about poor Alex. "Any clues?" I asked.

"Not one," he said tersely. Jack's frustration must be at epic highs. "This guy must be good." He paused before adding, "Hope Alex wasn't attacked by one of the mayor's so-called 'friends.'"

One of my eyebrows crept north as I glanced at the trio sitting at my table. "I'll ask," I said.

Before Jack could argue with me, I asked, "Bill, you know the mayor's son was brutally attacked earlier?"

Bill looked at me and nodded. "Wasn't us, if you're asking."

"Any idea who it was?" Bill shook his head.

"Nope." Antonio glared at Bill. "That is privileged information."

I shrugged. "Figured it was better than the chief of police hauling your asses in for questioning. No sense in my newly formed protection squad disappearing so soon after arriving."

Andy sighed, shaking his head. He knew Antonio irritated me, but he was a firm believer in not poking the bear. I, on the other hand, had never quite gotten the hang of remembering to keep my mouth shut in certain situations. Maybe something I should work on, but I'd save it for another day.

Out of the corner of my eye, I saw both Santino and Bill grin. Even they knew Antonio could be an ass. The fact made me relax; maybe they wouldn't be as hard to have around as I had feared.

"I'll be there as soon as I finish the paperwork," Jack said.

I could tell he was chomping at the bit to hear about the new guys involved in our little drama. "I'll have coffee ready."

After hanging up the phone, I turned to Antonio. "I don't answer my own phone?"

"No."

I stared at him for a moment, hoping he would expand on his answer, but he continued working on the paperwork. I looked down at the slim stack of papers on the table, wondering why they had to fill out anything. I mean, they had a paper trail? Wasn't that a complication in their line of work? Shaking my head, I looked over at Andy. He merely shrugged.

"It's better if we answer your phone," Bill said. "If the bad guy wants to know if you are home or alone, us answering lets them know someone's here. Solves a problem before it gets started."

I smiled my thanks at his answer. "Makes sense," I said.

"We have everything we need from you," Antonio said as he dropped his pen on the papers. "We'll get started."

Immediately, there was a flurry of Italian spoken between the three men. I had no idea what they were saying but decided they were discussing who was inside and who was outside. My thoughts were confirmed as they stood and, without a word, dispersed. Antonio had chosen the den to use as his guard post; Bill and Santino split the yard between them. There was silence in the kitchen as Andy and I looked at one another, unsure of what to do until Jack's arrival.

"Now that was interesting," Dad said.

I looked around for him, spotting him in the corner. Had he been there the entire time?

"Hey, Dave," Andy said. I looked at Andy, startled. Andy grinned. "Forgot I could see him, didn't you?"

Holy smokes, I had!

Dad met Andy's grin with one of his own. "Nice to be seen," he said.

"We should probably be quiet," I said. "I don't want them to hear our conversation."

Dad shook his head. "Don't worry about Antonio. He's so glued to his microphone and headset he isn't paying any attention at all to us."

"Yeah, I gather he is the boss," I answered.

"Don't think so. They all seem to be on equal footing," Dad said.

"You know Italian?" I asked, surprised.

He grinned. "On my side of life, language isn't a barrier. They were discussing where their positions would be for the first shift. No one seemed to be handing out orders, just confirming the best way to start."

"Huh. I thought Antonio was the leader, mainly from his attitude," I said. "Were you here the entire time?" I asked Dad.

"Yep. But stayed out of sight. Didn't want to distract you."

"What do you think of our merry trio?" I asked.

He thought a moment before answering, "Competent. They know their way around security issues. They're not thrilled with the woods out back but have a plan to deal with the problem. Logan will be pleased. I ought to warn you, though: they are fully armed."

I felt the shock waves hit, hard. Armed? I guess I had never considered that they would be armed. It gave me a jolt to know there were three armed men roaming around my property.

Andy nodded. "I noticed the bulges under their jackets."

"What? I didn't see anything!"

Andy grinned. "You were too busy being pissy toward Antonio. Give the guy a break. He's here to protect us."

"Well, I wouldn't want to have them as enemies." Dad laughed.

"Sweetie, right now, they are your best friends."

The doorbell rang. "That's probably Jack," Andy said, standing to make his way to the front door.

Antonio met Andy in the living room. Nodding, he followed Andy through the hallway.

Turning to Dad, I said, "This will take some getting used to."

He smiled. "I feel better knowing they are here."

I sighed. "Yeah, so do I."

I heard conversation. Then Andy and Jack walked in the kitchen. From the look on Jack's face, I figured he was not happy with the current situation.

"Peg."

I held up a hand to silence any further comments. "Sit down. I'll get you a cup of coffee. Help yourself to cookies." I pointed to the plate of mostly untouched goodies.

I made my way to the coffee machine, asking, "Strong?"

"I'm gonna need it," he said tersely. "That was a fast hour," I said. No way Jack had finished all his paperwork in ten minutes.

"No comment," he answered.

Conversation ceased as I waited for Jack's cup to fill with rich, dark coffee. Placing it in front of him, I reclaimed my chair. He watched me, waiting for answers.

Pursing my lips, I gathered my thoughts. "Here's the deal. Dad and Logan wanted better protection. You have to admit, after today's break in, they were one hundred percent correct."

Jack remained quiet, but he reached for his coffee. I took the motion as a good sign he wasn't going to murder me and rolled out the rest of my tale.

When I had finished filling in the gaps for him, Jack sighed and reached for a cookie. "Damn, Peg," he said, taking another sip of his coffee.

He didn't add any other comment. What could he say? I understood his dilemma. On one side of the fence was the fact Jack was an officer of the law and willingly allowing suspected mob guys into his beloved township. On the other side was the undeniable fact I needed more protection than the local police force could supply. Don't get me wrong; our local police force was a very professional outfit, but they weren't bodyguards. Jack understood the department's limitations; he just didn't like the situation. He wasn't alone; other than my dad, no one in the room was thrilled with my new friends now scattered around the property. Andy was relieved we had living guys protecting me, but their mob connections were uncomfortable to say the least.

I decided a change of conversation would help the uneasiness filling the room. "You find anything at all useful at the crime scene?"

Jack grunted. "Not one damn thing. We combed through every square inch of that property. It doesn't help the house is so far back from the road. Neighbors weren't any help either."

I drummed my fingers on the table, lost in my own thoughts. Why Alex? Why now? It didn't make sense.

"Peg?" Andy said.

Andy's voice dragged my attention to his face. "Yeah?" I asked him.

"Just a thought, but how many people are aware of your interest in the old murder?"

My eyes shifted to Jack's. Shrugging, he said, "Good question, Andy. I didn't think anyone other than you, me, Peg, and the mayor had any clue."

Andy thought a moment, then asked, "But how did the mayor find out?"

Jack shook his head, disgusted. "That's a problem I have not been able to solve. How he got wind of our poking around in the old files is still a mystery. Pisses me off to think someone in my own department would be a snitch."

A thought bounced in my tired head. "You don't think Mom could have somehow instigated the situation do you?" I looked over Jack's head to ask Dad.

Jack saw my line of vision and turned to see who I was addressing. His shoulders slumped when he realized he couldn't see who I was talking to, since it was a dead person. "I feel so left out of the loop!"

I ignored his outburst, but Dad grinned as he looked down at Jack's face. "Tell him I'm sorry he isn't capable of special sight right now."

I'm pretty sure Dad wasn't sorry one bit, but I was a little taken aback at the words "right now." I decided it was better to ignore the remark and waited for Dad to answer my question.

Seeing my concern, Dad said, "I suppose it's something I could look into, especially since I believe it's warranted. Under the circumstances"—he gestured to my living bodyguards—"I could leave you for a while to see what I find."

"I think it is worth the effort," I said. "Might help us decide how information is leaking."

"Take it easy, twinkle toes. I'm on it," he said, grinning. Suddenly, he was gone.

Andy smiled. "I like your dad."

"He's gone?" Jack asked.

Nodding, I said, "Yep. He actually may be able to unearth our snooper and snitch."

Jack thought about my comment, then said, "You know, he comes in handy. Who would suspect a ghost?"

Andy frowned. "Unless it is another ghost somehow giving out information."

The knot in my stomach twisted tighter. Andy saw my grimace. He reached for my hand and gave it a squeeze. "It will work out, Peg. I know it will."

I nodded but couldn't find anything to say.

Chapter 24

After Jack left, we had a quick dinner, watched a documentary on crocodiles, and went to bed. I was surprised how well I slept. I woke during the changing of the guard sometime in the middle of the night, but once I heard Italian being spoken in hushed tones, I was able to slip back into a deep sleep.

Andy decided to work from home the next day, which was fine by me. The more breathing people I had around me, the better I felt. The grand plan was to stay home myself, but I realized after digging around the freezer that a trip to the grocery was a must.

"I'm going with you," Andy told me, watching my grocery list grow longer. "You'll be gone too long by the looks of that paper."

Looking down, I realized he had a point. I had always organized my wandering through the local market according to the layout of the grocery store. Starting at the deli counter, I would methodically make my way down each aisle, checking off items as I went through the store. I despised shopping of any type, so I tried to make the ordeal as painless as I could manage. It had been a great plan of action, until they'd changed the entire layout so hungry shoppers were forced to mill around searching out items that once could have been found on autopilot. I hated to admit it, but I was surprised to find so many new foods I had never noticed. I guessed the game plan must work well for the owners of the stores.

Sighing, I said, "I know it's out of hand. I figured better safe than sorry: buy everything we could possibly need for a week or two. Keeps me from needing to go back anytime soon."

"Sound plan." He grinned. "But this could take hours by the looks of things."

I shook my head. "No way. My intention is to get in and out as quickly as possible." I studied the paper, then smiled. "Figure it should take about forty minutes."

The look of surprise on Andy's face made me laugh out loud. "I have my methods of speeding through the aisles."

Doubt covered his features. "Okay, but let's get going soon. I have a lot of work to plow through before lunch."

I glanced out the window and saw Antonio. "Should I offer them coffee?"

"No need. Some guy brought them supplies a few hours ago while you were asleep. They really have this guarding stuff down to a science."

I could hear the admiration in his voice, which was a slight change from his concern the night before. "Don't forget, these guys are the mob!"

He turned a light shade of pink, then said defensively, "I didn't forget, but you have to admit they are quite professional about their duties."

"No need to join their fan club," I snidely responded. "If I didn't need their expertise, I would never have them on this property!" I could feel my blood pressure going up, so I did a few deep-breathing tricks to pull it back down.

Andy opened his mouth to make his own cocky comment, but then the phone interrupted our argument. We looked at each other and then at the phone. The ringing abruptly stopped, and I heard Bill in the den talking quietly on our second phone. A few moments later he appeared at the kitchen doorway, smiling. "Your friend, the police chief, is on his way." He turned and went back to his duty station.

"What does Jack want this early in the morning?" I asked, looking down at my long list of supplies that were needed to survive. Coffee was a huge factor, since we seemed to be drinking gallons of the stuff recently.

"Um, Peg?"

I jumped at the sound of Bob's voice. I quickly scanned the kitchen and spotted him standing next to the dishwasher. "My God, Bob! What the hell!" I snapped.

"This is important, or I wouldn't be here," he snapped back.

I stared at him, shocked at his boldness. Whatever he was here about, it must be pretty important for him to have the guts to ignore my temper. I threw Andy a questioning glance. He nodded, indicating he could see and hear Bob.

"What's wrong?" I asked.

"Someone tried to kill Alex a few hours ago. I had to find Logan. He was able to control the situation, but it was close."

My mouth dropped open, and Andy's eyes grew as big as dinner plates.

"But he's in the hospital! Who tried to kill him? Didn't he have a guard?" I asked when I finally could think straight.

"Yeah, the guard thing," Bob mumbled. "There was a guy sitting outside his door when I first got there, but he left around midnight. Have no idea where he went."

"When did you contact Logan?" I asked, trying to mentally piece a timeline together.

Bob screwed his face up in thought. After a few moments of silence, he said, "Before the sun came up, I know for a fact. I was getting a bit nervous about the guard situation. Let's face it: I'm pretty limited in my ability to actually protect a living person." He looked down at the floor, embarrassed.

I took pity on him and said, "Bob, you're getting damn good at scouting around and finding out information we need. That's a long way from where you were a few short weeks ago."

He nodded but continued to stare at the floor.

"At least you were smart enough to get hold of Logan."

At the mention of Logan's name, Bob's head snapped up, his eyes glowing with admiration. "You should have seen the guy! He had the situation handled so fast!"

Obviously, Bob's fear of Logan was dissipating quickly. I nodded, saying, "He is full of surprises."

The doorbell rang. As Andy rose from his seat, I heard Bill's soft footsteps heading toward the front door. Andy followed suit. I could hear Jack's voice before he made it all the way to the kitchen.

"This is a hell of a mess!" he said.

"Calm down. Bob told us Logan managed the emergency. Alex gonna make it?" Andy said soothingly as he ushered Jack into the kitchen.

"Coffee?" I asked Jack as I headed toward the counter.

"God, yes. Thanks," he answered, plopping down into a chair. "I can't believe what a rat's nest this has become."

"Any idea what happened to the guard?" I asked, setting Jack's coffee in front of him. "Have you eaten?"

He shook his head. "Not hungry, but thanks."

Frowning, I asked, "You sure?"

"My stomach wouldn't allow food to enter at this point. The mayor is foaming at the mouth right now. We had Alex under a false name, so no one should have been able to find him."

"Well, someone damn sure did," I said.

Jack took a healthy sip of coffee and stared down into the cup.

"It's not your fault, Jack."

"I know, but it sure is unsettling. Peg, someone knew exactly where Alex could be found. They knew how to convince the guard to leave his post. Not a good sign."

I watched his face as he came to terms with the situation. "What does the evidence tell you?"

"We have a mole in the mix. I can't believe it, but it's the only answer."

"Well, I haven't told anyone, Andy hasn't, you are above reproach, and the mayor sure as hell wouldn't tell."

Jack frowned. "What if the mayor mentioned Alex's injuries to someone *he* thought could be trusted. That's feasible." He seemed to perk up at the thought the mayor could be the leak. Somehow, I didn't see the mayor as the problem; he was too savvy to allow any type of sensitive information to make it out of his office. Otherwise, the man would probably have been kicked out of office years ago or even landed in jail by now. I decided to keep my thoughts to myself and give Jack a few moments of relief from his guilt. Once his logic kicked into gear, he would realize his idea was wrong, and depression would make itself at home again in his mind. For now, give the guy a break.

Bob had been listening to our conversation with interest and suddenly frowned. Uh-oh, now what?

"Peg? Do you think your mom is involved somehow?" he asked.

I'd come to the conclusion that while Bob was squirrely as hell, once in a while he actually hit the nail on the head. His mention of my mother, yet again, made me shiver. I had to be honest, though, and we couldn't ignore the possibility. Glancing around the kitchen to see if Dad had returned from nosing around, I spotted Logan standing next to the window.

He turned to look at me, which made my hair stand on end. How in the world had he known I had spotted him? Creepy.

"Your father will return shortly. I believe I owe your friend"—he nodded in Jack's direction—"an explanation of my actions earlier this morning."

I raised an eyebrow. Logan wasn't the sort of fellow who owed anyone much of anything, especially an explanation. A small smile briefly appeared on his lips. "Or at the very least, an explanation of how the boy in question survived the intended attack."

"I wouldn't mind knowing that myself," I said. Hearing my words, Jack looked over at me in surprise.

"What?" he asked, confused.

"Logan's here to explain what happened to Alex," I informed him.

Jack's shoulders slumped. "We know what happened," he snarled. "The kid came too damn close to being killed!"

I decided not to respond, instead looking back at Logan.

Nodding, he said, "I understand his anger. The situation should never have occurred."

"What happened to the guard?" I asked.

He shook his head slowly. "I am unaware of the guard. There was no one sitting in the chair outside of Alex's door." He narrowed his eyes, deep in thought. I kept my mouth shut, allowing him time to think. I was getting pretty good at the mouth part—well, some of the time.

"What, or who, could have possibly convinced the guard to leave his station of duty?" he finally asked.

I shrugged. "No idea. Bribe?"

Logan stood straighter, as if he had heard voices and wasn't happy with who they belonged to at all.

A second later my parents arrived, with Mom screaming at Dad. Some things never changed.

"How dare you—" She stopped immediately upon seeing Logan. She clamped those lips together tighter than a drum and crossed her arms defiantly.

Dad had a firm grip on her arm, and it was easy to believe he had dragged her through the spirit world, kicking and screaming the entire way. Jeez.

Logan studied her face, glanced at my dad, then looked deeply into my eyes. "We have a problem."

The knot in my stomach got tighter. At this rate, I'd never have normal digestion again in my life.

"Is she the culprit?" I asked quietly. I felt an overwhelming desire to puke. I fought the urge, but it was a close call.

"She is not directly involved, but she is a problem."

"Elaine?"

At my question, Bob's head snapped up. He watched Logan carefully.

Frowning, Logan said, "I am not sure." He looked at Bob, saying, "I thank you for your vigilance earlier. Alex would have died without your decision to contact me."

Bob nodded, but the look of pride I expected did not appear. I frowned, wondering why. Could he be worried that Elaine had played a part in the attempted murder?

Jack's frustration overflowed at this point. "What the hell is going on?" he asked.

Andy opened his mouth to provide a quick answer, but Logan held his hand up for silence. Since Andy could see the gesture, he remained quiet and sat back in his chair.

"This is a damn three-ring circus. Dead people, living people, mob people." Jack threw his hands up in disgust.

Logan walked over to Jack and placed his hands on Jack's shoulders. Immediately, Jack's eyes widen. I grinned, knowing exactly the sensation he was feeling. He looked at me, asking, "Why can I feel hands?"

"Because Logan is helping you calm down. Those are his hands, so relax. You will feel great in a second."

Logan's capable hands began massaging Jack's shoulders. Within a minute, Jack's expression became peaceful. "Wow" was all he could manage.

Logan stepped back, and his gaze returned to my mother. "Nell, you have stepped beyond your boundaries this time."

She remained defiant, but I also saw an uneasiness settle around her eyes. She might not respect Logan, but she damn sure was afraid of him.

Logan's eyes found my dad next. "Dave, take her back. I have seen enough."

My dad's face registered surprise, but he nodded. Mom opened her mouth to argue, but Logan shook his head. Then they were gone, as quickly as they had arrived. I couldn't say I was sorry to see Mom leave, but I was stunned Logan had sent her away.

"Couldn't she have provided answers?" I asked.

Logan shook his head. "Any words she would have spoken would have been half truths—not lies but not true. I do not have time for her games."

I nodded. "Yep. I get it."

"Bob, please accompany me back to Alex. We have work to do," Logan said.

Bob nodded at Logan's words, and they both faded away.

I sat quietly reviewing the events of the last few minutes. They had been wild in one sense, but nothing had been resolved.

"They've gone, haven't they?" Jack asked.

Nodding, I said, "Yep. Surprised Bill didn't come out to see what the hell was going on in my kitchen." I gave a short laugh; it was all I was able to muster.

Andy smiled. "I'm pretty sure those three aren't thrilled with Jack's presence."

Jack nodded grimly. "And they damn well shouldn't be!"

"We are still at square one. We don't know how someone was able to approach Alex or how they knew where to find him," I said. "Logan didn't actually give us any answers."

Jack grimaced as he took a big sip of coffee. "Cold. Can you pop it in the microwave to heat it up a little?" He held out his half-empty cup.

Standing, I said, "I think you deserve a fresh cup."

Andy pulled a sheet of paper over and began drawing a diagram.

"What are you doing?" I asked.

"Trying to decide not only who the leak could be but also how information was leaked," he answered, head bent over the paper.

Jack and I watched as he drew lines that showed recent events, along with the people involved. After ten or fifteen minutes, he sat back and sighed.

"Jack, I hate to say it, but the leak is in your office," he said. "Sorry."

"Shit. I was hoping my gut instinct was wrong," Jack said as I handed him a fresh cup of coffee.

"How can you be so sure?" I asked Andy.

"I'm an engineer. This diagram shows all the people involved. Where the lines converge should show where the problem exists." We all sat there, staring at the piece of paper. Every line led back to the police department. "You sure you've given me names of everyone involved in the case?"

"Yep, you know as much as I do. I have gone over every person there, even the part-timers. I trust everyone," Jack said.

"Maybe one of the employees talked shop at home and information got out that way," I offered.

"No, they're all old-timers. They know better," he said as he drained the last bit of coffee from the cup. "I've got to get going. Alex isn't my only headache today. Some jackass trashed the high school sign last night. Ran right into the damn thing." He shook his head. "Probably a teenage prank." He turned to leave, saying, "I'll call later and see if your band of ghosts knows anything new."

Andy's cell phone rang as he got up to walk Jack to the door. He answered as they left the kitchen, and I heard him arguing with the caller. By the time he got back to the kitchen, he was furious. "I have to run to the office. Those morons can't find their way out of a paper sack."

"I'll be fine. I've got bodyguards, remember?" I smiled up at him.

He hesitated. "You sure?"

"Yep. Bill's in the den; the other two are outside. I'm guarded as well as Fort Knox."

"Don't go grocery shopping till I return. Promise?" I could see the worry on his face.

Laughing, I answered, "No way am I going out by myself. Even Dad trusts these guys."

Nodding, he grabbed his keys and stomped out to the garage. Once I knew Andy was gone, I cleaned the kitchen, thinking about our dilemma.

Who was the leak? For the life of me, I couldn't come up with an answer that made sense. I picked up Andy's diagram and studied it for a few minutes. There was something nagging at the back of my mind, but I couldn't grab hold of the idea. Shrugging my shoulders, I looked outside and watched my two guards talking. It was clear from their arm movements that they were discussing the best strategic areas to roam my yard.

The sun was shining, and I decided a little gardening would help settle my nerves. I quickly changed into grungy clothes, then grabbed the gardening tools from the garage. After a quick shout out to Bill about my change of plans, I headed outside to soak up some sun and work off my stress.

It was amazing how quickly weeds took control over any type of garden. One day you couldn't see any; the next they were monopolizing every square inch. As I methodically worked my way through the budding dahlias, my mind sorted through all the information I had gathered over the past few weeks.

Bob's and Elaine's murders had started this mess, and now with the attempt on Alex's life it felt as though the situation had come full circle. I could feel the answer floating around in my mind, but for some reason, I couldn't quite grab hold of it.

I sat back on my heels to survey my work. The dahlias were coming along nicely now that the weeds had been eradicated, and the basil was definitely in better shape than last year. I tilted my neck back to ease the aching muscles and noticed the Indians in the woods. Odd, since I could only see them when I was in danger. I quickly scanned the yard for my mob guys and couldn't detect their presence. My stomach tightened a bit, but I reminded myself these guys were pros and probably had hidden themselves expertly. I heard a noise behind me. Dread filled my entire body as I turned slowly to face the noise.

Chapter 25

"Hey, Mrs. S," Owen said, smiling.

"Owen! You scared me to pieces," I answered with a smile of my own.

"Just checking on you," he said, scanning the yard.

I stood up, dropping my spade onto the pile of now-dying weeds I would have to throw in the woods later. Owen's arrival gave me an excellent excuse to take a break. My aging body could only bend so much without paying for it later.

"Want a cup of coffee?" I asked, wiping the dirt from my jeans.

"No, thanks."

I looked up at him, expecting his easy smile to still be in place, and was surprised by his expression. "You okay, sweetie? You look a little worn," I said.

"It's been a busy few weeks," he said, "especially with you sticking your nose into long-forgotten murders."

I looked at him, surprised Jack had divulged our snooping. Hadn't Jack been antsy about too many people discovering our secret? I glanced back toward the woods. The Indians were clearly distressed by Owen's presence. They were watching him carefully, and a few of them were pacing. My frown returned, along with my headache. What the hell was going on around here?

"Here, would you help me move these dead weeds?" I asked Owen as I bent down to grab an armful.

"Mrs. S, don't worry about the weeds," he said.

There was something in his tone that made me halt my movement. Slowly, I straightened my body, looked up into his face, and froze. There was something about his eyes that made my stomach flip.

"You figured it out, didn't you?" he asked. "I knew you were getting too close."

It took a moment for me to find my voice, but when I did, it squeaked. So much for being superwoman. "What are you talking about?" Even I wasn't impressed with my response. The good guys in movies always had such clever remarks to make in these situations. Too bad this wasn't a movie script.

He cocked his head, studying my face. "You know exactly what I'm referring to, Mrs. S." The calm, cold, calculating tone of voice made me shiver. My thoughts were racing. Of course, the instant I'd seen the odd expression on his face, the whole mess had untangled for me. He had been Alex's teenage friend, and they had raised all sorts of hell in the township. He had made damn sure Alex had always been the fall guy; no one had ever suspected Owen's involvement. He was our township hero of sorts. But I also knew I had to keep him talking.

Unable to control my disappointment, I heard myself say, "Oh, Owen. What have you done?" Talk about motherly instinct kicking in at the wrong time! Or maybe it would save me. My mind told me to keep the conversation moving along, get him to admit everything. I told my mind to shut up. That type of maneuvering was way beyond my skill level.

He grinned. It wasn't the casual, carefree grin we were all used to from him. It was creepy as hell, and my skin crawled as I watched his face. Something glinted in the sunlight. Glancing down, I realized Owen had a knife in his hand. I moved to my right so I could have a better view of the woods. Yep, my Indians were still there, clear as a bell. Their agitation was increasing and so was mine. Nice to know that we were in sync with each other at this point. I still couldn't see Antonio or Santino; where were those guys?

Owen turned to see what I was looking at, scanning the woods carefully. Satisfied, he turned back to me. "There's no one there. Did you think the cavalry would rescue you?" he sneered. My heart just about stopped. "I took care of the guy out in the woods. Since when do you have security?"

"Owen Wells! Behave yourself!" I snapped. "What the hell has happened to you?"

Glancing back into the woods, I noticed Logan was now among the small tribe of protectors. He looked grim, which did nothing to help my nerves. I heard *Keep him talking* in my head and nodded slightly to acknowledge I had gotten the message. Strangely, once I spotted Logan, I honestly believed everything would work out somehow.

Looking back into Owen's face, I said with as much calm as I could muster, "Why not explain the entire situation to me?"

He was turning the knife handle around in his hand, searching for the most comfortable position to hold the damn thing. My stomach twisted a bit more, which wasn't helping me.

"I've never told anyone." He paused. "Alex knows more than he should but only because we were hanging out together in high school." His contempt for his old friend showed plainly. "But it didn't last past graduation. That kid was a mess by then. I should have put him out of his misery long ago, but it was too entertaining watching him self-destruct." His disgust with Alex was obvious. It made me sick to my stomach.

He looked over my shoulder, lost in his twisted memories. I took a quick glance back at Logan. He nodded encouragingly. I sighed, which brought Owen's attention back to me.

"Why don't you start at the beginning?" I asked. "Tell me what went wrong?"

"Wrong? Nothing went wrong!" he snapped. "I loved leading a double life." He paused. "I had everyone in the stupid township fooled! It was great!"

"What about your family?"

"What about them? I've run circles around them for years," he answered.

"Do they have any idea?" I asked. I could see his family in my mind. Hard working, pleasant folks. His mother and I had been in the PTA together; his dad and Andy had played golf a few times. They seemed normal, so how had they produced the man now threatening my life?

Cocking his head in thought, he said, "I think, deep down inside, they've always known." He shrugged before saying, "They aren't my problem; I can control that part of life."

"When did you start misbehaving?" I asked. It was a stupid question, and I expected him to laugh, but for some reason, he seriously answered my query.

"Do you remember the Dahmer case?" he asked. After my quick nod, he said, "I was just a kid, couldn't have been more than six or seven. The FBI was all over their property, and the local news focused on the story nonstop. I was fascinated by the attention the guy was getting. It was the talk of the township." He stopped, lost in his own thoughts as his mind strolled down wacko memory lane. My stomach was churning, but I kept my mouth shut. I sneaked a quick peak at Logan, who nodded encouragingly. Great, where were my rescuers?

He paused, then said, "No one noticed how interested I was in the story. Why would they? I think my parents honestly thought I was too young to pay attention."

Totally immersed in telling his story, he ignored my intake of air. God, it was creepy.

"My reading skills were minimal at that age, so I listened to all the news reports when my parents were too busy to notice. As time went along, my abilities increased. I remember going to McDowell library and searching for any articles about Dahmer." He stopped and looked at me. "You know how the old library had a second story?" I nodded. "It was a great place to hide. Nobody bothered you up there as long as you stayed quiet."

He was absolutely correct. There had been old, worn chairs that you could sit in for hours. While you had still been able to hear the hustle and bustle downstairs, somehow it hadn't seemed to invade your mind upstairs.

"I miss that library," he said. "The new one sucks. Who the hell designs a library with no place to be secluded? Stupid." He stopped again, memories obviously flooding his mind.

I wondered if I could make it to the house before he caught me, but a voice in my head said, *No. Stay calm and listen to him.* Glancing back at Logan, I knew he wanted me to draw out the conversation as long as possible. I had to trust he had reinforcements on the way; why else keep me stuck listening to Owen?

My legs were beginning to go numb, so I shifted my stance. The movement brought Owen's attention back to me. "Why don't you sit down? It will be easier in the long run," he said.

I looked at Logan, who nodded, and I smiled up at Owen. "Thanks, sweetie." He smiled back and helped me sit next to the edge of the garden. I didn't know what was creepier: his absorption with his crimes or his kindly helping me get more comfortable.

"I started doing minor stuff, you know? Stealing cash from Mom's purse, just to see if she would notice." He looked down at me, astonished. "You know what? She thought she was either misplacing money or forgetting what she bought." He shook his head. "What a stupid bitch."

A memory of my own surfaced. At a PTA meeting, his mother had been stressed out about how much money they were spending. With tears in her eyes, she'd told me she had gone over receipts and couldn't find where it could possibly be disappearing. Her fear had been that her husband was cheating. I looked at Owen and, in that flash of memory, wanted to slap the self-satisfied expression off his face. The pain and agony he had caused his mom made me furious. I held my hands tightly in my lap to control the urge.

"I eventually started breaking into houses. Just for fun, not taking anything expensive. I spread out my range of activity so I wouldn't get caught." He smiled. "Back then, a lot of people here in Bath never locked their doors, especially during the day. But I wanted a bigger challenge, so once I got my driver's license, I went to Cuyahoga Falls, Akron, and even Hudson."

Out of the corner of my eye, I noticed a flurry of activity in the woods but couldn't decide exactly what they were all doing back there. I hoped to hell they were forming up for some type of rescue. It was about damn time.

"The part I enjoyed the most was fooling everybody around here. I became the best student, best athlete, and most polite teenager ever to exist! It was exhilarating to know that I had pulled the wool over everyone's eyes."

His creepy grin was back in place. My heart was pounding, but I forced myself to remain still. It took everything I had in me; let's face it: courage was not my strong suit.

"My one mistake was taking Alex with me the night I went to the Bradleys'. I knew I was going to murder those idiots, but he had no idea. What a jackass the kid was as a teenager. His dad was becoming a big shot, but he was scared of his own shadow. I could talk him into just about anything." He stopped. "But it's been fun controlling him like a puppet all these years." He shook his head. "Too bad it's about to end. I'll have to find new entertainment."

"You have no guilt over any of this?" I asked quietly.

"Guilt? Are you kidding? If people are stupid enough to let me kill them, why should I feel guilty?"

I frowned. "That's how you honestly feel?" His explanation made no sense to me, but would anything he said actually have sanity involved?

Laughing, he said, "I became a cop so I could learn how to avoid being caught as my hobby became more complicated. Four years of learning how to catch bad guys actually is a great way to discover how *not* to show your hand. I've been able to smudge the edges of investigations, learned how not to leave any DNA at the scenes and ways to outsmart even the FBI." His smug tone set my temper off again, but I knew Logan would have a fit if I blew up now.

Suddenly, my neck hairs tingled. Bob was on my right, Dad on my left. Even though I knew physically they couldn't help, having them there sent a wave of relief through my body. Owen must have noticed a difference, because he cocked his head at me. "What's up with you?" he asked suspiciously.

I shook my head, afraid to try speaking. Well, really I was afraid I'd puke if I opened my mouth.

"Peg, keep him talking," Dad said. "Help is on the way. Logan got hold of Andy, who called Jack. The kid's shifting too much for your protection guys to get a good shot. Just hang in there, sweetie."

I didn't acknowledge his words and hoped like hell he knew I heard him.

"God, Peg. I'm so sorry," Bob said. "I wish I could help you more. I would never have guessed this kid was the one who murdered us. Logan's working on a solution."

Poor Bob. He finally had found out who had killed him, and now he was here to watch the little shit try to kill me. I wondered where Elaine was through all this drama. Funny how your mind worked when you were in a pickle.

"Did you hear something?" Owen asked, looking around the yard. "Someone talking?"

I raised an eyebrow but didn't answer him.

"Shit," Dad muttered. "I forgot that some nuts can hear us."

Oh, that was great. Crazy people could hear ghosts? So was I crazy? Stood to reason, given my present circumstances. I noticed the knife twisting in Owen's hand again. He was agitated, and I needed to keep him bragging about his life of crime.

"Did you?" he asked again.

I shook my head and tried looking confused. It must have worked, because after a quick glance around the yard, he continued talking. The knife, however, was still twirling around the palm of his hand. I was beginning to sweat, and I swear I'd never had to pee so bad in my life.

"When I'm finished here, I've got to head back over to the hospital. Alex has become a liability and needs to be taken care of for good." He stopped as a confused expression covered his face. "I can't believe the little bastard's still alive."

Ah, yes. Bob saved that little bastard, you asshole.

Owen looked down at me. "Remember the day I was in your house?"

I nodded.

"I knew you and Jack were up to something the moment I saw him down

in the basement looking through files. I put in a call to Akron PD letting them know something was up about that case. They will jump through hoops to protect Bennet Hayes." He paused a moment, then said, "You have to hand it to the jackass: he's become very powerful around here."

"What I can't work out is how the hell you two stumbled onto the fact Alex wasn't the killer. I know the little coward didn't spill the beans. I was starting to go through the papers on your kitchen table when I heard you coming in from the laundry room."

"How'd you get in?" I couldn't believe I was able to ask a coherent question at this point. This kid scared me to death.

His easy laugh returned. "Piece of cake. Back in high school I stole house keys from all my friends. Figured they'd come in handy someday." He paused, looking at me. "But since you were home, I had to come back to see if you had anything written down telling me how much you knew."

Shock waves of understanding rippled through my body. That was why the Indians had seen the intruder before! They had seen Owen the first time and couldn't decide if he was welcome or not.

"So how did you know it was me?" he asked.

I shrugged. I wasn't about to tell him anything.

He smiled. "It doesn't really matter. I just didn't want to learn I had left behind DNA or some other type of evidence. I was still learning the ropes back then." The knife became still, and he shifted his weight. Instinctively, I knew this wasn't a good sign. "But it doesn't matter at this point."

"When I tell you, duck," Dad said. I nodded.

Owen's arm stopped in its upward arc. "Are you sure you didn't hear anything?"

I remained stone still. Let the son of a bitch figure it out for himself.

After a moment, the arm continued to rise. "Sorry, Mrs. S."

"Duck!"

I fell forward into my garden's rich soil. A shot rang out, and Owen's body hit the ground next to me. I could hear and feel the thud of impact. A sob escaped my lips.

"Peg!" Andy's voice rang through the yard. I could not only hear people running toward me but could also feel the earth vibrate with their feet pounding the grass as they did.

I didn't want to move, much less sit up. Jack grabbed one arm, Andy the other. With me stumbling between them, we made it to the house and into the kitchen. They gently sat me down in my chair. Logan told them to put my head between my knees. That accomplished, the world stopped spinning. After an eternity, I was able to slowly sit upright.

"Son of a bitch. I could hear the dead guy!" Jack said.

"I need to pee." Andy laughed. "Come on, old girl. I'll get you there."

Chapter 26

Drinking a soothing cup of hot tea helped my nerves. Well, to be honest, it was probably the whiskey Andy had added to the cup that settled me down more than the tea. But I was feeling much better by the time the cup was empty. I looked longingly down into the bottom as Andy laughed. "No more right now," he said. "No sense in getting you snockered."

"I still can't believe it was Owen!" I said, pulling the blanket that Andy had wrapped around me even tighter.

"We have guys going over his apartment," Jack said. "The little jerk saved trophy items from each crime. There's enough evidence there to have put him away for many lifetimes if we hadn't shot the bastard." Jack said through gritted teeth, "I trusted that kid!"

"We all did," I said. "Remember, it was part of his plan."

I had filled them in on Owen's secret life. While it had been a relief to solve Bob's and Elaine's murders, the fact another homegrown kid had gone bad hit us hard. I looked around the kitchen and smiled. Bob, Dad, Logan, Andy, and Jack had protectively gathered around me.

"What took you guys so long to arrive? I was out of ideas. If Owen hadn't been so eager to share some of his adventures, my goose would have been cooked long before help arrived."

Logan shook his head. "I was busy working in Owen's head."

I frowned. "Owen's head?"

Logan nodded. "You obviously understood my messages to you?"

I nodded.

"Owen could also understand the communications I was sending to him." He paused. "I am positive he has been able to receive negative input most of his life. It has been normal for him to 'hear' information, so when I connected with his mind, he was comfortable following the advice he heard." He shrugged. "Even before I began to suspect Owen, I strongly believed whoever was the culprit had had help from our side of life, encouraging him in his crimes."

My eyes narrowed. "You never shared that tidbit. Or the fact you ever suspected Owen."

"The information would not have helped your investigation. There was a strong possibility it would have hindered." Meeting my eyes, he continued, "I take responsibility for your situation, but there was no other way to bring the true criminal forward. Remember, if someone appears to be too perfect, they usually are far from perfect."

I frowned, thinking hard. Finally, I asked, "So I was bait?"

Logan's eyes left mine, and he gazed out the window. "Possibly."

It was apparent he wasn't going to offer any further information, so I decided to change my focus. "Bob, where was Elaine during this fiasco?"

He shook his head sadly. "No idea. Can't find her or your mother. Sorry."

I glanced back at Logan, wondering if he would add any comment to this development, but his eyes remained glued to my backyard.

I rearranged the blanket for more warmth, looking at Jack. "Pretty good shot. Thanks."

His face grew beet red, and his eyes left mine, the floor becoming the focus of his attention. I frowned and asked, "What?" "I haven't fired a gun in years. Well, except at the firing range. I was

sweating bullets, and my hands were shaking so hard I was afraid I'd hit you."

"But you made the shot," I said.

He shook his head. "Never in a million years would I have been able to hit Owen squarely in the head."

My frown increased. "So who shot him?"

"Antonio grabbed my gun, aimed, and fired. I've never seen anything like it. He didn't hesitate even a second. Dirty Harry couldn't have done better." He shook his head as he spoke.

Ah, the mob guys. In all the excitement, I had forgotten them. Looking around, I asked, "So where is the mayor's finest protection squad?"

Andy grinned. "They got out of here as fast as they could. Once they phoned the mayor about Owen, they skedaddled pretty quickly. Owen

208

knocked Santino out like a light. Guess he thought Bill was the only guard here."

No surprise they'd left so quickly. With all the cops currently milling around the property, they had probably been sweating. As much as I hated to admit it, the mayor's mob squad had come in handy.

"Why didn't he use the gun he had on him?" I asked.

Jack laughed. "Ballistics from my gun wouldn't raise any questions later; his probably would sound off alarm bells all over the state."

"Good point," I answered, grinning.

"Uh, I have a question," Bob said.

I nodded for him to continue.

"How'd you know you were in trouble?"

Good question. I sat thinking for a moment before saying, "When I could see Logan's friends in the woods, I wondered what was happening. I had realized a few days ago I could only see them when I was in danger, but when Owen appeared, I was confused. I've known that kid his entire life, and I wasn't consciously leery of him one bit."

I sighed, thinking of his family. His poor parents. Would they understand or be devastated?

"Consciously?" Andy asked. "Does that mean deep inside you knew something was off concerning him?"

I pursed my lips, thinking about his question. Finally, I shook my head. "Nope, not that I'm aware of really. It would be nice to say I had an inkling, but it wasn't until I saw that horrible expression on his face that it all fell into place." I shuddered at the memory. I hoped I wouldn't have nightmares over this mess.

Logan turned to face me. "I am pleased we have concluded this situation. Thank you for your help."

I shrugged. "Don't think I had a choice in the matter. But at least now it is over and done. I can have my life back now."

Smiling, he shook his head and said, "Mrs. Shaw, we have only begun."

Before I could respond, Logan was gone. Damn it to hell. What did he mean?

I looked at Andy and realized he had heard Logan's comment. By the expression on his face, he wasn't any happier with Logan's parting remark.

Jack saw our faces and asked, "What's going on?"

"I think Logan wants us to continue cleaning up messes around here. I'm not thrilled with the prospect."

Jack sat quietly for a moment. "You know, Peg, it could be a bonus to have a little help from your friends." He held his hands up before I could respond to his ridiculous idea. "Think about it. They walked you through this chaos, and we caught a serial criminal. From the calls I've gotten so far from our detectives, we have been able to solve over a dozen cases these past few hours. By the time they are finished combing through Owen's apartment and all his trophies, we may have closed the books on over twenty or thirty cold-case investigations, half of those being unsolved murders."

I sat listening to Jack, fuming. My midlife plan did not include stumbling into dangerous predicaments. Eventually, I wanted to enjoy being a nice, plump grandma—baking cookies, babysitting, and vacationing with Andy. I had no intention of allowing these past few weeks to become a new pattern in my life.

Bob's voice interrupted my anger. "Peg, I want to thank you for helping me. You haven't only solved my murder; you also gave me the courage to step away from Elaine's bitterness."

I looked up at him, giving him a small smile. I had to admit that watching Bob thrive helping Logan had been interesting. Who knew dead people could change so much?

"I knew you would succeed!" someone new said.

I turned my head toward the new voice and spotted Nana grinning widely.

"How long have you been here?" I asked, feeling a bit of anger rising.

"Simmer down, sweetie. It all worked out, eventually."

"Nana, I could have been killed!" I answered hotly.

"Oh, that," she said with a flick of her hand. "There's worse things."

My mouth fell open. "Nana!"

"Well, it's true!" she defended herself.

I dropped my head into my hands. I loved her, but let's face it: too much of Nana could be harmful to my health.

"It ended well," she said. "Plus, I knew you were the perfect person to help."

I raised my head to face her. "Why? Why in the world would you ever think I was the person to help?"

She grinned. "Because you don't like change. I knew you would get the job done, if only so you could resume your boring life. I told you a little variation in life is good."

I shook my head. "This was too much."

"I disagree. You are pretty good at this stuff. Just wait till next time; you'll see."

"Next time?" I shouted. "There won't be a next time!"

Grinning, she faded.

Andy had sat quietly, waiting for what he could hear of my conversation to cease. Concern covered the features of his handsome face.

I sighed. "Nana thinks there will be a next time. No way."

Jack cleared his throat before saying, "Consider helping again." Seeing my expression, he hurriedly said, "Maybe not as crazy as this one, but possibly we do need more help from their side."

"I think this would be a good time for Peg to get some rest," Dad said. "It's been a long day."

"I want a hot bath, another hot toddy, and my bed," I said.

"See you later, Peg," Bob said, fading from sight, waving slightly.

Dad was standing near the window. He glanced at the woods, then back at me. "I love you. Remember, we can communicate now. Call my name when you need to talk."

Tears sprang to my eyes as he slowly faded, his smiling face warming my heart. Andy lifted me from the chair. "Come on, old girl. Let's get you settled in a hot tub."

Tired, I decided to worry about my mom and Elaine another day. I snuggled in Andy's arms as we walked down the hall. He had better not forget the whiskey in my tea!

About the Author

Sue Hawley is the mother of five adult children who is determined not to have empty nest blues. She lives with her husband in an old farmhouse in Bath, Ohio. Hot Flashes/Cold Cases is her debut novel.

Letter to Readers

First and foremost, I want to thank you for reading Hot Flashes/Cold Cases.

My hope is that you enjoyed Peg Shaw's adventures as much as I enjoyed writing them. The idea sprang from basically nowhere and started simply with the question "What if menopause could cause a woman to start seeing ghosts?"

I was experiencing the joys of hot flashes myself, which had an irritating habit of occurring at the most inopportune moments. The more the idea swam around my mind, the funnier it seemed. Peg Shaw was born, followed by Bob, Elaine, Nana, and all the others.

Each character appeared all by themselves and I seldom knew why they decided to join the story, but I've learned to let them have free reign. I feel privileged they have allowed me to tell their stories.

Bob is my all-time favorite spirit. I love his enthusiasm, even when he trips on his own personality. I have a real soft spot for him; he makes me smile every time he pops in to create his own particular type of mayhem. He's more of a hero than he realizes.

I have great respect for Logan. His wisdom, power and sense of responsibility are what makes him important to me.

I would enjoy hearing who your favorite characters are. Drop me a line at suehawleyauthor.com and tell me who captured your heart and why.

Sue Hawley

PS – If you enjoyed this book, I would love it if you go to Amazon and post a review.

PSS – Do you want me to notify you when a new book is published? Send me your email address and I will add you to the list to be notified when Peg and the Deadsville gang have a new release.

52711972R00125

Made in the USA
Lexington, KY
20 September 2019